OTHER BOOKS BY LJ ROSS

Holy Island

Sycamore Gap

Heavenfield

Angel

High Force

Cragside

Dark Skies

Seven Bridges

The Hermitage

Longstone

The Infirmary

THE MOOR

A DCI RYAN MYSTERY

LJ Ross

"O, beware, my lord of jealousy;

It is the green-eyed monster which doth mock the meat it feeds on."

—William Shakespeare, *Othello*

PROLOGUE

Saturday, 1st June 2019

"*This is Tyne Radio Drivetime Classics, broadcasting across the North East…*"

Samantha O'Neill took an involuntary step away from the disembodied voice on the radio, stumbling backward into a solid wall of fur. The horse let out a half-hearted whinny and craned its neck to see what all the fuss was about, while the girl's head swam with the ripe scent of manure, warm and cloying on the summer air. The walls of the tiny makeshift stable were closing in, as though the muddied tarpaulin would engulf her, choke the very life out of her.

Dark spots swam in front of her eyes and she started to shake.

All the while, Boy George was singing balefully about karma and chameleons.

"*This is Tyne Radio…*"

She surged forward to end the offensive sound, groping for the switch with clumsy fingers.

But her arm froze, falling away in mid-air.

Fractured, blurry images from the past played around the edges of her mind as the door to her memory was quietly unlocked. Her body swayed as it remembered the same jingle she'd heard on a different radio eight years ago, and her heart pounded as she tried to snatch at the wisps of memories long forgotten. Tears fell in salty tracks down her cheeks as she heard the sound of her mother humming as she washed dishes. She could see her clearly now; a slim young woman in stonewash jeans with deep, rich red hair worn in curls down her back. She remembered Esme O'Neill as she had been, through the eyes of a child who had watched her from behind the wooden slats of her play pen.

"*This is Tyne Radio…*"

Samantha's breathing began to hitch, coming in short sobs as she remembered the caravan door opening, before the monster stepped inside. She heard harsh, angry words, then the sharp slap of flesh hitting flesh. There was a struggle; something crashed. A child was crying, frightened by the noise and something else, something much worse.

Then, a dreadful stillness where nothing stirred but the tinny sound of the music floating on the air.

"Mama! Mama!"

She saw her chubby arm reaching through the wooden slats, trying to grasp her mother's lifeless hand as it lay outstretched on the linoleum floor.

"Mama," Sam whispered.

The memories faded, and ordinary sounds filtered back through her foggy brain. Outside the stable tent, the men and women of *O'Neill's Circus* continued to set up camp on the moorland. She heard their occasional burst of laughter as they went about their business, oblivious to what had just happened to change her life irrevocably.

The horse wandered over to nuzzle her neck, sensing her disquiet.

"Shh, Pegasus," she managed.

Long minutes passed until she scrubbed both hands over her face and stood up from where she'd fallen. All around, the moor bustled as people raised a series of brightly-coloured tents from the ground. She heard her father's voice carrying on the air, barking orders as the Big Top rose in an elegant sweep of red and white.

Sam watched it happen from the shadows, heard the back-slapping cries as they hurried to secure the lines, and the occasional curse when one broke free. These people were her family, she thought. Theirs was an extraordinary world of magic, choreographed to entertain the masses—and, so long as the circus belonged to an O'Neill, hers would be the ruling family. Her father was the final arbiter of disputes, playing Solomon to every money quarrel and drunken brawl laid at his feet. By rights, she ought to tell him what she had remembered and thus break a lifelong taboo by speaking her mother's name. For as long as she could remember, Charlie O'Neill had never spoken of his inconstant wife, long dead to him now.

But others had. The circus had whispered about the woman who'd left her man and child to run off with a rich country-man with a big house. Esme O'Neill had disgraced her family and dishonoured her faith. She wasn't fit to be remembered, this woman whose character had been so maligned.

Except, none of it was true. Sam knew that now.

Her mother had not left them, she had been taken.

It was a heavy burden, this new knowledge. If she spoke out, it would be tantamount to betrayal; unthinkable and unforgivable. Fear curdled in her belly as she thought of her father's anger and of the uproar that would follow if she went to the police. But she could not ignore what she had seen, and she could not allow others to continue as they had for so long, believing her mother to be unworthy.

She knew what she must do.

Heart heavy, she turned away and melted back into the shadows.

CHAPTER 1

Sunday, 2nd June 2019

Thirty miles north of the city of Newcastle upon Tyne, Detective Chief Inspector Maxwell Finlay-Ryan watched a flock of birds swoop across a cloudless Northumbrian sky. Sunday mornings were made for this, and it had been far too long since he'd been able to enjoy a quiet moment of reflection and contented idleness while he watched the world go by. Life as a murder detective didn't lend itself to lazy lie-ins or meandering walks along the riverbank but, at the none-too-gentle insistence of his sergeant—and his wife—he'd agreed to take some time off and recharge his batteries.

He was giving serious thought to the prospect of depleting them again by joining his wife in the shower, when the front door bell rang.

"Foiled again," he muttered, and trotted downstairs, telling himself he'd quickly dispatch whichever political campaigner or religious missionary was presently darkening his door.

But, when he yanked the door open, the rebuff died on his lips.

A girl of no more than eleven or twelve stood on the porch step, a backpack hanging over one shoulder. A tanned, freckled face was framed by a crop of reddish-brown hair that had been stuffed beneath an ancient baseball cap, and her jeans were caked in mud and God only knew what else. Ryan had no time to finish his assessment before the girl tipped up her cap and fixed him with a direct, green-eyed stare.

"Are you the bloke from the news?" she demanded.

Ryan raised a single black eyebrow and folded his arms across his chest.

"That depends," he said. "Who's asking?"

She shuffled her feet, which were clad in scuffed trainers that might once have been white.

"Look, I need to know if this is the right place," she said, unconsciously mirroring his stance. "You look like him."

Ryan's lips twitched.

"Like who? Because, unless it's James Bond, I'm not sure I'll be flattered."

She flashed a smile, which was gone just as quickly.

"Detective Chief Inspector Ryan," she said. "I saw him—I saw *you*—on the news a while ago. You're supposed to be the best."

"At what?"

"Catching killers."

There was a short, humming silence as Ryan took a closer look at the girl's face and saw what he'd missed the first time around. Beneath the bravado and oversized hat, there was something else.

There was fear.

"Where are your parents?" he asked, peering towards the driveway to see how she'd made it this far. "Come to think of it, how did you find out where I live?"

She smiled again.

"You can find out most things, if you ask the right people," she said, and ducked beneath his arm to scuttle inside the house, bringing a strong aroma of horses with her.

* * *

"Hey!"

Ryan let the front door slam shut and hurried after the girl, just as Anna came downstairs and caught a flash of movement headed in the direction of the kitchen.

"What's going on?" she asked.

"Monkey on the loose," Ryan threw over his shoulder.

Anna let out a muffled laugh and followed him into the kitchen, coming to a surprised halt as she was met with a girl of around ten, who had wasted no time in helping herself to a chair at their large breakfast table and was eyeing the bowl of fruit in the middle with hungry eyes.

"Who's this?" she asked.

"Good question," Ryan growled.

"I'm Samantha," the girl said, watching them closely. "You can call me Sam, if you like."

"That's a pretty name," Anna said, and offered her the bowl of fruit. "Have we met before?"

Sam's shoulders tensed as the woman drew near, then relaxed again. There was a kind look in her eyes.

"No, you don't know me," she mumbled, reaching for an apple. "I came—I needed to see *him*. It's important."

She flicked a glance across to where Ryan remained standing a safe distance away, tall, raven-haired and, to her eyes, everything a hero was supposed to look like.

"You still haven't told me how you found this address," he said.

"It doesn't matter how," she shot back, between loud bites. "I need your help. My mum's been murdered, and I want you to find out who did it."

Anna and Ryan exchanged an eloquent look.

"You're telling me your mother was murdered? When did this happen?"

All suspicion forgotten, Ryan took a seat while Anna melted away to put the kettle on. Moments like these called for coffee and, in the girl's case, strong hot chocolate.

Sam began to fiddle with the cuff of her sweatshirt, picking at the fraying edge.

"Eight years ago," she said.

Ryan did the maths.

"You would have been…two, or three?"

"Two," she nodded.

He ran a hand over his jaw and sighed. It wasn't that he didn't believe her, exactly, but it was hardly a compelling case so far.

"Okay. Tell me your mum's name, and why you think she was murdered."

Sam wrapped her fingers around the enormous mug of hot chocolate Anna set in front of her.

"Thanks," she mumbled, and took a fortifying sip before continuing. "She was called Esme. Esme O'Neill. But her real name was Esmerelda."

Ryan didn't so much as flinch, although he'd never investigated a victim with so whimsical a name before.

"Esmerelda O'Neill," he repeated. "Go on."

"My daddy and everyone told me she ran off," she explained. "They said she'd left me when I was a baby and I'd always thought…Everyone said she was bad, but now I know it wasn't her fault. I know she never left me."

"How do you know?" Ryan prodded.

"I remembered what happened," she replied, in the kind of tone that implied it was obvious. "Yesterday, I remembered while I was mucking out Pegasus' stable. I saw what happened."

"You…saw your mother being killed?" Anna murmured, and reached across the table to touch the girl's fingers in sympathy.

Sam nodded, and blinked furiously against unexpected tears. The woman's hands were tender, as her mother's had been, and she smelled nice.

Ryan gave her a moment, then spoke carefully.

"This would have been back in 2011," he said. "Do you know what time of year? Anything else that might help me to understand?"

Sam looked at him from beneath the rim of her preposterous hat with such aching sadness that Ryan felt his gut twist.

"It happened the last time we were in Newcastle," she said. "We haven't been back since, but…I think we always used to come in June."

"We?" Anna asked, taking the words out of Ryan's mouth.

"*O'Neill's Circus,*" Sam said. "My great-grandfather started it. I think we used to come to Newcastle every year, but this is the first time we've been back since…since she died."

She'd almost said, 'since she left', but that wasn't true. Not now.

"I remember how it happened," she continued, in as firm a voice as she could muster. "She was strangled. I was there but, when I try to think of *who*, I can only see a shadow—"

She broke off suddenly and set the apple core on the table, bearing down against the memories which threatened to crowd into her mind again.

"Will you help?" she asked, compelling him to listen. "*Please?*"

Ryan gave a short nod.

"It's my job," he said simply, and was rewarded with a smile that would have lit up the darkest sky.

CHAPTER 2

"Make way for the Yorkshire Pudding King!"

Detective Sergeant Frank Phillips' humble declaration greeted Anna on the doorstep a short while later. In deference to the milder weather, his stocky body was showcased in a pair of khaki cargo shorts that looked as though they'd survived both world wars, and a blinding pink shirt embroidered with a pattern of tiny green palm trees. He'd rounded off the ensemble with a liberal sprinkling of Old Spice.

Rendered momentarily speechless, Anna had no time to warn him of the unexpected addition to their lunch party before he stepped inside, wiping his comfortable Hush Puppies on the hallway mat.

His wife followed, with the long-suffering air of one who had seen it all before.

"Anyone would think you'd never eaten a roast dinner," Detective Inspector Denise MacKenzie grumbled, leaning in to bestow a quick peck on Anna's cheek as she shrugged out of her summer jacket. "I had to strong-arm him away from the bacon, this morning."

Anna gave herself a mental shake.

"Ah, there's something I should mention—"

But Frank was already making his way towards the kitchen and, a few seconds later, they heard his booming voice carry along the hallway.

"Who's *this*?"

* * *

Sam's eyes widened as another man entered the kitchen. He was older than Ryan; short and tough-looking with a boxer's physique—not that he looked particularly dangerous at that moment, dressed in a flamingo-pink shirt and shorts that revealed pale, hairy legs that clearly weren't accustomed to regular sunshine.

"Frank, meet Samantha O'Neill," Ryan said, watching her with the ghost of a smile. "Sam, this is my sergeant and good friend, Frank Phillips."

"I don't want to speak to anybody else," she scowled. "I only want to talk to *you.*"

Phillips was affronted.

"Story of my life, that is," he grumbled. "All the lasses love a pretty boy."

Sam drank the rest of her hot chocolate, to hide a smile.

"Well, hello!"

MacKenzie set her handbag on the kitchen countertop and made a discreet assessment of the girl, who stared at her with wide eyes.

"This here's Samantha," Frank said, moving across to sniff at the meat roasting in the oven before looking out bowls and a whisk to get started on the Yorkshire pudding batter. That was their little tradition, he thought—he would make his legendary puddings, if Anna made the gravy to pour on top of them.

While Phillips set about washing his hands, the girl glanced between them in a mixture of hope and confusion.

Ryan kept his voice light.

"Would you like me to call your dad?" he offered.

She shook her head, firmly. Until she knew which of them was responsible for her mother's death, nobody at the circus could be trusted.

Including her father.

"Is there anyone else?" Ryan asked. "A grandparent, or an aunt or uncle?"

Sam's lip wobbled, only slightly.

"No," she whispered. "There's nobody else I want you to call."

There was an infinitesimal pause, then Ryan nodded.

"In that case, why don't you stay for lunch while we figure out what to do next?"

* * *

Phillips polished off the food on his plate and paused briefly, twiddling his fork before reaching across to claim the last slice of beef. Unfortunately, he was beaten to it by the lightning-swift jab of another fork belonging to the young interloper sitting beside him.

Catching sight of his outraged expression, Sam shrugged.

"You snooze, you lose," she told him, and smiled toothily before shovelling the meat into her mouth.

Phillips folded his arms across his paunch with grudging admiration.

"You've got some competition there, Frank," MacKenzie chuckled. "You must be slipping."

Phillips' eyebrows flew into his receding hairline as he watched the girl snaffle the last of the cauliflower cheese, too.

"Don't know where she's putting it all," he exclaimed. "Skinny as a rake, that one."

"I've got a fast metabolism," Sam told him, and glanced meaningfully towards his thicker waistline. "It slows down a lot, when you get old."

Phillips' jaw dropped.

"Why, you cheeky little—"

Ryan laughed, and judged it the appropriate moment to step in.

"Got a minute, Frank?" he asked, and bobbed his head towards the adjoining room.

* * *

"I'm tellin' you, that one's trouble," Phillips said, as soon as the door to Ryan's study was closed.

Ryan leaned back against the desk and crossed his legs.

"She's hungry and, if I'm any judge, she's scared."

Phillips relented a bit, thinking of the shadows beneath the girl's eyes.

"Aye, well," he said, clearing his throat. "What's she doing up here, anyhow? Why didn't she call 999?"

"I don't know. She turned up on my doorstep," Ryan said, with a shrug. "Barged her way in and told me her mother had been murdered eight years ago and that she wants me to find her killer. Not only that, she claims to be a witness."

Phillips sank into one of the easy chairs.

"If all this happened eight years ago, she can't have been more than a bairn," he said, with a troubled expression.

Ryan nodded.

"Well, that's a turn up for the books," Phillips said, after a moment. "I thought this place was supposed to be hard to find?"

Ryan let out a bark of laughter.

"Only for hardened criminals," he said, dryly.

"So, what are you going to do?"

Ryan didn't think he was referring to the security breach.

"Same thing I always do when a murder is reported. I'm going to look into it."

Phillips scratched the weekend stubble on his chin.

"Thought you were having a few days off?"

Ryan smiled.

"No rest for the wicked, so they say."

"That must make you Old Nick, himself," Phillips quipped, but he knew better than to argue. "Howay then, I'll fire up the coffee machine."

CHAPTER 3

When Phillips stepped back into the room, he found Ryan hunched over a desktop computer, having already accessed the Missing Persons Database remotely using his police credentials. He looked up when a mug of steaming coffee was placed in front of him.

"Thanks. How are they getting on, back there?"

Phillips thought of how the girl had jumped up to help him clear the plates from the table before joining Anna and Denise in the living room, where he'd left them chatting like old friends.

"They're thick as thieves," he said.

Ryan nodded, turning his attention back to the screen.

"I've already searched existing records for an 'Esmerelda O'Neill' but there's nothing on the system. I'm looking into Missing Persons, now."

"Esmerelda?" Phillips asked. "Sounds like a Romany name but the lass looks Irish, if you ask me."

In fact, with her red curls and cat-green eyes, it made him wonder whether that's how Denise might have looked, at a similar age.

"There's no record of homicide and no record of any missing person having been reported with that name," Ryan said, interrupting his train of thought. "Samantha was told her mum had run away with another man, but she's adamant that isn't what happened."

Phillips pulled a face.

"Aye, but you know what kids are like. Maybe she made up a tall tale, to take the edge off the truth. Nobody wants to think their mum upped and left them, do they?"

Ryan looked back at the empty screen, then brought up another database.

"I have to check," he said, more to himself than anyone else.

But there was no record of an Esme—or an Esmerelda—O'Neill registered for tax, National Insurance or at any known address. She had no criminal record, either. He might have been forgiven for wondering whether the woman had ever existed, until another search finally flagged something.

"Here we are," Ryan said, with a measure of relief. "Esmerelda Marie Cleary, born in Lincoln on 17th March 1987."

"She was only young," Phillips murmured, from his position behind Ryan's left shoulder. "That would have made her twenty-four, back in 2011."

Ryan nodded.

"There's a record of marriage here, too," he continued. "To Charles Michael O'Neill, at St Andrew's Church in Newcastle on 14th June 2008."

He spent another few minutes collecting any other information that was readily available, which did not prove to be much, until he swung around in his chair to face Phillips with serious eyes.

"No record of her death, no record of divorce or re-marriage, either," he said. "I'd need to get one of the analysts to dive into any bank records or vehicle registrations but it's looking as though she's dropped off the grid."

They both turned as they heard the unmistakable sound of a child's laughter wafting through the cracks in the door.

"Canny kid," Phillips said gruffly, having forgiven her earlier transgressions. "There's still a chance her mam could be alive and well with a new family somewhere. If she belonged to a travelling circus, maybe she just flew beneath the radar and that's why the records are a bit patchy. It's possible, isn't it?"

"Anything's possible."

But Ryan was focused on other possibilities, and he swung back around to the computer. His fingers flew across the keyboard and then drummed the edge of the desk while he waited for the search results to appear.

When they did, his face became shuttered.

"Look at this, Frank."

Phillips peered at the screen again, skim-reading the results of Ryan's search of cold case murder files for the Newcastle area in or around June 2011.

He stopped when he reached one entry, in particular.

"Ah, God," he breathed. "Do you think that's her?"

Ryan thought of the child seated at his table next door and hardened his heart. If he allowed emotion to creep in, he would be unable to do the job that was required of him now.

"Unidentified female, Caucasian, age range eighteen to thirty," he read aloud. "Discovered in a shallow grave in the woods near Bolam Lake by a hiker on 4th July 2011. Red hair, approximately five feet seven inches tall."

Phillips read the remaining information in the summary for himself, which included a pathology report detailing a body having been found in an advanced state of decomposition. It had, however, been possible to identify a crushed trachea, indicative of death by violent strangulation.

"You said the girl saw this happen?" he said, softly.

Ryan sighed.

"Yeah," he said heavily. "And there's something else to consider, Frank. If she saw them, maybe somebody saw her, too."

* * *

Charlie O'Neill narrowed his eyes against the glare of the mid-afternoon sun as he watched the circus come together. Every tent, caravan and stall had been erected in accordance with an agreed layout approved by the Local Council, and every nut and bolt had been checked, double-checked and would be triple-checked before the day was out. Tomorrow, there would be a grand opening and the scent of toffee apples and fried meat would thicken the air for the next ten days until they packed it all away again and moved on, clearing a path for the next travelling fairground that would come to entertain the town.

His town, he thought.

He'd been born in Newcastle, at a house his parents used to own, until they'd decided to emigrate to hotter climes. He couldn't blame them; in fact, he'd welcomed the news. His father had been the ringmaster of *O'Neill's* for over thirty years and had shown no signs of slowing down or stopping, until a stroke left him partially immobile and speech-impaired. No longer able to command the same respect as before, he'd been forced to stand aside for a younger and abler man. Some people would frown if they heard him say that, but it was just the way of the world. Strength was required of a leader, especially in their business. Weakness was a chink to be exploited, and, if he didn't guard against it, the circus would soon carry a different name. That was the price of power, Charlie realised. While you had it, you were invincible. When you lost it, you were just another crippled old bastard people used to know.

Might as well enjoy it, while it lasted.

He tugged a pack of cigarettes from the back pocket of his jeans and stuck one in his mouth. All the talk of nicotine causing cancer held little sway with him: he'd smoked since he was nine years old and had no intention of stopping now. What would be the point? He'd only look like a health-crazed nonce from the city, and that would never do.

Talk of the city made him think of the people beyond the moor, and he felt an uncomfortable tug of recognition. The Town Moor was a large area of common land in the centre of Newcastle, bigger than Hyde Park or Hampstead Heath—maybe even bigger than Central Park in New York, although he'd never been. It was surrounded by middle-class suburbs and, over the rolling fields, he could see the city skyline rising above the line of trees which marked the perimeter where the moor met the road. He heard the thrum of traffic as people made their way home, having enjoyed the remaining hours of the weekend before returning to their humdrum, nine-to-five jobs on Monday.

Tossers.

For all that he'd been born within the bells of St Nicholas' Cathedral, Charlie felt no particular loyalty to his home town, or to its people. So long as they came to the circus after work or at the weekend, so long as they spent their money on popcorn and candy floss, he didn't care what they did with the rest of their time.

He took a long drag of his cigarette, then blew out the smoke in an elaborate swirl. He watched it melt into the summer air and wondered if he had done the right thing in coming back here. If things had been different, wild horses couldn't have dragged him within ten miles of Newcastle. But he had other people to think of; a circus to support. He could no longer take decisions solely for his own benefit, however much he hated the sight of the place.

Everything reminded him of *her*.

If he allowed himself to think of it, he might remember meeting Esme for the first time, all those years ago. He might think of how she'd looked on their wedding day at the church less than a mile from where he now stood.

But he would not think of it.

It was enough that he saw her likeness every time he looked at his daughter, who grew more like her mother with every passing year.

No, he would not think of it—or of Esmerelda, wherever she was, now.

CHAPTER 4

"Sam?"

When Ryan's quiet voice interrupted their conversation, three female faces looked up from a lively game of Scrabble. He watched the light drain from the girl's eyes and was sorry for it.

"She's really dead, isn't she?" Sam whispered, and blinked away tears.

She'd known it all along, but still hoped to be wrong. She'd wished it was all a horrible nightmare, some kind of fantasy she'd created in her own mind, but she saw the truth reflected in Ryan's blue-grey eyes, long before he spoke the words.

"There is a woman who matches the description you gave us," was all he would say. "Nothing is certain until we've done some tests—"

"You mean, like, DNA?"

Beside her, MacKenzie smiled.

"Yes, exactly," she said.

"In that case, why don't you take a sample from me now and send it off to the science boffin who does the testing?"

Despite the circumstances, Ryan found himself holding back a smile as he thought of how Tom Faulkner, their senior crime scene investigator, would react to being called a 'boffin'.

On reflection, he'd probably love it.

"I'm afraid it's not quite that simple," he said, taking a seat near to where she sat cross-legged in front of the coffee table. "Legally, you're a minor, and there are certain rules about that. We'd need a parent or guardian to be present, for starters—"

Once again, she cut Ryan off with the kind of breath-taking ease Phillips could only hope to emulate.

"I'm also a witness, aren't I?" she said. "Don't you need to eliminate me from your list of suspects? Here, I'll volunteer a sample."

With that, she plucked a chunk of hair from beneath her cap and held it out, roots and all.

"Ah, now, just a minute—"

"Technically speaking, she *is* a witness," MacKenzie pointed out.

"She was two years old at the time." Ryan raised a single, disbelieving eyebrow. "I hardly think she'd be high on our list of suspects, do you?"

"Well, I'm not calling my dad," Sam told him. "He must be one of your prime suspects and I've already said, I don't want him to know where I am."

Ryan frowned.

"Now, hang on a minute," he said. "Even *if* I agreed to accept a DNA sample from you for the purposes of the investigation, that doesn't mean your father isn't entitled to know where you are."

"Yes, it does," she argued. "What if he killed her? Or, if it wasn't him, it could have been anybody else at the circus. We all live in the same place and, when the word gets about that I came to the police, one of them might come and find me. They all know where I live, don't they?"

Ryan looked around the other faces in the room and was exasperated to find himself outnumbered. After all, the kid had a point.

"Okay, let's assume there's a case to investigate." He held up his hands. "You'd have to go into protective custody, at a safe address—"

"I'm not going into care!"

"Nobody's saying that," Anna soothed, and looked meaningfully towards her husband.

"She can't stay here," Ryan said, with as much authority as he could muster in the face of rising panic.

"Of course, I can't stay here," Sam said, and looked at him as if he were dopey. "I came to you because you're the one in charge—"

The other three in the room snorted in unison.

"Everybody knows you," she continued. "That means they'd know where to look, if somebody wanted to find me. I need to stay somewhere no one would think of, with somebody totally *average*. You know, somebody who wouldn't stand out in a crowd or attract attention. Not good-looking, just ordinary. A nobody. Like him," she said, pointing squarely at Phillips, who was perched on the edge of the sofa beside his wife.

He came to attention with an outraged grunt, almost falling off his perch.

"Well, I've never—!"

"She does have a point," Ryan mused, and crossed one leg comfortably over the other. "You do blend in, Frank."

"I'll blend you, in a minute—"

"Now, now," his friend said, mischievously, and looked at the woman seated beside him. "What do you say, Mac?"

All eyes turned to the person who made the final decisions in the MacKenzie-Phillips household. Denise put a gentle hand on her husband's knee and looked into the girl's small, expectant face. She wanted to find something there to give her pause, to remind her of why she never became involved in the lives of those she helped, but found nothing except the trusting eyes of a child.

"If the Chief Constable will sign off on it, I'll make up the spare bedroom for tonight," she said slowly. "But let's be straight from the start, Sam. If there's a case to investigate about your mum, then I'm more sorry than I can say, and we'll do all we can to help you. But my husband is anything but an 'average nobody', and neither am I. We expect good behaviour and a measure of respect while you're staying with us."

The girl nodded vigorously.

"You'll hardly know I'm around. I promise."

MacKenzie smiled, while Phillips looked to the heavens and wondered what he'd let himself in for.

* * *

"Boss?"

Charlie half turned.

"What is it, man? I'm busy."

He wasn't, especially, but he couldn't face a conversation with his younger brother just now. His twin had been born only three minutes after him, but it may as well have been three decades, for they were worlds apart. The name sounded right—their father had demanded good, strong names for both his sons—but 'Duke' didn't match the awkward, clumsy man who spent his days clowning around, making people laugh.

"It's important," he insisted.

Charlie swore viciously and ground his cigarette into the soil beneath his feet before turning and spreading his muscular arms.

"Well? You've got my attention."

"It's about Sam," Duke said, refusing to be intimidated. "I can't find her anywhere."

Charlie huffed out a laugh.

"Is that all? You know she does this every time we come to a new place. She'll have gone for a wander around the town."

Duke remained troubled and looked up at the sky, which was a bold wash of warm amber as the sun began to fall into the horizon. Soon, it would be dark.

"She left an extra bucket of feed beside Pegasus," he persisted. "The stall's been mucked out, but she gave him twice the usual amount. Why would she do that?"

Charlie was losing patience.

"Look, I don't have time to worry about why the bloody horse has two buckets of feed. We've got a meeting later and it's important. I don't need you losing your nerve and screwing this up for both of us."

Duke said nothing, but continued to look at him with sad, clown eyes.

"Fine," Charlie spat. "Go and look around, if it makes you feel better, but I'm telling you she'll trot back soon enough—probably with an armful of clobber she's nicked from some poor sap. I want you back here, with or without her, by seven."

"And, if it's without her? What then?"

But Charlie had already turned away.

CHAPTER 5

"Where are we?"

On the drive home, Phillips had counted eighty questions from the youngster sitting in the back seat. This was the eighty-first.

"Kingston Park," he replied testily, as they passed through the comfortable residential neighbourhood on the western edge of the city. "Although we're thinking of moving soon, aren't we, love?"

"Frank needs more room for his ties," MacKenzie chipped in, with an affectionate smile. "And I'd like to be nearer the sea."

"Are we close to the sea?" Sam asked, with a trace of excitement.

"Not far," Phillips replied. He almost went on to say he'd take her, one day, but stopped himself just in time. The lass wasn't going to be with them long, and it wouldn't do to get too attached.

MacKenzie silently agreed, although it went against the grain.

"Nearly there," she said instead, and a moment later they turned into a cul-de-sac lined with smart, semi-detached houses built sometime in the seventies and eighties.

"I don't know how you can stay in one place for so long," Sam said, as she unfastened the seatbelt they'd bulldozed her into wearing. "Don't you get bored?"

MacKenzie shook her head as she opened the car door.

"I like to visit new places, but there's nowhere like home."

The girl let the word roll around on her tongue and wondered what 'home' might feel like. Hers had been a transient, often volatile existence, and the caravan she shared with her father was just a place to sleep.

"Shoes off, please!"

She toed off her scruffy trainers at Phillips' insistence, then padded through the hallway towards the kitchen.

"She's like a homing pigeon, that one," he muttered, and MacKenzie smiled.

"Hungry?" she called out.

"Always!" two voices replied.

* * *

"Will you be alright in here?"

Half an hour later, Sam heard Phillips' rumbling voice behind her but couldn't quite find the words to answer. She stood on the threshold of a beautiful room which boasted an enormous double bed decked in soft covers and fluffy pillows. There was a dressing table and a stool in the corner, with a mirror on top. The curtains at the window were a delicate, buttercup yellow and caught the last rays of the evening sun.

"It's just the spare room," he continued, starting to feel a bit worried. "I know it's not much, but—"

"It's lovely," she said huskily. "Are you sure you don't mind me sleeping here? I don't want to mess it up."

Phillips almost reached out to ruffle the girl's hair, before stopping himself again.

"Don't be daft, make yourself at home," he said. "Towels are in the cupboard, here, and there's a bathroom just next door you can have to yourself. You might fancy a bubble bath, before bed."

She turned to look at him.

"Thank you for having me to stay," she said. "I know you didn't want to, but I'm grateful all the same."

Phillips cleared his throat.

"W'hey, it's not that I didn't *want* to, lass—it's just that you've got your own family, haven't you? Your dad must be getting worried, by now."

She gave him a small, tight smile.

"I don't think so," she said.

"Aw, now, I'm sure that's not—"

"You don't know him," she interjected. "He's a hard man, Mr Phillips."

"Frank."

"What?"

"You can call me Frank," Phillips said. "None of that 'Mr Phillips' stuff. Makes me think of my granda'."

"Oh. Was he not very nice?"

Phillips sighed.

"He was a man of his time," was all he said, choosing not to discuss the less attractive aspects of his grandfather's character.

"My dad's a bit like that," she said knowingly, and sank onto the edge of the bed, clutching her cap. "He doesn't hug or play games. He's too busy for any of that. But I get to look after the horses."

"You like horses, eh?"

"I love them," she said, before her face fell again. "I'm going to miss Pegasus. He's big and gentle and he's my favourite. My dad's always said I can keep him, when he gets too old to perform."

"You'll see him again soon," Phillips said, and hoped it was true.

But she shook her head.

"Not until I know who killed my mum," she said, matter-of-factly. "I don't trust any of them, now."

Phillips sighed. A hasty call to the Chief Constable had bought them some time, until the morning, but Sandra Morrison had been less than impressed by the whole situation and had already put a call through to her counterpart in Social Services. The girl wouldn't be happy when she found out, but their hands were tied.

"We'll go down to the station tomorrow and put it all in writing, in a proper statement. For now, try to get a good night's sleep," he said.

MacKenzie took that as her cue to step in.

"Here we are," she said brightly, and laid out some soft cotton pyjamas. "They'll be a bit big for you, I'm afraid, but if you put these on after your bath, I'll wash your clothes and dry them in time for tomorrow morning."

Sam held the pyjamas close to her chest.

"Thank you."

* * *

As the last checks were made on the Big Top and the sun finally slipped off the edge of the world, Charlie O'Neill opened the door to his caravan and stepped inside. He found it spotless, as always, which was how he preferred things to be kept. Cleaning was women's work and he'd impressed that ethos upon his daughter, as soon as she'd been old enough to lift a mop.

"Sam?" he bellowed.

He pulled a can of beer out of the small fridge and took a grateful swig. He wasn't a big drinker and never had been. That was another kind of weakness and he preferred to have his wits about him. All the same, a bit of Dutch courage never hurt anyone.

"Sam?" he repeated, wandering through to the tiny second bedroom with its cabin-sized bed. Theirs was one of the largest caravans, as befitted his status, but nobody would ever describe it as spacious.

He found the room deserted and the bed neatly made.

He stepped inside and cast sharp eyes around the four walls. He was about to take another swig of beer, when his eyes fell on the empty space beside the door where her backpack should have been.

"Shit," he muttered.

If he went out looking for her now, he'd be late for his meeting. On the other hand, if he didn't, what kind of father did that make him?

The only kind he knew how to be, he thought, and drained the last of his beer.

* * *

Five miles northwest of the circus, Sam lay snugly beneath the covers in MacKenzie and Phillips' spare bedroom. When Denise stuck her head around the door, she found the girl curled up tight in the foetal position, only the top of her head visible beneath a mountain of covers and cushions.

"Poor little mite," she murmured, and shut the door softly behind her.

"It'll be a hard day for her, tomorrow," Phillips said, when she joined him downstairs. "We need to know all the ins and outs about what she remembers, and Social Services will want to move her somewhere else, too."

MacKenzie tucked her feet up onto the sofa beside him.

"I worry for her, Frank," she said. "If she's telling the truth and the DNA results come back with a positive match tomorrow, we've got a murder investigation on our hands. It's most likely to be someone the victim knew, which makes it likely that Sam knew her mother's killer."

And they knew her.

Phillips reached across to rub her feet. Since her attack, MacKenzie's leg had never been the same and, by the end of a long day, her feet ached.

"All these years she couldn't remember what happened, so they probably stopped worrying about it becoming a problem. Now she's done a runner, that'll put the wind up."

They fell silent, considering the ramifications of that.

"She told me her da' was a hard man," Phillips continued, keeping his voice low. "If he's involved, we could have a fight on our hands keeping the girl safe."

"Let's hope he isn't," MacKenzie whispered. "For her sake, let's hope she doesn't have to live with the horror of that, too."

CHAPTER 6

Monday, 3rd June 2019

The new day dawned bright and cloudless, a bold blue canvas against which passing aeroplanes blazed frothy white trails as they made their way to foreign shores. Ryan and Phillips watched them from the boxy confines of the Northumbria Police Constabulary Headquarters, through the single, grubby window of their Chief Constable's corner office.

"Let me see if I understand the situation correctly," she said, in deceptively calm tones. "A girl—a *child*—you've never met turned up on your doorstep, Ryan, and you didn't think to call Social Services immediately?"

He held his ground.

"No, ma'am. Samantha O'Neill reported a murder, which falls within my remit. I took a brief statement and corroborated certain basic facts to establish whether she was…" He paused, searching for a delicate way to put it.

"Telling the truth, or pullin' a fast one," Phillips put in, helpfully.

"Thanks," Ryan muttered.

"Don't mention it," Phillips returned.

Sandra Morrison sucked in a long breath, then let it out slowly. She prided herself on being a fair woman, not given to displays of irrational behaviour or emotional outbursts. That same restraint had cost her a marriage and countless friendships over the years, but it had also enabled her to rise swiftly through the ranks of a police hierarchy that had—until more recent times—been largely geared in favour of her male counterparts. On the whole, she didn't regret the choices she had made, and she was usually able to predict the actions of the staff she was responsible for leading.

Usually, being the operative word.

The two men standing before her represented two of the best murder detectives the Criminal Investigation Department had to offer; not merely in their own district but on a national level. Ryan and Phillips could not be more different, both in looks and in temperament, and there had been times when they had taken her by surprise. However, she wouldn't have described either of them as a 'soft touch', and she said as much.

"I wouldn't have pegged either of you as the type to take in waifs and strays," she said, to nobody in particular.

Ryan merely cocked his head.

"The girl's a witness to murder," he said. "That changes things."

"Possibly," she corrected. "Only if the DNA results prove the unidentified female is her mother."

"They're due back today," Ryan said. "I've asked Faulkner to put a rush on it."

Morrison leaned an elbow on the edge of her desk and propped her head on her hand. She could have probed him about why he'd felt it necessary to authorise an express forensic service on a cold case but, since the deed was already done, there seemed little point in quibbling over it.

"Where's the girl?" she asked.

"MacKenzie's introducing Samantha to some fine dining, in the staff canteen," Phillips joked. "She's been no trouble, so far."

Morrison thought she heard the beginnings of affection in his voice and was troubled. She glanced up at the clock on the wall.

"The rep from Social Services will be arriving any minute now," she said crisply. "Let's be clear about something, Frank. I allowed the girl to stay with you last night because it was so late in the day and both you and Denise are fully DBS-checked—but that was a one-off. Social Services will need to assess the situation and decide whether she should return to her family or go to a foster family in a secure location while an investigation is ongoing."

Phillips was defensive.

"She's a canny lass and all that, but I'll be just as happy to see her go back home," he said.

"Just as well," Morrison returned.

"She seems adamant she won't return to her father," Ryan put in. "Even without the spectre of murder hanging over her head, Samantha obviously doesn't want to go home. The prospect of her father being a prime suspect didn't faze her at all, which is highly unusual. That should be enough to give us pause."

"There doesn't seem to be much love lost," Phillips agreed. "Maybe she'd be better off somewhere else."

Morrison made a sweeping gesture with her hand.

"It's not our decision to make," she said. "You've known the girl for two minutes, so you can't possibly know what she feels or doesn't feel about her family, or indeed whether your skills will be required at all. Don't get carried away by sentiment."

"Has the father reported her missing, yet?" Ryan asked, mildly. "It's been nearly twenty-four hours. Has he rung the Control Room to make a report?"

Morrison hesitated, then acknowledged the point with a wry smile.

"No," she muttered. "He hasn't."

* * *

"Why do you keep looking at him like that?"

Trainee Detective Constable Melanie Yates jolted in her seat in the staff canteen, and turned a slow shade of red.

"Like what? I wasn't—"

"You keep looking at that man, over there," Samantha insisted, between mouthfuls of bacon and baked beans that had spent so long sitting on the counter they resembled congealed orange gloop.

"Look," she said. "He's walking over, now—"

"Finish your breakfast, Sam," MacKenzie said firmly, earning a grateful smile from Yates, whose burgeoning attraction for Detective Constable Jack Lowerson was the worst kept secret in Northumbria CID. The man in question was presently helping himself to a cup of coffee from one of the industrial vending machines lining a wall on the other side of the room and was, thankfully, oblivious to their conversation.

"He's not bad," Sam continued, blithely. "I like Ryan, better, though. He's taller and has black hair and nice eyes. But I guess he's already married."

Her last observation was delivered with a distinct measure of child-like resentment, and both women laughed.

"He's a little old for you, don't you think?" MacKenzie teased.

Sam shrugged, and bit into another slice of toast.

"If you like him so much, why don't you just tell him?" she asked, bringing the conversation neatly back around to Yates, who wished the ground would conveniently swallow her alive.

"I can see we're going to need to give you a little fast-track introduction to the Girl Code," MacKenzie said.

"What's that?"

"I'll tell you later, but it involves keeping schtum about certain matters of the heart."

"Oh," Samantha said, wisely. "You mean because the one over there doesn't know Mel likes him?"

Yates wondered if it were possible to die from acute embarrassment, and was almost relieved when Lowerson arrived, effectively putting an end to the conversation which had revolved exclusively around him.

"Hello," he said, sliding into a chair beside Samantha. "I'm Jack."

"So that's your name," she said enigmatically, earning herself two hard stares from the other women at the table.

CHAPTER 7

On the marina at St Peter's Wharf, on the banks of the River Tyne, Fred Marsons was not having a successful morning. In fact, it would be fair to say he was not having a successful year, nor a successful life, by many standards. He was a man of forty-seven but could easily pass for twenty years older, thanks to a life marred by hard drink and drugs. Those vices had cost him all he held dear: his family, his friends, his health, his home, and every job he'd ever had. He had no fixed address, had few of his own teeth, and his jaw had partially eroded, leaving him with a perpetual hangdog expression he could do nothing to change.

Many well-intentioned people had tried to help him claw back his identity over the years but, in truth, he hardly remembered the man he had once been. Young Fred used to like playing football, he remembered, and had loved a girl called Alison. They'd had a child, whom he hadn't seen in more than twenty years. People didn't understand how he could have let it happen, why he had fallen so far or how he could put his addiction before his own kin.

The same questions, every time, from different mouths.

Because it was a sickness, he'd tell them, that's why. A disease that wormed its way into the soul and fed off the weakness it found there. It made a mockery of the pain and suffering he locked away in the depths of his heart and numbed it all, so he could pretend it wasn't there, but it was. It festered away, rotting his mind. He knew all about it, understood his own reasons for poisoning his body, all the whys and wherefores, but he was too far gone to care. Even thinking about how bad it was made him hanker for the next hit.

"C'mon lad," he mumbled to the dog, who loped alongside him as he shuffled towards the large dumpsters on the far side of the marina.

He happened to know that the Council had scaled back their collections and were not due to empty the big ones until the end of the day. If he was lucky, he might find something worth saving. On the other hand, the weather was warm, which did not bode well for the task that lay ahead.

"Stay," he told the mutt, who plonked his bum down on the tarmac.

With considerable effort, Fred heaved the metal lid upward and swore volubly when he discovered the smell was even worse than he'd expected.

Stoically, he set an old plastic crate on the ground which he planned to use as a step to propel himself up and over the side. He retched a few times and spat the stench from his mouth as he drew closer and the odour grew even more potent. It was like mouldy fruit and something else...something meaty.

Fred curled his gnarled fingers around the rim of the dumpster and boosted himself up, intending to hoist himself over the edge. He never made it that far because, as soon as his chin rose above the rim, he spotted the cause of the foul smell.

The body lay in a bloodied heap atop a mountain of rubbish, its arms and legs twisted like a rag doll and its face barely recognisable—but it wasn't that which caused Fred's arms to buckle and his grip to loosen, sending him crashing to the floor.

It was the maggots.

He'd never liked maggots.

* * *

While Fred Marsons vomited into the water at St Peter's Wharf, Samantha O'Neill stared mutinously at the unsuspecting woman from Social Services, who'd been dispatched from Head Office to assess her needs. Having tried and failed to achieve that goal for much of the morning, she'd appealed to Ryan for help.

"What's the problem?" he demanded, wearing the look of a man who had better things to do with his time than spend it running through the corridors of CID on a fool's errand.

"I told you before," Samantha hissed. "I only want to speak to *you*. And maybe Frank or Denise," she tagged on, thinking of the police couple who had shown her kindness without seeming to need much in return. "But definitely not *her*."

The look she shot towards the woman was so venomous and mistrustful, Ryan could have laughed.

But he didn't.

"First of all, we don't say 'her' or 'she'. This is *Mrs Carter* and she's here to help. Listen to me, Sam. If you want me to take your report seriously, we have to play by the rules. That includes making sure you have somebody here to take care of your interests. You need an appropriate adult to act as a guardian when we take a statement from you and, since you don't want me to call your father or anyone else you know, Mrs Carter has kindly agreed to help us out."

Samantha remained unconvinced.

This was how it started, she thought. Nice-looking men or women came along and said they 'just wanted to chat' and, the next thing you knew, they'd whisk you away to some hell-hole in suburbia to live with a foster family who already had children with names like 'Poppy' or 'Henry'.

She shuddered at the thought.

"I don't care what her name is," she insisted. "I don't trust anyone from the Council."

"Why don't you just have a seat over here," Mrs Carter said, a bit desperately. "We can have a nice chat."

Samantha sent Ryan a smug look, as if to say she had just been vindicated.

"Why can't Frank be the thing you said—the responsible adult?" she asked, and Ryan's eyes danced with mirth as he thought of the many responses that came to mind when answering that question, none of which he could say.

"He can't be the *appropriate* adult because he'll be taking your statement," he said. "DS Phillips and I will be acting in our formal roles. The law says you need somebody with you to make sure your rights are being respected and that we're acting in line with our duties and responsibilities when we take down what you tell us. That person needs to be someone who isn't with the police."

Sam's shoulders slumped, and she glanced again at the mousy-looking woman who appeared to have come to the station dressed entirely in beige.

"Fine," she conceded and, when she noticed Ryan's meaningful look, even found her manners. "Thank you for agreeing to be the appropriate adult, Mrs Carter."

He smiled.

"Let's get this show on the road, then."

CHAPTER 8

Samantha found herself seated in an uncomfortable foamy armchair inside the 'Family Room', which strongly resembled the waiting area of any GP or dental surgery in the land. Usually, it was the province of grieving families, and Ryan had taken no small amount of pleasure in clearing away the stacks of leaflets littering its low coffee table touting bereavement and funeral services, alongside 'healing yoga' and acupuncture. Stretching and whale music were all very well and good, but they wouldn't bring a victim's family the peace that only justice could deliver.

With that in mind, he looked across at the child who was relying on him to find justice for her mother and found himself wondering whether it would be a stretch too far, this time.

Not if he could help it.

"Here you go," he murmured, and handed her a mug of hot chocolate. It was a Vending Machine Special, but something was better than nothing.

"Your wife made a better one," she told him, with her usual forthrightness.

"She makes most things better," Ryan agreed. "Are you ready to start?"

She nodded, and he seated himself in one of the chairs beside Phillips. The woman from Social Services was already making extensive notes from her position next to Samantha and was using a pen emblazoned with the slogan 'I am PAWfect' alongside a picture of a fluffy white cat, which he tried his best to ignore.

Ryan recited the date, time and names of those present for the camera, which had been set up on a tripod in the corner to record the interview.

"Now, before we begin, I need to make sure you understand that it's very important you tell us the whole truth, Sam. Do you understand what I mean?"

"Yeah, you mean I'm not supposed to lie."

Ryan nodded.

"I won't," she told him. "I'm just going to tell you what I remember."

"Alright then," he said. "We can also stop at any time. If you need to take a break, use the loo or have a drink of water, just say so, it's no problem. Okay?"

She gave him a hesitant smile and blushed slightly because he'd said the word 'loo'. It seemed incongruous coming from a man like him.

"Okay," she nodded.

"Great," Ryan said. "In that case, let's start at the beginning. What prompted you to come to my house on Sunday?"

Sam found that, when it came down to it, her mouth was suddenly dry. She took a hasty sip of her drink, scalding her tongue in the process.

"I was mucking out Pegasus' stall on Saturday afternoon," she began. "He's one of the horses in my family's circus."

"O'Neill's?" Ryan asked, for the benefit of the tape.

"Yeah, that's the one. Anyway, I turned on the radio to listen to some music and suddenly I felt a bit weird. My head started to hurt, and I felt sick, like I was going to throw up or something. I was going to turn the radio off again, but that's when it happened."

"When what happened?"

"I remembered," she said, softly. "It was kind of like watching a movie. I could see my mum beside the sink in our caravan, except it was years ago. Anyway, she was listening to the radio and I think it was the same station."

She paused, squeezing her eyes shut.

"Yes, it was the same station," she repeated. "I remember the jingle."

"Which one?" Phillips asked, looking up from where he was taking a careful record of what she told them.

"The one from Tyne Radio," she replied. "There's a kind of jingle and then the presenter says, 'This is Tyne Radio'."

She hummed a couple of bars, and Phillips recognised the jingle straight away; they'd listened to it on the car radio as he and Denise had brought her to CID Headquarters that morning. It must have been awful for the girl to hear it, but she hadn't breathed a word. He'd assumed she was pale because of something like car sickness, or the stress of having to make a statement at the police station, but instead, the radio had triggered the worst memory of her young life and he'd been to blame for it. The knowledge left him feeling guilty and oddly bereft.

He looked back down at the notepad on his lap.

"So, you remember your mum was beside the sink, listening to the radio," Ryan continued, steering Samantha back to the story. "What else?"

She licked her lips.

"I was in my cot or maybe a play pen," she said. "I'm pretty sure, because I remember the wooden slats. I could only see what was happening through them."

Ryan nodded.

"You were in the kitchen?"

"It's the same caravan we have now. There's a little kitchen area, with a built-in table on one side and a sofa on the other," she explained, and thought of how different it was to Ryan's stone-built house, or Phillips' comfortable semi. She looked between them but found only quiet patience reflected in both pairs of eyes.

"It's open-plan," she said. "From what I can remember, the play pen must have been right in front of the sofa. I can draw a picture, if you like."

Ryan smiled.

"Thanks, maybe we can do that later. You were saying your mum was at the sink doing the dishes and listening to the radio. Do you remember what happened next?"

"The door opened," she whispered, and her face paled as she forced herself to think of it. "I remember the monster came inside. It had white hands."

Phillips looked up at that.

"When you say, 'white hands', do you mean the skin colour or that they were wearing gloves?"

Sam screwed up her face in a monumental effort to recall the image.

"I—I'm sorry, I'm not sure," she said, miserably.

"It's okay, pet," he said. "Just tell us what you can."

She took another sip of the hot chocolate.

"It's all a bit blurry, but I know they were fighting. At first, it was just words—then I think it got worse. Something crashed, maybe one of the plates beside the sink. Then the words stopped. It was just the music and a kind of gurgling sound…"

"Do you need to stop?" Mrs Carter asked gently.

Her stomach was starting to heave, the memory churning like acid, but Samantha shook her head. It needed to be told.

"The—the white hands were around her neck. My mum was tugging at them and choking, then they both fell to the floor and I could see her legs thrashing around, kicking out to try…to try and get away. I couldn't see her face and—and the radio kept playing, really loud—"

"Was it a man or a woman?" Ryan asked, very casually.

"Man," she answered instantly, then frowned. "At least…I-I thought it was, but I can't see the face. I'm sorry…"

She brushed away tears and Ryan handed her a box of tissues.

"No need to be sorry," he murmured. "We don't have to do this all in one go."

"I want to tell you," she insisted, and blew her nose loudly. "You don't understand. All my life, people have told me my mum was bad and that she never loved us. They told me she left to be with somebody else and that she's probably had other children, by now. And—and I believed them, until I remembered. I remembered it all."

Phillips swallowed a constriction in his throat and stared fixedly at the notepad on his lap.

"Ah, how about his height?" he asked, and if Ryan heard a catch to his friend's voice, he said nothing.

Samantha ignored the tissues and wiped the sleeve of her jumper beneath her nose, trying to remember.

"Um—they seemed really big, but I don't know if that's because everybody seems big when you're little," she said, miserably.

Ryan shook his head, but it was by no means a negative gesture. In a few short words, she had summarised an entire criminological textbook on the problems of eyewitness evidence, especially coming so long after the event. It was well established that, in the eyes of a victim, an aggressor was often perceived to be twice or three times the size they turned out to be in reality.

As soon as the thought crossed his mind, Ryan began to wonder what height Charlie O'Neill came in at.

"What happened after your mother and…the monster, fell to the floor?" he asked.

Samantha finished her drink and set it back on the table.

"I saw her hand lying there, on the floor," she said, and regretted the sickly-sweet liquid lining her stomach as she thought of it. "Her fingers were sort of curled up and she wasn't moving. Then, her hand was just…gone. I don't know where it went."

Ryan glanced towards Phillips, who pulled an eloquent face. It was an odd recollection, by any standard.

"You mean you can't remember what happened next?" he asked. "Did the monster take her out of the same door they came in?"

"No," Samantha said slowly. "I can't remember seeing anybody leave through the front door. My mum was there one minute and then just…gone."

Ryan wondered whether to put it down to the long passage of time.

"Did she have anything in her hand, Sam?"

She tried to visualise it, but her mind was shutting down, no longer willing to cooperate while it waged a battle to protect a young soul that had been through too much already.

"I can't remember."

Ryan sensed there wasn't much time left and turned to the question that was uppermost in his mind.

"Just one last question for today, Sam. Do you remember what your mum was wearing when all of this happened?"

She looked up at him and yawned, feeling exhausted all of a sudden.

"Um, yeah, she was wearing light blue jeans—really tight ones, all faded at the knees—and a pink top, a bit like the colour Frank was wearing, yesterday."

Phillips looked up and winked at her, to bring a smile.

"She had good taste," he said.

"Why do you want to know what she was wearing?" Sam asked, trying to see inside Ryan's mind.

"Just one of the routine questions we need to ask," he said breezily. "We'll probably need to ask you some more questions tomorrow, if that's alright?"

She nodded.

"Did I do okay?"

Ryan gave her one of his best smiles, the kind he reserved for special occasions.

"You're a very brave person," he said quietly, and the other two in the room nodded their agreement. "You're doing the right thing, Sam, reporting this to the police."

"Do you promise to find who did it?"

Rocky ground, Ryan thought. There were very few promises he could make, in his business.

"I can promise you I'll do everything in my power," he said, and meant it.

"We all will," Phillips added. "It's a scary thing, coming to a place like this, having to tell a hard story like that to an old codger and a handsome bloke like me."

He paused, waiting for her to laugh, and, when she did, the whole room brightened.

"What happens now?" she asked.

"We've sent off that DNA sample you gave us," Ryan said. "While we're waiting to hear back, we're going to go and speak to your dad and some of the other people at the circus."

She became tense.

"Are you going to tell him where I am?" she asked, urgently.

Ryan shook his head.

"No, for the present, we have agreed to treat you as a protected witness," he said, nodding towards the woman from Social Services. "We're going to start investigating."

"Where am I going to stay?"

"You're going to spend some time with Mrs Carter," Ryan said, and his tone brooked no argument. "She's going to talk to you about some special support services we have for people who have experienced traumatic events—"

"I'm not speaking to any quacks."

Phillips couldn't help the roar of appreciative laughter that burst from his mouth.

"They're highly trained people!" Mrs Carter protested. "Child psychologists, grief counsellors—"

Samantha looked unimpressed.

"Let's cross that bridge when we come to it," Ryan suggested, to avert any further argument.

* * *

A short while later, Mrs Carter took the girl for a late lunch at the infamous Pie Van, a mobile café known affectionately as 'cholesterol on wheels' to the police staff who were its main clientele. In the leftover silence, Ryan turned to his friend, who had been noticeably quiet during the interview.

"Everything alright?" he asked.

Phillips made a show of tucking his pen back into the breast pocket of his suit blazer, to buy himself a few seconds.

"Fine," he lied, then thought better of it. They'd known each other too long for him to fob Ryan off with social pleasantries. "We've just never had a case quite like this, before. Funny, after all these years, the job can still catch you off guard."

"We'll do our best for her, Frank, same as always."

"Aye, I know, but...she seems all on her own."

Ryan sighed inwardly.

"You can't save them all," he murmured and, in the next breath, realised he was a hypocrite. He lost sleep, trying to save people. He spent his days trying to avenge the dead, whose names and faces lived on in his deepest psyche, tormenting him.

"There must be hundreds—no, thousands, of kids who've seen things like that," Phillips said. "Children out in war-torn countries who see their parents blown to kingdom come, kids who go through...well, more than either of us ever had to."

"That's all true, but we haven't met them," Ryan said. "It's easy not to think about it until one comes and knocks on your door."

"And then eats you out of house and home," Phillips chuckled.

"I'm already used to that, with you around," Ryan grinned, and clapped his friend on the back. "Chin up."

Phillips drew in a deep breath and nodded.

"Aye," he said, and turned back to business. "What d'you make of what she said?"

"I think her account ticks two major boxes for us," Ryan said. "Firstly, she remembered what the victim was wearing. She said her mum was wearing light blue jeans and a pink t-shirt. Well, the body they found back in July 2011 was still clothed, and the pathology report lists a pair of light blue jeans and a pink t-shirt."

Phillips turned away to look out of the window. It overlooked the car park outside and, across the tarmac, he spotted the girl's red head bobbing up and down as she chatted to the bloke who ran the Pie Van.

"Too much coincidence," he murmured. "It has to be her mam."

Ryan nodded grimly.

"Secondly, her description of what happened to her mum is consistent with strangulation, which was listed as the cause of death," he continued. "The odds are stacking up in favour of this being a match."

"Are the DNA results in yet?" Phillips asked.

Ryan took a moment to check his messages, then shook his head.

"Nothing yet," he said. "They should be in by the end of the day but, while we're waiting, I think it's high time we paid her father a visit."

Phillips needed no further bidding.

"This should be interesting," he muttered.

CHAPTER 9

As the sun reached its highest point in the sky, Detective Constable Jack Lowerson steered his car eastward along Walker Road and through the old streets of Newcastle, with its rows of 1950s pre-fabs that had once housed the shipbuilders and miners who had made up the majority of the city's workforce. After those industries died, many of the communities were forgotten; fractured and laid to waste, like the skeleton yards which still lined that part of the river as it curled through the city towards the sea. But there was plenty of pride in these streets, and the kind of grit and determination no amount of money could buy.

The kind he'd been forced to learn, through hard experience.

"Penny for them," Yates asked, from her position in the passenger seat where she'd been covertly watching the emotions dance across his face.

Lowerson kept his eyes on the road.

"I wasn't thinking much," he said. "Just wondering what we'll find when we get down to the wharf."

The report had come in from the Control Room less than half an hour ago but the details had been scant; all they knew was that a body had been found inside a dumpster underneath one of the fancy apartment blocks lining St Peter's Wharf, an area that had been redeveloped and now attracted yuppies, investors and high-rollers who liked to moor their boats in its marina.

"I can hardly wait," Yates joked, as he parked the car along one of the side streets near the water.

"Nobody said it would be a glamorous job," came the surly rejoinder.

Yates stared at him for a long moment, wondering how long it would take for the 'old' Jack to return. He'd been through hell and back, there was no denying it, but life moved on and it was time he did, too. If he would only take the trouble to ask, she might have told him that she'd been through her own share of problems, and they could have helped one another.

Instead, he seemed content to wallow in his own self-pity.

"You know, it wouldn't hurt you to crack a smile, sometimes," she snapped. "The job's hard enough without having to partner up with Mr Miserable, day in and day out."

With that, she slammed out of the car and began to make her way down to the marina, which had been cordoned off by the first responders.

Lowerson watched the sunshine bouncing off her hair as she stormed down the street and started to tell himself that she was out of line talking to him like that, but innate honesty gave him pause.

He could have made an effort to smile more often.

He caught his reflection in the rear-view mirror and saw a man in his early thirties with an old man's eyes. On the surface, he looked just the same, but inside…inside was hollowed out, nothing but a shell of the person he used to be.

Maybe she was right.

It was time to come back to life.

* * *

On the other side of town, Ryan and Phillips made their way through the affluent streets of Jesmond, with its sprawling Victorian villas and leafy parks, towards a large area of pastoral land known as the 'Town Moor'. It comprised over a thousand acres of common land with suburbs on all sides: Spital Tongues and the city centre in the south, Gosforth in the north, Kenton Bar in the west, and Jesmond to the east. A border of trees lined the edge of each field before it met the road, but it was mostly open land to allow the Freemen of Newcastle to graze their cattle if they wished.

"I remember coming to The Hoppings when I was a nipper," Phillips remarked, as the circus came into view.

Ryan knew it was a famous funfair and a local institution in these parts, but he had never been.

"The Hoppings arrives at the end of June, doesn't it'?" he said, and indicated to turn, following signs for 'CIRCUS PARKING'.

Phillips nodded.

"Aye, the fair comes during the last week in June. The circus is separate, and it used to come at the beginning of the month," he said. "I wonder why it stopped."

Ryan navigated his car across tufts of bumpy grass and thought back to what Samantha had told them.

"If we're right and, more importantly, if Sam is right, her mother died eight years ago when the circus was visiting Newcastle," he said. "She also told us the circus hadn't been back since then, so maybe therein lies the answer."

Phillips made a rumbling sound of agreement.

"Maybe somebody didn't want to come back, for fear of raking up trouble with the law."

"Or maybe they didn't want to jog a little girl's memory," Ryan murmured, peering through the windscreen at a sea of tarpaulin tents decorated in cheerful shades of yellow, blue and red. From the outside, the circus looked jovial, its colourful flags beckoning people to come and leave their cares behind. But it was the inside that concerned him, the grey underbelly nobody could see.

"Come on," he said. "Let's go and find out what made the circus roll back into town after all these years."

* * *

They had arrived before the circus opened to the public, which they quickly understood to be a blessing in disguise, given the scale of things on the ground. Temporary structures of all kinds had been organised in a simple formation, with the main arena—the Big Top—in the centre, with ten smaller tents surrounding it offering old-fashioned curiosities including a hall of mirrors and a tarot tent run by somebody called 'Psychic Sabina', whose name was painted in large lettering on the front.

Two boys were vigorously polishing the brasswork of a vintage carousel to a golden shine, and a Ferris wheel was juddering into life. Food and drink stands were dotted here and there and, as they made their way from the designated parking area, Ryan and Phillips could see a line of twenty or so caravans and motorhomes set back from the rest, which they judged to be the living quarters of those who worked for and travelled with the circus.

"Posh caravans," Phillips said with a low whistle. "Y' know, I was thinking about getting one and taking Denise for a tour around the Highlands and Islands, next summer. Arran's meant to be beautiful."

He pointed out a particularly swanky-looking number in jet-black, with a racing-green stripe. Having grown up loving his caravan holidays as a child, Phillips knew a good one when he saw it.

"Why don't you just stay at a B&B?" Ryan suggested, never having stayed in a caravan in his life. "Wouldn't it be cheaper and less hassle?"

Phillips gave him a pitying look.

"You don't understand," he said. "It's all part of the *experience*."

"And trying to reverse a caravan along a narrow country lane is part of the experience, is it?"

"All part of the fun," Phillips assured him, and nearly broke out in a sweat just thinking about it. He'd ask Denise to do the tricky manoeuvres, he decided. She was a far superior driver, but would it take some convincing for her to forego a spa hotel in favour of an apartment on wheels.

That was a challenge for another day.

"We're not open yet!"

The topic of caravanning was interrupted by a loud shout, and they both turned in reflex. A man of around Ryan's age loped across the grass towards them dressed entirely in yellow and white, bearing a strong resemblance to a giraffe running over the plains of Africa.

"Sorry," he said, as he drew near. "We're not open yet. The first show isn't until four-thirty, but the gates open at three-thirty if you want to get seated or have a go on the coconut shy."

Ryan checked his watch, which told him it was a little after two.

"Thanks," he said. "Actually, we're here to speak to Charles O'Neill. Do you know where we can find him?"

Duke gave them both a searching look. They looked like they could handle themselves, especially the older one, but the taller one had 'police' written all over him.

"What d'you need to speak to him about?"

Ryan retrieved his warrant card and held it out for inspection.

"I'm Detective Chief Inspector Ryan and this is Detective Sergeant Frank Phillips. We're conducting some enquiries Mr O'Neill might be able to help us with."

They watched the man's pupils widen, then he ran an agitated hand through his messy brown hair.

"Um, right. Okay. Charlie's in the Big Top for a rehearsal. Shall I go and get him?"

"What's your name, son?" Phillips asked, before he could run off to warn anybody of their arrival.

"Duke."

"Have you got a last name, Duke?"

"O'Neill."

Ryan's ears pricked up.

"We understood Charles O'Neill to be the owner of the circus—what's your relationship?"

"Yeah, dad transferred it all to Charlie," Duke replied, without any hint of malice. "He's better at managing everything."

"You're brothers, then?"

"Yeah, he's older, by three minutes."

Which meant that Duke was Samantha's uncle, Ryan thought, and she'd told him there was nobody else she could turn to.

Interesting.

By now, Duke was skipping from foot to foot in his eagerness to get away, an action made all the more ridiculous thanks to the garish polyester yellow and white clown suit he was wearing. It came complete with a giant flower lapel that squirted water, big red boots, pristine white gloves, and a neon green wig he'd tucked underneath his arm.

They assumed it was too early for the stage make-up and giant red nose.

"Why don't you lead the way?" Ryan said, gesturing him forward.

"Right, yeah. Let me just—"

"So, it must be a hard job, trying to make people laugh all the time?" Phillips asked, overriding him with a gentle hand on his lower back as they walked towards the Big Top.

Duke shrugged his skinny shoulders.

"Um, yeah, I s'pose."

Phillips tried again.

"What made you choose that over becoming Dangerous Duke, the cannonball guy?" he asked, with a friendly wink.

That elicited a short laugh.

"Actually, I wanted to be an acrobat," he admitted, a little sheepishly. "But dad didn't think…ah, well, it was a long training course and I was needed here, to help out."

Why d'you want to prance about like a monkey? Is that what you are, boy? his father had said. *Are you a monkey? Why can't you be more like your brother?*

Duke was walking quickly across the grass, so Ryan deliberately slowed his own stride to counteract it.

"I suppose you know your brother's wife, Esmerelda?" he asked, catching the man off guard.

Duke tripped over a tuft of grass, though whether it was thanks to his over-large shoes or a sense of disquiet, they couldn't tell.

"Why do you want to know about Esme?" he asked.

"You know her, then?" Ryan asked, as they approached a side entrance to the Big Top. It consisted of a hidden flap in the tarpaulin, cleverly concealed at the seams so he might never have seen it.

"Yeah, I knew her," Duke muttered.

With that, he threw back the tarpaulin and ushered them into another world.

CHAPTER 10

Back at St Peter's Wharf, Lowerson and Yates stood over the body of what had once been a man. The forensic team had beaten them to it, setting up a large protective tent and photographing the remains *in situ* before carefully transferring the body onto a wide sheet of thick black plastic which would, they knew, become a kind of shroud when it was taken to the mortuary.

In the early days, Lowerson might have admitted to feeling slightly nauseated by the sight of a body in decay, particularly when it had been left alongside the usual day-to-day household detritus that people threw away for very good reason.

However, he prided himself on having overcome such paltry complaints.

As if to contradict that assertion, his stomach gave a violent lurch, and, when he glanced at Yates' stony profile, he was mortified to see that she looked cool and calm by comparison.

"Male, approximately forty years old. Looks like he suffered severe head trauma and multiple lacerations to the face and torso," she said, with as much detachment as she could muster. "Hard to tell the extent of the damage or how long it's been out here but, given the concentrated areas of insect infestation—"

Lowerson took a couple of deep breaths through his teeth.

"It's probably a gangland kill."

Yates ran her eyes over the body and wondered how he could tell.

"You mean because it was dumped in the bin?"

"Nah, because somebody's taken the tips of his fingers," Lowerson said, eyeing the bloodied stumps that were blooming in shades of yellow and green. "They do that to make it harder for us to identify the body. Same reason his face is messed up. I bet we don't find any wallet or keys, either."

Yates looked back down at the body.

"Huh," she said, feeling disappointed she hadn't seen it for herself. "I guess there's always something new to learn."

"Same goes for all of us," he said, and broke into a smile as Faulkner approached them dressed in his perennial garb of white polypropylene overalls, hood and mask, which he tugged down briefly to greet them.

"Hi Jack, Mel," he nodded to them both. "What've we got here, then?"

"You tell us," Lowerson said, and took a strategic step further away. "But it looks to me like an execution kill."

Faulkner nodded.

"Yeah, I'm no pathologist, but I'd say you've got at least ten major stab wounds there, alongside blunt head trauma. I'd also put money on the poor bloke having died elsewhere, before being transferred to the bin."

"How can you tell?" Yates asked, with genuine curiosity. "Not enough blood?"

Faulkner nodded.

"Yeah, wounds of that kind would normally come with significant blood loss, whereas there's hardly any blood inside the dumpster or anywhere around it. I've got the team going over the surrounding area now, so maybe we'll get lucky and find something useful."

"Anything so far?" Lowerson asked. "Any personal belongings?"

The body had been found completely naked, except for a pair of soiled black Y-fronts. It was a long shot, but there was a chance the CSIs might have stumbled across a discarded wallet amongst the assortment of old cardboard boxes and food waste.

"No such luck, I'm afraid," Faulkner said, apologetically. "It'll take a while longer to finish going over the area here, so you never know. I'll keep you posted."

They thanked the Senior Crime Scene Investigator and then stepped outside the forensic tent, breathing deeply of the fresh air outside.

"Thank God," Lowerson muttered. "It smelled awful in there. Like…"

"Over-ripe pumpkins and charcuterie meat," Yates decided. "If they were spread over a dead body."

His nose wrinkled.

"Yates, did anybody ever tell you that you have an elegant turn of phrase?"

She smiled.

"All the time, Jack. You're just a bit late to the party."

* * *

Back at CID Headquarters, the temporary truce Ryan had negotiated between Samantha and her social worker had collapsed in spectacular fashion during his absence.

"I'm not going!"

Samantha positioned herself in the corner of Chief Constable Morrison's office, between an overstuffed bookcase and a plant stand which held a fern that had seen better days. It would have been better to be near the door or the long window on the other side of the room, but both potential exits were blocked by Mrs Carter and DI MacKenzie, respectively. The Chief Constable remained seated at her desk, attempting to deploy the kind of parental tone she'd heard mothers and fathers use to restore order to a volatile situation in the playground.

"I'm sorry, Samantha, but the rules are clear—"

"Yeah, well, your rules are stupid," the girl said. "I don't understand why I have to go and stay with some dodgy family in the middle of nowhere—"

"They're lovely people, and they live in Gosforth," Mrs Carter said, in an exasperated tone. "They already have a couple of kids you might like to play with. They're called Freddie and Myla—"

"I knew it," Samantha intoned.

"—and they'll keep you safe while the investigation is ongoing."

Sam looked across at the woman from Social Services and knew that she was only doing her job. She probably signed up to help disadvantaged people straight out of university, thinking she'd make a difference to the world. Maybe she did, sometimes. Or maybe she just got a kick out of people telling her what a good person she was, doing such a hard job.

But this wasn't about her not having any clothes to wear or food to eat, or any of that other stuff. It was about finding out which one of the people she'd grown up with was responsible for murder. She wanted to know which of them had lied to her all these years and, even worse, smeared her mother's memory.

This was about *betrayal*; something Mrs Carter apparently knew nothing about, with her cat pens and her beige jumpers.

"Why can't I stay with Frank and Denise?" she asked.

Morrison sighed heavily.

"We've already been through this, Sam. It's inappropriate for you to stay with police officers, especially those involved in the investigation. There are short-term foster families ready and willing to help."

Sam was incredulous.

"How can it be wrong to stay with *police officers*?" she demanded. "I thought the police were fully vetted and checked as part of their training and stuff? If it isn't safe to stay with them, it doesn't say much for the service, does it?"

The three women looked amongst themselves in varying degrees of shock. Morrison was dumbfounded, Mrs Carter was frustrated and MacKenzie…

MacKenzie was impressed.

In a couple of sentences, Samantha had undermined the police bureaucracy and found its tender spot, with a bold childish logic that was hard to refute. All the same, rules were in place for a reason, and it would be all too easy to grow attached to the little cat currently spitting and snarling in the corner.

"The Chief Constable's right," she said quietly, and moved closer to the girl before leaning down so they could talk eye to eye. The action put pressure on her bad leg, but MacKenzie ignored the pain, deeming a little girl's wellbeing to be much more important.

"I don't have the clearance to look after you, neither does DS Phillips. There are protocols to follow, while we concentrate on finding out what happened to your mum."

MacKenzie had a kind, persuasive manner that worked more than nine times out of ten with difficult members of the general public, but not today, apparently.

"I want to speak to Ryan," Samantha demanded. "I want to hear what he has to say."

Morrison wondered whether she ought to laugh or cry about the fact that the word of a single man would outweigh three equally well-qualified women in the eyes of this little girl, then she realised the men in her family circle had probably taught her to respect male authority.

Perhaps, during her time with them, she'd come to respect female authority, too.

"Ryan isn't here," she said firmly. "Even if he were, he would agree that this is the proper course of action. A foster home is the safest place for you at the moment, unless you want to go back to your father?"

That was an effective threat, as far as it went, but the girl had another weapon up her sleeve.

"If you force me to go to a foster home, I'll run away," she said, very softly. "*I mean it.* You won't ever know where I've gone."

MacKenzie heard total resolve in the girl's voice and felt her heart begin to hammer against her chest.

"Ma'am, could I have a word in private?" she asked, turning to Morrison.

"No, I think we've spent more than enough time talking about this."

"Ma'am, I believe the witness may be a flight risk," MacKenzie tried again. "If she absconds from the foster home, she'll be in danger."

"The *witness* is a ten-year-old girl," Morrison snapped. "The protocol is clear in situations like these. You know that, Denise."

She looked past MacKenzie and gave a short nod towards Mrs Carter, who pasted a condescending look on her face.

"I know it can be hard to stay objective," she crooned, patting MacKenzie's arm in a manner that set her teeth on edge. "But, don't worry, she'll be *very* safe with us."

She turned back to Samantha.

"Come on, missy. Let's go."

CHAPTER 11

Ryan and Phillips followed Duke O'Neill inside the Big Top, which was the centrepiece of *O'Neill's Circus*. They walked along a wide inner corridor that followed the curve of the enormous red-and-white-striped tent. The PVC-coated tarpaulin of the tent provided the outer wall on one side, whilst the back of four large sections of tiered seating provided the other.

"How many exits are there?" Ryan asked, as they dipped inside.

"Apart from the main entrance, there are three side exits," Duke explained. "We just came through Exit B. There's one exit for each section of seating, so it helps with crowd management and keeps the Health and Safety Officer happy, otherwise everyone would try to push through the main entrance if there's an emergency."

He hesitated, as if unsure which way to go.

"Let's go this way," he decided.

The stacks of tiered seating had been set up to face the central arena in four sections marked 'A' to 'D'. As they made their way along the corridor, they could see that the back of the steel scaffolding rose well above ten metres and disappeared up into the roof of the tent to maximise audience capacity. A series of lights shone at intervals along the corridor, guiding the way as their footsteps crunched softly over the grass floor. At that time of day, daylight still leaked through the edges of the tent's outer wall but, after dark, they imagined it would be poorly lit.

"Must be able to fit a thousand people in here," Ryan remarked, rapidly re-assessing any quaint notions he might have held about the scale of the operation—the space was more akin to a serious concert arena than a country fair.

Duke shrugged.

"Yeah, we can seat up to eighteen-hundred," he said, and carried on striding along the corridor, his banana-yellow outfit serving as a beacon through the relative gloom. "It's usually a sell-out show."

Suddenly, an enormous explosion rocked the tent, the sound bouncing around the walls like a pinball.

"What the—?" Phillips jumped.

"It's just part of the rehearsal," Duke told him. "Come and see."

When they reached the end of Section B, he turned right and led them along a smaller gangway separating that section of seating from the next. As they moved out of the shadows, the central arena came into view, bright spotlights illuminating it with powerful beams shining down from the uppermost scaffolding. Row upon row of empty seats provided the backdrop to a circular arena in the middle of the tent, around which a track had been etched out and covered with wood shavings and where, they assumed, horses would run. Overhead, sleek men and women dressed in old-style leotards swung through the air, their flight between the high swings timed to perfection so that they dodged a towering burst of flame that erupted from a giant flame-thrower positioned on the floor of the arena below. A wide net had been set up as a safety precaution, but Ryan and Phillips barely noticed it; their eyes drawn instead to the dance being played out above their heads.

"Amazing, isn't it?"

Duke stood beside them to watch the end of the acrobatic display. He'd seen it countless times, but it never grew old.

"It's incredible," Ryan murmured, but dragged his eyes away to scan the surrounding area through force of habit.

The main structure of the tent appeared to be supported by four enormous poles which, on closer inspection, consisted of two pairs connected by a bar at the top. These poles provided the base units for the rest of the show, and extensive high-level rigging had been erected around them including a long walkway and several smaller platforms. He watched as one of the male acrobats swung back up to one such platform and a pair of arms flashed out of the darkness to catch the swing, allowing the acrobat to dismount in safety.

"Look at that," Phillips nudged his friend, and they watched a woman on a unicycle make her way along a tightrope, almost overbalancing before she corrected herself at the last moment.

"You almost fell on your arse!" somebody bellowed, taking the words out of his mouth.

They scanned the arena until their eyes fell on a man standing in the centre, decked out in a red dress coat and tight black trousers tucked into polished black riding boots. He held a loudspeaker in his hand and Ryan knew instinctively that this was the man they were looking for.

The ringmaster.

"Marco! You were a couple of seconds out on that last turn," Charlie called up to the rooftop. "Keep on like that and you'll end up in the net!"

A stream of what sounded like French or Italian profanities wafted down from the ceiling.

Charlie laughed to himself and was about to turn away when his keen eye spotted the three spectators standing in the aisle. As Duke had done, he made a lightning-quick assessment of Ryan and Phillips, coming to similar conclusions.

"Take a five-minute break!" he called out to the performers, and stepped into the epicentre of the arena, where the spotlight circled him in a blazing halo of white light. If the police had come for him, they'd have to come all the way.

They were on his turf now.

* * *

Since he showed no intention of coming across to greet them, Ryan and Phillips made their way towards the owner of *O'Neill's Circus* via a safety gate at the end of the gangway. Duke lolloped behind them, his clown feet squeaking loudly as he went.

"Charlie, this is Detective Chief Inspector Ryan and Detective Sergeant Phillips," he said, as they stepped beneath the blazing lights. "They want to talk to you."

At first glance, the brothers appeared similar. They were both around average height with wavy, mid-brown hair, but that's where the similarities ended. Where Duke was verging on thin, Charlie had a hard, muscular physique. His skin was tanned and tattooed down to his wrists, whereas his brother was pale and freckled. They both had greenish-brown eyes, but only one set was sharp and calculating.

"Oh yeah?" Charlie said, and reached inside the breast pocket of his immaculate red coat for a packet of cigarettes. "What about?"

Phillips watched him retrieve a cigarette and had a fleeting sensory memory of when he used to smoke, too. His fingers began to twitch, so he shoved them inside the pockets of his trousers and reminded himself sternly about things like emphysema and, even more terrifying, what MacKenzie would say if she caught so much as a whiff of smoke on his breath.

"We're from Northumbria CID," Ryan was saying, and watched the brothers' faces for any reaction.

There was none.

"Nobody's died that I know of," Charlie said, with a negligent shrug. "We only got here on Friday night, so we wouldn't know what's been happening around these parts. Would we?"

He turned to his brother, who shook his head vigorously in agreement.

"No—no idea."

Ryan smiled thinly.

"We'd like to ask you some questions regarding Esmerelda O'Neill," he said. "We understand you were married in June of 2008, here in Newcastle. Is that correct?"

Charlie's face was frozen in surprise, the name conjuring up an icy blast from the past. He deliberately relaxed his muscles again and took a long drag of his cigarette before answering.

"Yeah, I married her," he said, then let out a harsh laugh. "She's got herself in trouble with the law, has she? Well, she better not be thinking she can palm anything off on *me*," he growled, jerking a thumb towards his chest. "That privilege ended when she walked out the door, eight years ago."

He remembered it. He remembered everything.

"Can you tell us when you last saw Mrs O'Neill?" Ryan asked, deciding not to mention murder, since the penny didn't seem to have dropped for either man. Besides, he hadn't received DNA confirmation of a match between Samantha and the unidentified female, so it was best to play his cards close to his chest for the time being.

Charlie dropped his cigarette to the floor and ground it out with more force than necessary.

"Look, why d'you want to know?" he asked, making no attempt to hide his irritation.

When no answer was forthcoming, he shook his head.

"The last time I saw Esme was on 3rd June 2011. It was a Friday and she was in the caravan seeing to the baby. I left in the morning to look over the rigging and, a few hours later, Duke came running up to tell me somebody'd found the baby alone in the caravan, bawling her eyes out. That's the last any of us saw of her and, far as I'm concerned, a cat's a better wife than she was."

His brother put a hand on his shoulder in silent support, but Charlie shrugged it off with an angry jerk.

"I don't know where she is now, and I don't care," he continued, thumbing another cigarette from the packet.

"Did you ever hear from your wife again? Do you know where she went?" Phillips asked.

"Yeah, I know," Charlie sneered, and the flame from his lighter danced in his eyes. "She went off with some bloke. She took a bag of clothes with her and left a bit of paper telling me she'd found someone who'd treat her like a bloody princess."

He blew out a stream of smoke and dared them to question it.

"Have you heard from your wife at all, since then? Did you make any efforts to contact her?" Ryan asked.

"Why would I want to chase after her?" Charlie roared. "Esme didn't give a shit about us, so why would I want to sit down and talk to her about it? I'm well shot of her."

"Did you keep the note she left you?" Ryan refused to be swayed by the outburst.

"I got rid of it, along with rest of her junk," Charlie said, bitterly. "Look, you're wasting your time over Esme. If she's gone missing, it's probably because she's run off with the next mug and they're living the life down on the Costa del Sol."

Phillips had been listening carefully and came to the conclusion that Charlie O'Neill was an outstanding showman. To all the world, he was the injured party; a man abandoned by a wife who was flighty and unreliable. But, throughout their conversation, not once had he mentioned that his ten-year-old daughter had run away. For all he knew, Samantha might have been kidnapped—or much worse.

A wave of protective feeling washed over him for the little girl, and he looked at her father with renewed contempt.

"Didn't you think to call the police, when your wife went missing?" Phillips asked, pointedly.

Charlie shook his head.

"I keep telling you, Esme didn't go missing; she just had a better offer."

Duke had been standing quietly by his brother's side, but now he spoke up.

"They're CID, Charlie," he murmured. "They must think something's happened to her."

Ryan had been occupied checking a recent e-mail from the forensics team on his smart phone. A couple of lines from Tom Faulkner confirmed what they already suspected: the DNA belonging to the unidentified female was a match to Samantha's. He couldn't say it was good news—knowing that the little girl had lost her mother in the worst possible circumstances could never be a cause for celebration.

But it did mean he could re-open the murder investigation with renewed vigour.

"Well?" Charlie demanded. "Is he right?"

Ryan slid the phone into the back pocket of his jeans and, when he looked up, his eyes were flat and cold.

"I apologise if I was unclear," he said. "As her next of kin, we have a duty to inform you that the body of Esmerelda O'Neill has recently been identified. It was discovered in July of 2011, but we were unable to make a positive identification at the time. I'm sorry for your loss," he added, as a matter of good practice. Charlie O'Neill didn't seem the type to shed many tears over the news, but you could never tell.

"We've re-opened the investigation into her murder, and we'd appreciate your co-operation. Both of you," he added, with a nod for Duke, whose face quivered beneath the scrutiny.

"I can't believe it," he breathed. "I never thought—is she really dead?"

"Of course, she is. He said as much, didn't he?" Charlie bit out.

Ryan and Phillips exchanged a glance, while Duke began to stammer an apology.

"S-sorry, Charlie. This must be awful for you—"

"How do you know it was her?" Charlie asked, cutting across his brother. "How come you've only just identified some woman as being Esme, if the body was found back in 2011?"

Phillips looked at the man with barely concealed dislike. Even if they believed his story that he had spent the last eight years thinking his wife had simply been unfaithful, the news that she had been murdered ought to have softened his hatred for the dead woman.

Instead, Charlie appeared completely unmoved.

"Sometimes, identification can be difficult if a victim is found without any personal possessions or if their DNA isn't already on our database. Your wife had no criminal record, Mr O'Neill, so we had no profile to cross-check when her body was found. It might have helped if she'd been reported as a missing person," Ryan said, without rancour.

"I already *told* you, I thought she'd run off with some bloke," Charlie bit out, and then a thought struck him. "Hang about, if you didn't have Esme's DNA, how come you managed to identify her now? I haven't seen any *Crimewatch* appeals with Esme's picture, and I've never had a copper knocking on my door asking me to come and identify any bodies."

Ryan told himself to tread carefully. He couldn't lie, but Samantha was in protective custody and one misstep could put her in danger, if they weren't careful.

"Unfortunately, by the time Esme's body was discovered, it was in an advanced stage of decomposition and we were no longer able to identify her through photographic methods," he replied. "Thankfully, we were able to trace a DNA connection."

Charlie looked at Ryan with sharp eyes. His general disposition was to believe he could take anyone, be they man, woman or beast. At first glance, this one had 'toff' written all over him, from his expensive brown suede boots to his fancy haircut. He was athletic but not a fighter—not like the shorter one, who looked as though he'd gone a round or two. All the same, appearances could be deceptive. There was a look behind Ryan's glacier-blue eyes, like a volcano that was dormant but liable to erupt at any moment.

There was something else, too, and it struck Charlie like a thunderbolt.

He knew where Samantha was.

"Where's my daughter?" he snarled, balling his hands into fists. "Where the hell is she?"

Ryan's face didn't alter. O'Neill was no fool; it was only a matter of time before he put two and two together and came up with the right answer. There was only one person whose DNA they could possibly have used to make the match.

"She's safe," he replied, simply.

Charlie found himself caught between an inclination to strike out and a fatalistic sense that there was nothing he could do to change a course of events that was already in motion. Behind them, circus staff were starting to gather, their chatter rising to a low hum that buzzed in his ears like flies.

"Where did you find her?" he asked.

Ryan shook his head.

"She found us."

"Why?" Duke asked, plaintively. "Why would she go to you? Why wouldn't she want to stay here?"

"You tell us," Phillips replied, and the other man fell silent.

Charlie's eyes swept over the figures standing around the arena chatting, smoking, and casting curious glances towards the four men beneath the spotlight. He'd chosen an exposed position because he wanted his crew to know he was fearless when it came to dealings with the police, but now he wished they weren't crowding around like vultures, ready to pick at the scraps.

He flicked the stub of his cigarette away.

"I want my daughter back," he said, in an ominous tone. "I want her home within the hour or I'm making a complaint to your Chief Constable—or whatever useless jobsworth is taking up a chair down at the station."

Phillips felt his hackles rise.

"Samantha's under the care of Social Services and the police, now," he said.

He'd protect her with his own hands, if he had to.

"What for?" Charlie burst out, drawing interested looks from the gathering crowd. "What does she have to do with anything?"

"Her interests are being properly represented by a guardian, while the investigation into her mother's murder is ongoing," Ryan said, declining to comment further.

He would not discuss the details of an active investigation, especially not with the man who was his prime suspect.

"She doesn't need a guardian," Charlie stormed. "She's got her father."

"And an uncle," Duke added, with a rare show of bravery.

"Who didn't even report her missing," Phillips pointed out, taking the wind out of their sails.

"Now look, you little pr—" Charlie began, then checked himself. It was a sensitive moment in all their lives, and he couldn't afford to piss off the police. It was bad enough that word would get about that they'd visited him, today.

He wasn't looking forward to having that particular conversation, later.

"What's that, son?" Phillips said softly, cupping a hand to his ear. "I didn't quite catch it."

Duke put a restraining hand on his brother's arm.

"C'mon, Charlie. We need to get ready for the show. There's nothing you can do now, anyway—"

O'Neill threw off his brother's hand and pointed a finger in Phillips' face.

"I want her back by the end of the day. If Samantha isn't in her own bed by tonight, I'll kick up such a stink, you'll wish you'd never met her."

"I'll never wish that," Phillips murmured, after the man had stalked away.

* * *

Once the police left, the whispers started.

Esme was murdered.

Did you hear?

Esme was murdered.

News spread across the moor like wildfire, and those who had known her were caught between denial and shame. How they'd crowed about her, over the years. How the other women had cursed her name, after claiming to be her friend.

Those women were ashamed to think of it now; sickened to recall how little effort they'd made to help Samantha, a little girl who kept to the shadows and was easily forgotten. They'd been happy to ignore her, since she looked so like her mother.

The mother who'd been murdered.

But why wouldn't Sam come home? they wondered. *Why had she gone to the police?*

The circus crew lived by an unspoken code while they travelled the length and breadth of the country and beyond, bringing laughter and entertainment to the masses. Problems and disputes were solved within the community. Not everybody who sold candy floss or juggled apples was of travelling stock, but all members of the circus, whether young or old, knew it and abided by it.

Especially if their father was the ringmaster.

Sam had broken this cardinal rule and had placed her faith in outsiders. Worse still, the police.

What did she know?

They began to look at Charlie with fresh eyes. Their leader, the man they trusted, was under suspicion from more than one quarter and they started to wonder if there was a grain of truth in it.

While they watched him, O'Neill went about his business the same as before. He felt their eyes boring into the side of his face, like hot irons searing into his skull.

And while they thought of him, he thought of Esme.

Esme.

What Samantha had done enraged him, the betrayal slicing like a knife. What had prompted her to forget all she'd ever learned, to flout every rule, and seek out the pigs?

What did she know?

CHAPTER 12

"Are you hungry?"

In the large, open-plan office belonging to the men and women of CID, Lowerson looked up from his desk for long enough to shake his head at Yates.

"Nah, I wolfed down a cheese sandwich earlier," he said, distractedly. "You go ahead."

"Um, okay. I was thinking about having a drink after work, since it's…Monday," she finished, lamely. "Want to join me?"

"I'm doing Dry June," he replied. "No alcohol for the whole month, I'm afraid."

She pulled a face and wondered why she liked this man. He was an uptight, conservative, vegetarian teetotaller, who wore shiny suits and too much hair gel. She also strongly suspected he whitened his teeth on the regular.

Nothing like Ryan, who probably laughed in the face of hair gel.

He was married, as Samantha had so charmingly reminded her, and therefore strictly 'Out of Bounds'. Not that he'd ever look twice at another woman; a fact that became glaringly obvious when one was introduced to his lovely wife.

She studied Jack over the top of her desktop monitor.

He might be all those things, but Jack was also kind, loyal, intelligent—and she admired his aptitude for the job. He was universally liked by small animals and children, and they were the most discerning of all.

"I thought it was Dry January?" she said.

"Yeah, I forgot—so I'm doing it in June, instead."

Melanie Yates rolled her eyes. At times like these, she wished she had a sister or even a mother she could talk to; some kindly person to offer helpful snippets of advice and a friendly ear while she vented her frustration.

As if the Universe had heard her plea, MacKenzie walked into the room.

"Catch anything big?" she asked, sliding into one of the desk chairs beside them.

Not yet, Yates thought.

"Working on it now," she murmured.

"Yeah, we caught one this morning," Lowerson chimed in, oblivious to any subtext. "White male, maybe mid-forties or thereabouts, looks like a gangland kill. We've transferred the body over to the pathologist and Faulkner's team are analysing the samples now, so we can check if he's already on our system."

"No identifying markers?" MacKenzie surmised.

"None," Lowerson said. "His face was completely caved in and they took all of his clothing, too."

"Sounds like a professional hit," MacKenzie remarked.

"Yeah. We'll keep digging and hope for a stroke of luck. You're the SIO on this one, so just let us know how you want to play things."

MacKenzie considered the young man sitting in front of her. Jack Lowerson had been through more during his time with Northumbria CID than many of his more senior colleagues, and he had the scars to prove it. Still, he couldn't command his own investigations until he was promoted up the ladder, something that relied upon being able to demonstrate what the pencil-pushers liked to call, 'real life examples', which he couldn't do unless his commanding officer gave him enough freedom to acquire them. Years ago, when she was finding it hard to break through the barriers, Ryan had gone out of his way to provide her with the opportunities that enabled her to be promoted.

Now, it was time she thought about doing the same.

"How about it, Jack? The rules won't allow you to be appointed as the Senior Investigating Officer in a murder investigation, but how about *Acting* SIO? All of the other seniors are busy, including myself, so it seems a reasonable use of resources," she said. "Report to me at the end of each day and I'll stay on hand, if you need to run anything past me."

Lowerson sat up straight in his chair.

"I'm not ready," he said automatically.

"You've been ready for a while," she argued. "It's time for the next step, wouldn't you say?"

Lowerson looked towards Yates, as if for divine intervention.

"Don't look at me," she laughed, holding both hands up. "I think you'd do a great job. Just don't expect me to call you 'Guv', any time soon."

His face fell.

"How about 'boss'?"

"Keep dreaming."

MacKenzie leaned back in her chair, watching the pair of them with an indulgent, almost maternal expression. She glanced at the white, standard-issue plastic clock on the wall, which told her it was just after four o'clock, past the end of their shift.

"Why don't you two go and celebrate the temporary promotion?" she suggested, with a sly wink for Yates. "That's reason enough to fall off the wagon for an hour or two, wouldn't you say?"

But Lowerson would not be swayed.

"I've got a bit of paperwork to do here," he said, in an overly formal voice that befitted his new position of responsibility. "Thanks anyway."

Yates looked crestfallen, so MacKenzie considered it her civic duty to step into the breach.

"Well, if you won't, I will," she said. "C'mon, Mel. Let's go and see if that good-lookin' barman is working this evening. The one that looks like a long, tall glass of pinot grigio. Course, if you tell Frank I said that, I'll call you a dirty liar."

Since Yates knew it was all for her benefit, the smile she gave was warm and genuine.

"What barman?" she said, deadpan.

With a parting sigh for the back of Lowerson's head, MacKenzie bundled her friend out of the office.

CHAPTER 13

The sun shone brightly through the avenue of trees lining the road, sending dappled light streaming across the car windscreen as Ryan and Phillips made the journey back to Police Headquarters. On days like these, it was hard to do the job they had sworn to do; to set aside the beauty that was all around them and focus instead on the worst side of humanity. It took a toll, one that couldn't easily be measured, and it was part of Ryan's job to look out for the signs that it was becoming too much; either for himself, or for his team.

He glanced at his friend, who had become withdrawn since they'd left the circus.

"Don't let O'Neill get under your skin," he murmured, breaking the heavy silence. "He's arrogant and aggressive, but we've seen his type before."

Phillips shifted in his seat.

"Aye, and worse," he agreed.

As always, Ryan's patience was the catalyst. The quiet air he carried around him like a forcefield managed to be both comforting and unsettling at the same time, drawing Phillips out of his solitary reverie.

"When I think back on some of the characters we've known and some of the God-awful things they've done, I often think it's a wonder we haven't turned into a couple of crackpots," he said.

"Speak for yourself," Ryan shot back, to make him laugh.

"True enough," Phillips admitted. "You're well past saving."

Ryan smiled and made the turn onto the Coast Road, heading west towards Wallsend and Police Headquarters.

"The thing is, I've met countless types like Charlie O'Neill. I knew them from the old days, when I was a kid. Some of them were my mates and some…well, some of them ended up in prison."

"Does it play on your mind?"

Phillips blew out a gusty breath.

"It can help to know the right people," he admitted, thinking of when Denise had been kidnapped by a dangerous killer and he'd called in every favour he could. "But, aye, it doesn't sit well to know that the boys I used to scrap about with are rotting away while I'm living the good life."

"You call picking over dead bodies 'the good life'?" Ryan said, with a raised eyebrow.

"It beats the nine-to-five," Phillips grinned, then grew serious again. "It beats being on the dole or living at Her Majesty's Pleasure, like some of the lads I used to know."

"Free will," Ryan said. "They were free to make their own choices, just as you were, Frank. Don't beat yourself up for having made the right ones."

Phillips looked across at his friend's hard profile, silhouetted against the passing landscape, and thought that life had taught him a lot since the first day he'd walked onto the job. But, beneath all that experience, there remained the beating heart of an idealist, one who expected people to make the *right* choices and was disappointed when they didn't. Ryan hadn't known what it was like to live hand to mouth; hadn't known the shame of needing to beg, borrow or steal. It didn't make him uncaring; in fact, Maxwell Finlay-Ryan was one of the kindest people he knew. It didn't make him naïve or unrealistic, either. A grown man of his years, having seen what he'd seen, was long past being either of those.

But it did make him a perfectionist, one who demanded everything of others that he demanded of himself—and, sometimes, the bar was just too high.

Phillips cleared his throat.

"The problem is, son, what's the 'right' decision? We live by the laws of the land; we enforce them every day. If we don't, the place would go to rack and ruin. I joined the police because I wanted something different for myself—I wanted law and order and stability, and I've made a good life," he repeated. "But who's to say all those others made the 'wrong' decisions? If they were starving hungry with bairns to feed, they'd have done anything to put food in their mouths. Was it wrong?"

"And what about the other ones?" Ryan argued. "The ones who didn't have a good reason to lie, or steal, or maim, or kill? We've seen their kind, too."

Phillips nodded.

"That's true," he agreed. "Take whoever killed Samantha's mam. What kind of low-life would kill someone, right in front of a baby girl?"

Ryan simply shook his head.

"I can't answer that yet," he said. "But we're going to find out, Frank—and, when we do, they're going to feel the full force of the law."

Phillips thought of the little girl who was, by now, in the safe-keeping of a nice foster family who would care for her until they found the answers she so desperately needed. He felt a pang of regret that she wouldn't be staying with them for longer, making her way through his supply of smoked bacon and stottie cakes, no doubt.

"Are you going to be alright?" Ryan asked, reading his mind. "Once this is all over, it won't be our decision whether Samantha goes back to her father. She might have to, and I need to know whether you'll be able to cope with that."

There were a hundred things Phillips might have said, denials he could have made, but he fell back on the truth.

"I see a bit of myself in her, at that age," he said. "As for her father, I've got no respect for a man who'd let his own flesh and blood wander about the streets, where anything might happen to her. It's a wonder she made it up to your house on Sunday, without getting lost or in some kind of trouble," he said, his voice rising slightly in outrage.

But then, he relaxed again.

"Aye, I care what happens to the lass—we all do. But if you're asking whether I can keep a cool head about it while we're trying to find who killed her mother, you can trust that I will. Besides, she's better off where she is, at least for now."

It was all the reassurance Ryan needed.

"Yes, at least we know she's somewhere safe."

* * *

Ryan's equilibrium didn't last long.

Almost as soon as he turned into the car park at Police Headquarters, his mobile phone began to ring, filling the car with a tinny rendition of the soundtrack from *Back to the Future.*

"You changed your ring tone!" Phillips exclaimed.

"Only slightly," Ryan muttered, and brought the car to a hasty stop. "They're both Spielberg films, after all."

He caught it on the last ring.

"Ryan."

Phillips watched the expression on his friend's face and grew worried as it changed from polite enquiry to the focused look of a man who had just been given bad news.

"When did this happen?" he demanded, while Phillips strained to hear the voice on the other end of the line. "Right. I'm at the office now, so I'll call you back in five minutes. I want a full-scale search of the vicinity set up, immediately."

As soon as he heard *search*, Phillips' blood ran cold.

"What is it?" he asked, when Ryan hung up a few seconds later. "What's happened?"

Ryan scrubbed a hand over his face, then let it fall away.

"It's Samantha," he said bluntly. "She's absconded from the foster home. They have no idea where she is."

Phillips felt his stomach flip.

"What? How—how could they let it happen?"

"She's not under arrest," Ryan said. "They're only human. But I agree, I don't know why they weren't keeping a closer watch. MacKenzie told us the kid threatened to run, that she argued with Morrison but was overruled. They should have known it was a risk."

Phillips was already imagining the worst.

"O'Neill knows there's a murder investigation going on, and it doesn't take a brain surgeon to figure out that Samantha's our star witness."

"The only witness, aside from whoever killed Esme," Ryan agreed. "And the whole circus has probably heard about the investigation by now, not just the O'Neill brothers."

Phillips closed his eyes briefly, praying for calm.

"She's out there, on her own, while somebody could be looking for her," he whispered. "They'll be worrying she'll remember who it was, if she's already remembered enough to come to the police. What can we do?"

Ryan slammed out of the car and Phillips scrambled to follow him.

"We get a search underway and hope we find her before anybody else does," Ryan rapped out, striding towards the automatic doors at the front of the building. "There's no time to lose."

CHAPTER 14

T*he Shipbuilder* was a former working men's club that had been gentrified over the years so that it now boasted a gastro menu and muted décor, to meet the increased footfall its landlord was now enjoying since Northumbria Police had recently moved its headquarters to the area. As part of its refurbishment programme, the pub had appointed new staff with a careful eye, and MacKenzie and Yates could only applaud their efforts as they looked on from their position atop the faux-industrial stools set out along the polished bar.

"I didn't know you could get forearms like that," Yates remarked, over the rim of a very nice glass of Malbec.

MacKenzie made an appreciative noise.

"My Frank isn't far off," she said, her voice softening. "But it's high time you went out and had a bit of fun, Mel. There's no use hanging around for Jack; he's liable to take twenty years before he gets his act together."

Unconsciously, Yates' shoulders slumped.

"I know you're right," she muttered, and took another slug of wine. "The worst thing is, I was the idiot who kept turning him down before…well, before he met Jennifer. You know the rest."

She certainly did, MacKenzie thought. Their former Detective Chief Superintendent, Jennifer Lucas, had crashed into their lives like a wrecking ball the previous year, leaving hearts and minds torn apart in the process. Lowerson's own mother had finally put an end to it—and her—but she couldn't quite work up the sympathy to mourn the woman's death or to empathise with his mother's actions. The only person she felt sorry for in all of it was Jack, whose worst crime had been to try to find happiness.

"Maybe he needs a little more time," she said, cupping her hands around her own glass. "He's probably still dealing with the fallout of all that carnage. It's a lot to take in."

Yates nodded.

"You're probably right," she said. "But what do I do in the meantime? Every morning, I have to tell myself to stay professional, but nothing helps."

"You've got it bad," MacKenzie said, and rubbed a hand on the girl's back.

Oh, to be young again.

"Need a top-up, ladies?"

They both sat up a bit straighter in their seats as the barman came to rest his improbably large forearms on the bar beside them.

"Haven't seen you in here, much," he said to Yates.

"I—ah, no. I've been busy."

"Chasing criminals, eh?" he said, turning up the charm a notch. "It makes me sleep better at night, knowing there's dedicated people like you keeping the streets safe."

MacKenzie took a hasty sip of wine, to cover a laugh.

"Uh, thanks," Yates managed.

"What's your name, Chief Inspector?" he asked, and MacKenzie almost choked.

"Oh, no, no. I'm just a trainee detective," Yates replied, and a slow flush spread across her face. "Um, Melanie. I'm Melanie."

"Well, Melanie. I'm Dante."

MacKenzie wondered if a person might expire from repressed laughter.

"Dante?" she couldn't help but say, and he gave them both a sheepish smile.

"Well, actually, I'm called Dennis—after my grandad—but I'd never get a date if I told Melanie that, would I?"

Yates' eyes widened.

Date?

"So, how about it, beautiful? Would you risk going out for dinner with a bloke called Dennis? You can still call me Dante, if you like that better."

He looked at her with such longing, she felt it would be rude to refuse.

"I—okay," she said.

"You've made my day," he declared, and wrote his number on the back of one of the paper napkins sitting in a caddy nearby. "Give me a call whenever you're ready to hear my tales of daring on the high seas, and the time I was almost mauled by a Great White Shark."

"Really?"

"Nah, but I fell into a river, once. I'll tell you all about it, over a curry."

* * *

While Yates navigated the baffling world of romance and dating, Ryan and Phillips headed directly to Chief Constable Morrison's office, which was on the executive level at Police Headquarters. As his long legs ate up the floor, Ryan made a series of calls to his colleagues in local police divisions to arrange for immediate assistance in conducting a search, while Phillips concentrated on keeping up with his friend, without rupturing his vital organs.

They arrived at Morrison's door and Ryan rapped a knuckle against the wood.

"Come in!"

When they entered the room, they found Sandra Morrison had been appraised of the situation and had already anticipated their response.

She held up her hands, palms out, in a gesture of peace.

"Before you start, let me tell you I've just spoken with Social Services," she said, to save time. "They're very apologetic, but it's quite common for newly fostered children to abscond. They're usually picked up very quickly because they try to make their way home."

"Samantha's social worker told me she went missing within an hour of arriving at the new place," Ryan said. "But it took the family several hours before they decided to tell us. Why?"

Morrison waved a hand towards the visitors' chairs arranged in front of her desk, which both men ignored. She set her jaw and walked around to the front of her desk.

"I don't know, Ryan. People are human, and they make mistakes," she said. "Maybe the family thought she'd come back."

"A mistake is one thing," he said. "Negligence is another."

"Placing blame isn't going to help," she said. "The priority is to track her down and bring her in."

"What then?" Phillips asked. "Put her into another foster placement? She'll only run again."

"You don't know that," Morrison said, but had to admit it was a strong possibility. And, if anything happened to Samantha in the meantime, she didn't like to think what the press would have to say about it.

"I know the DNA results came back on that DB," she said. "I know we've got a murder investigation on our hands and that means there's an even stronger possibility that what Samantha says she remembers is a version of the truth. But it's still not a smoking gun and there's a chance Esme O'Neill ran off, just like everybody says she did—"

"Ma'am, with respect—"

She overrode the interruption.

"Haven't you considered the possibility that the woman left as her husband describes, to be with some unknown lover, and that person is responsible for her death? It may not have anything to do with *O'Neill's Circus*."

Ryan had considered the possibility—and rejected it.

"You didn't see the girl's face when she came to my door on Sunday. You didn't hear her describe the scene. It was too vivid to be a figment of her imagination."

Morrison knew that Ryan was adept at reading people; it could be a royal pain in the arse, most days, because it meant you couldn't get away with anything less than the whole truth. But that didn't mean his judgment was infallible.

"I want you to bear it in mind, that's all. In the meantime, Samantha's still the only witness you have and she's out there, in a strange city, on her own. I want a full-scale search set up."

"Already underway," Ryan confirmed.

"She can't have much money," Morrison thought aloud. "That limits her options, significantly."

Phillips thought that it also limited a little girl's ability to buy things like food, if she needed it. Outside, the air was turning cool as the wind picked up and night began to set in. He thought of all the people who were homeless, unable to pay for a warm shelter or a bed for the night, and he bore down against the sense of helplessness that seeped through the defences he'd carefully built.

"Do you want to alert the press?" Morrison asked, and Ryan found himself unusually torn by indecision. On one hand, the added exposure on the nightly news or on the radio might lead to Samantha being found more quickly; then again, it might not. Instead, it could lead to numerous false sightings and, crucially, would alert any nefarious characters to her disappearance and further jeopardise her position.

It was an uncomfortable choice, but he made similar ones every day.

"We should get it all over the news," Phillips said, beating him to it. "We'll have every parent in the North East looking out for her."

"As well as others we'd rather not have looking for her," Ryan reminded him.

Phillips swore roundly, and wished for a cigarette.

Another thing Charlie O'Neill had to answer for.

"We can't take the chance, Frank," Ryan continued. "There's still time to find her, before nightfall. If she hasn't resurfaced by sunset, we'll contact the press team and go public. That gives us"—he paused to check the time—"more than two hours."

Morrison nodded.

"You'll call me, if there are any developments."

It was not a request.

CHAPTER 15

Having been recalled from her sojourn at *The Shipbuilder,* MacKenzie sent Yates home and joined Ryan and Phillips in their hunt for the missing child. With his usual lightning speed, Ryan had set up an incident room and was treating Samantha's disappearance with the same focus he would give any murder investigation or serious crime befalling the city or its people. Teams of local police were patrolling the neighbourhood where she was last seen and had gone house to house to find out if there had been any sightings. The same approach had been taken at the nearby Gosforth High Street, where there was any number of shops and restaurants whose CCTV might have caught her movements on camera.

Unfortunately, all of these steps took time, energy and resources that were already stretched thin.

"There are some bus stops close to where the foster family live," Phillips said, poring over a dog-eared map he'd laid out on the conference table. "Gosforth Metro station is nearby, too. We could try to get hold of the CCTV from around there."

"I've already been in touch with the metro and bus companies," MacKenzie said. "The upside is, everybody is willing to help. The downside is, it's going to take hours, at least. It'll be tomorrow before any of the footage comes through and even longer before we'll have had time to go through it all."

None of that came as a surprise; it was the same story every time.

"Let's think about this," Ryan said, moving to stare out of the window with unseeing eyes. "Where would Samantha go?"

Where she felt safe.

He quickly put a call through to Anna, on the off-chance the girl had turned up on their doorstep, but pocketed his phone a few minutes later.

There'd been no sign of her.

"Let's get a squad car to check along the roadsides and bus routes up into Northumberland, anyway," he said. "She could be on her way."

Over the next hour, reports streamed in from local police, hospitals, local businesses and transport officials, and their message was the same: nobody had seen Samantha O'Neill. Outside, a light rain began to fall as night closed in and Ryan knew the time had almost come to contact the press.

"Frank? There's a chance Samantha has gone back home, to the circus. They wouldn't tell us, if she did; I'm almost certain. We need to check for ourselves."

Phillips grunted his assent.

"It's familiar," he said. "She might have thought it was better than the alternative. Let's go."

* * *

Samantha had not gone back to her family's circus, either.

The fact Ryan and Phillips were making two visits in one day was enough to set tongues wagging but, when Charlie O'Neill found out the reason for their unexpected arrival, he considered it a gift in his favour. A dramatic scene followed, where he'd bemoaned the loss of his daughter, as if he'd entrusted her into police care—conveniently forgetting his own lax approach to parenting in what Ryan considered to be a hypocritical masterstroke of public relations.

After a full search of the circus and its grounds, with particular focus on the stable tent and the caravans, they'd retreated empty-handed into the night, their ears ringing with threats of hard-hitting exposés about police incompetence being printed in the *Daily Mail.*

"I'll put a call through to the media liaison," Ryan said, as they left the moor for the second time that day. "We can't put it off any longer. In the meantime, you might as well go home with MacKenzie. You look dead on your feet."

Phillips didn't bother to argue, because he felt wrung out. It was odd that emotional turmoil could be more taxing on the body than a good spar in the boxing ring.

"If you need me—"

"I'll call," Ryan finished for him. "Go and get some sleep. I've got all the local street charities watching out for her around town, in case she decides to sleep rough."

Phillips looked out at the passing skyline of the city.

"She's out there, somewhere beneath the same sky," he said. "I hope to God she's alright."

"Me too, Frank," Ryan said softly. "Me too."

* * *

Beneath that same sky, another person thought of Samantha and wished they knew where to find her.

It would be so easy, they thought. *So simple to break her neck, then throw her in the river. Or, maybe one good whack around the back of the head would do it. They could drive out somewhere remote and bury the body—or, better yet, stage things to make it look like the kid had been attacked by some passing nonce.*

It would be so much simpler than getting rid of her bitch of a mother.

The thought was so tantalising; maybe they'd just take a little drive and see what they found.

CHAPTER 16

Phillips and MacKenzie said little as they made their way home, both occupied with the unspoken task of scanning the streets for a red-haired little girl in a baseball cap.

But there was no sign of Samantha.

"I let her down," MacKenzie said huskily, as Phillips turned off the car engine a short while later. "I should have known this might happen. I tried to warn Morrison—"

"Hey, hey," he said, as he reached across to grasp her hand. "You did what was right, we all did. You can't blame yourself."

"Well I *do*," MacKenzie said, in a rare show of emotion. "If anything's happened to her, Frank, I'll have Samantha on my conscience until the day I die."

Alongside all the others she carried around like ghostly talismans, just as Ryan did; as they all did.

"Ryan said he'd call, the moment there was any news," Phillips said, as they stepped out of the car. "He's a man of his word."

"Right enough, he's probably still at the office or searching the streets himself," MacKenzie agreed. "He cares about that wee girl as much as we do."

Phillips fished around his pockets for his house keys.

"He puts on a good show," he said. "But underneath, he's all mushy peas."

MacKenzie found herself laughing despite it all and turned to him, right there on the doorstep.

"Never change, Frank Phillips."

She tugged him forward to bestow a lingering kiss.

"What was that for?" he managed, once he could think clearly again.

"For being wonderful," she said, and stepped inside the house.

* * *

As soon as she entered the hallway, MacKenzie's body went on full alert.

She threw out an arm to warn her husband, who opened his mouth to protest and then clamped it shut again when he saw what she had seen.

The coats they kept neatly on a rack against the wall had fallen to the floor in a heap, bearing an uncomfortable resemblance to a body. Faint muddy footprints trailed across the carpet in the direction of the kitchen, where a light burned.

"I turned off all the lights when we left this morning," MacKenzie whispered. "I think there's an intruder. Call for back-up, Frank."

Phillips thought of calling the Control Room but, in times of crisis, there was only one person that came to mind.

He pressed the speed-dial number for Ryan, who answered after the first ring.

"Son, we've got a situation here," he said in an urgent undertone. "An intruder may still be in the house. I need a squad car, soon as possible."

"Consider it done," Ryan said. "I'm on my way, too. Get out of there, Frank."

But MacKenzie had already toed off her boots and was taking the first slow, silent footsteps towards the hypnotic glare of the kitchen light.

"*Denise*," he whispered.

MacKenzie held up a hand in a signal for quiet, while she listened for any small movements to indicate they were not alone. Sweat prickled the skin on the back of her neck as she remembered another hallway, at another time, when she'd been taken unawares.

She'd sworn it would never happen again.

All the same, fear made her body tremble and, even though Frank was with her, she fought the urge to run.

Phillips followed behind, his eyes scanning the empty living room as they passed by the open doorway. His natural inclination was to go ahead of MacKenzie, so he would take the brunt of any attack that might befall them, but he knew his wife would not thank him for the chivalry. She was a strong, capable woman who had her own demons to slay; if he persisted in trying to fight them for her, she'd never be able to rid herself, once and for all.

And so, he followed her lead.

As they rounded the corner of the stairs and the kitchen doorway came into view, they saw that their intruder had really gone to town in there. Milk, jam and toast crumbs littered the countertop, and cupboard doors stood ajar, as if somebody had been searching for hidden treasure. And they'd found it.

There, on the breakfast bar, stood the remains of what had once been Phillips' special shortbread assortment, carefully selected and transported from Fortnum & Mason after a recent trip to London. Thirty individual biscuits with delicate flavouring he'd been looking forward to savouring over the coming weeks, reduced to little more than dust.

Total carnage.

"If I ever find who did this," he said, shakily.

MacKenzie hushed him, and moved back out into the hallway, following her nose. The living room was mostly untouched, despite there being several items on display that might have attracted the eye of any would-be burglar.

"Call off the cavalry, Frank," she murmured, and slowly relaxed as she started to climb the stairs.

"We haven't checked everywhere, yet," he said. "They might still be lurking somewhere."

Covered in crumbs.

MacKenzie continued to climb the stairs. At the top, she turned along the landing and made directly for the spare bedroom at the other end of the passage, while Phillips' heavier tread creaked on the stairs behind her.

Gently, she pushed open the door and felt relief wash over her, strong and heady.

"Careful, love—"

"I think we've found the culprit, Frank."

* * *

Samantha was curled in the middle of the bed, fast asleep.

Her clothes lay in a bundle on the floor and, without thinking, MacKenzie scooped them up to be washed for the next day.

"The little—"

"Shh, Frank, let her sleep."

The flashing blue light of a squad car blazed through the curtains from the street outside and they hurried downstairs to forestall their colleagues' entry.

"False alarm!" Phillips said, in a stage whisper, as Ryan let himself through the front door. He was flanked by a couple of local bobbies who, at his quick instruction, retreated in mild disappointment.

"Everything alright?" Ryan asked, closing the front door behind him.

MacKenzie and Phillips looked between themselves, then led the way through to the kitchen to pour a tall glass of something fruity.

"It's Samantha," Phillips said, and Ryan came to attention.

"You've heard something?"

"Seen something, more like," MacKenzie drawled. "Samantha's sleeping in our spare room, upstairs."

Ryan looked up at the ceiling, automatically.

"What? How the hell did she get in here?"

"No idea," Phillips said. "There's no sign of any broken glass, so she must have palmed a spare key when she was staying with us, yesterday."

Ryan's lips quirked. It seemed they had acquired Newcastle's own version of the Artful Dodger.

"I'm glad she's alright," he said, with feeling.

With no leads on her whereabouts, he'd been worried.

"She must feel happy here," he said. "But Morrison won't like it, and neither will Social Services. There's still a question of protocol, regardless of what happened today. They'll want to put her in another foster home; maybe even the same one."

They took a collective sip of wine and enjoyed its medicinal qualities as they thought of what could be done.

"What if she stayed here?" MacKenzie suggested, very softly.

Ryan frowned.

"What do you mean?"

She licked her lips and set the glass back on the counter.

"I mean, what if we kept it quiet that Samantha's staying here with us? It seems she won't run away, so long as we play our cards right. As the kid said herself, we're not high profile enough to tip off somebody who might be looking for her."

Phillips made a sound like a *harrumph*.

"Go on," Ryan said, and leaned back against the counter. It had been a very long day and it wasn't over, yet.

"Morrison will take some convincing but, if we can get her to understand that Samantha might run again, she'll agree. Failing that, we can paint a very vivid picture of what the press would say if she went missing for a second time."

Ryan had to admire the sheer audacity of it.

"You're suggesting a kind of...undercover childcare arrangement?" He nodded slowly. "We'd have to tell her father she'd been found; we owe him that, but we don't need to tell him her exact location. Of course, somebody would need to be here to look after her, here at the house."

"I don't mind—"

"I'll do it—"

Phillips and MacKenzie spoke in unison, as Ryan looked on in surprise.

"I don't have a heavy caseload at the moment," MacKenzie said, silently ticking off the various cases she'd need to hand over to other colleagues. "I can take some time off."

"It's settled then," he nodded. "We'll square it with the Chief, tomorrow."

From her crouched position on the stairs, Samantha grinned broadly.

* * *

By the time Ryan made it home to the picturesque village of Elsdon, it was the early hours of the morning. Anna had left the hallway light on for him, as she always did, so that he would never return to a darkened house. It brought a smile to his face as he dragged his weary body through the door, which widened when he realised that she was still awake and burning her own midnight oil.

"Anna?"

She looked up from a pile of open textbooks spread out across the kitchen table, her dark hair shining in the lamplight as she researched local Northumbrian folklore. As an academic historian, it was her business to delve into the past and try to make sense of it, whereas his was to ensure their future was something they could be proud of, too.

"Hi," she said, warmly.

He said nothing, only reached down and plucked her from the chair and into his arms for a thorough kiss.

"That's better," he said, long moments later.

"I don't know where you get the energy," she said, the history books forgotten.

"Oh, I always have the energy," he growled, and, quick as a flash, tipped her over his shoulder into a fireman's lift.

"Ryan! Put me down!"

"Nope," he laughed, and took the stairs two at a time.

* * *

Later, when Anna lay with her head on his chest, Ryan trailed slow fingers up and down the slim column of her spine.

"I guess you found Samantha," she said, sleepily.

"Yeah," he said, and then shook his head in disbelief. "That kid is a constant surprise. When Frank and Denise got home, they found her waiting for them. She'd let herself in, cleaned out the shortbread—"

"Uh-oh," Anna laughed.

"You should have seen Frank's face," Ryan said, and let out a rumbling chuckle. "She wiped out his prize biscuits, then tucked herself in for the night."

Anna looked up at his face in the half-light of the bedroom.

"She's not shy, that's for sure."

"You can say that again," Ryan said, with a smile. "She's a tough little thing. Brave, outspoken…it's easy to forget how young she is."

Anna nodded, thinking that the same thing could have been said of herself, at that age.

"She's seen a lot."

Ryan leaned down to brush his lips against the top of her head, which was dishevelled thanks to his earlier efforts.

"What'll happen to her now?"

Ryan heaved a sigh.

"She's going to stay with them, until the investigation is over."

Anna was surprised.

"Will Morrison allow it?"

"I hope so," he replied. "It's unorthodox but, in this case, it seems to be the best option."

Anna was silent for a moment.

"She's a sweet little girl," she said eventually. "I hope…well, I hope they don't end up getting hurt."

Ryan looked down at her in confusion.

"You think she'd take off, or steal something?"

Only their hearts, Anna thought.

"I don't think she'd do anything deliberately," was all she said. "But that doesn't mean she won't end up hurting them, anyway."

Ryan let that sink in, and then turned to the topic that had been playing on his mind ever since Samantha had burst into their lives.

"Does it make you wonder about having kids?" he asked.

"Of course," Anna replied, without hesitation. "We've always said we'll have a family, one day—if we can. But, right now, I'm not sure…" she trailed off. "How do you feel about it?"

"I love you," he said. "I can't wait to have children with you, but there's no rush, either."

Anna breathed a sigh of relief.

"That's exactly how I feel," she said. "Let's enjoy it being just the two of us, for now. There'll be time enough for changing nappies and midnight feeding."

"Sounds wonderful," he said, pulling a face. "But, so long as they look like you, I can handle anything."

Anna smiled against his chest and let herself be lulled to sleep by the sound of his strong heartbeat, just as their children would too, one day.

CHAPTER 17

Tuesday, 4th June 2019

The following morning, Phillips and MacKenzie awoke to the sound of pots and pans clattering in the kitchen downstairs.

"What the—?" MacKenzie exclaimed. "Frank, go and see what on Earth's happening down there."

Phillips rolled out of bed and reached for a jazzy dressing gown he'd acquired some years ago during a memorable trip to Las Vegas. It was all black but featured a pattern of tiny dancing Elvises in white flared suits.

When he padded downstairs and into the kitchen, he found the place under new management.

"What's all this?" he asked, lifting a mute arm towards the broken egg-shells lying discarded on the kitchen counter next to an open packet of bacon.

Samantha looked across from her position beside the hob, where she was kneeling on a chair she'd dragged through from the dining room.

"I thought you might like some breakfast," she said, shyly.

But Phillips was more concerned about naked flames and gas appliances.

"Did your dad let you use the hob, at home?"

She gave him a lop-sided smile.

"Course he did. How else am I supposed to cook dinner?"

Phillips looked down into her upturned face, then ruffled her hair.

"Thanks for all this, pet, but we don't expect you to cook for us. In fact, while you're here, why don't you let us take care of you, eh?"

She looked crestfallen.

"Don't you like scrambled eggs and bacon?"

His stomach grumbled loudly, just at the mention of it.

"Is the Pope Catholic?" he replied, with a grin. "I'll get the plates."

* * *

Later, after an extensive clean-up operation, MacKenzie and Phillips sat down at the table beside Samantha.

"Sam, we need to talk."

The girl looked between them and swallowed, already anticipating what was to come. They were about to tell her that it was no use; she'd have to go back into care and there was nothing they could do about it.

"I'm sorry about taking your keys," she whispered. "I promise, I put them back in the drawer in the hallway, where I found them."

That cleared up that mystery, MacKenzie thought.

"It's okay," she said. "We're happy to know you're safe, but it was wrong of you to run away from the foster family; they were very worried. In fact, we all were."

Samantha blinked in surprise. In her whole life, nobody had told her they'd worried about her.

"You were?"

"Well, of course we were!" Phillips boomed, and patted her arm. "People care about you, lass. Don't go running off like that again, alright?"

She nodded.

"I'm sorry," she said, and then took a deep breath. "Are you sending me back?"

She focused on a spot somewhere above their heads, as she waited for the hammer to fall.

"Well, actually, we wondered if you'd like to stay here for a while."

Samantha's face broke into a smile.

"Really?"

"Aye, but we'll need to set some ground rules," Phillips said, folding his arms across his paunch. "First of all, there'll be no quaffing of the shortbread biscuits without leaving one for me and Denise. Agreed?"

Samantha giggled, then nodded.

"Agreed. Anything else?"

Their faces grew serious.

"Yes, Sam, there's something else. Something very important," MacKenzie said, quietly. "It concerns your mum."

She looked between them and read twin expressions of sympathy.

"It was her, wasn't it?" she whispered.

Phillips cleared his throat.

"Yes, love. It was. We're so sorry."

Samantha's eyes filled with tears and her lip wobbled.

"I already knew she was dead, but…but…"

MacKenzie could stand it no longer, and she threw her arms wide open. The girl sobbed and buried her face against the warmth of her shoulder, purging herself of the grief that racked her small body. Watching them, Phillips knew they'd stepped over an invisible line and they wouldn't be able to step back again.

They could only move forward.

* * *

Later that morning, MacKenzie took Samantha back into Police Headquarters for further questioning. Once the worst of the tears had passed, anger had followed, bringing with it a determination to help find the person responsible for her mother's murder. While she tried to remember any small details that could help them, Phillips made his way across town to one of the less convivial spots on a murder detective's map: the mortuary.

He met Ryan by the side entrance and together they made the journey into the bowels of the Royal Victoria Infirmary.

"How'd you get on with Morrison?" he asked, as they walked along the long, uncomfortably warm corridor in the hospital basement towards a set of secure double doors.

"Fine, once she came around." Ryan was cagey, thinking of the difficult conversation he'd had with their Chief Constable earlier that morning. "She's a reasonable woman."

Phillips gave his friend a knowing look.

"Well, whatever she said, you obviously convinced her otherwise. Thanks, lad."

"Don't thank me too soon," Ryan muttered. "She also said that, if anything went wrong, she'd come down on the pair of us like a tonne of bricks."

No idle threat.

As they reached the double doors, Ryan keyed in the entry code to the mortuary—the province of Doctor Jeffrey Pinter, Chief Pathologist attached to Northumbria CID.

"Morning!" he called out, from somewhere behind one of the enormous, dank-smelling immersion tanks on the other side of the room.

Ryan and Phillips tugged on their visitors' lab coats and scrawled their names in the log book.

"Morning, Jeff," Ryan said, and Phillips grunted, trying not to focus on the waxy outline of what had once been a heavily overweight man. "You look busy."

Pinter emerged around the side of the tank, his face full of smiles despite having just had his hands in places Phillips would rather not think about.

"Suspicious death, came in the other day," Pinter explained, with a shrug of his bony shoulders. It was an unfortunate coincidence that, thanks to a lack of Vitamin D and poor genetics, the pathologist bore a strong resemblance to most people's notion of the Grim Reaper. Luckily, his cheerful personality made up for whatever physical deficiencies he might have had.

"Ah, do you have a minute to go over that old report we spoke about on the phone?" Ryan asked, nose wrinkling as he passed by the tank.

"Of course. Why don't you come into my office?"

They followed him through the main mortuary workspace and along a short corridor leading to a number of private examination rooms, as well as Pinter's personal office.

Inside, a single, uninspiring strip light perfectly complemented the overall ambiance of the room.

"Couldn't you get an artificial plant, or something?" Phillips asked. "I know it's a mortuary, but you could still spruce the place up a bit!"

Pinter looked around the stark, white-washed space and saw a clean, orderly environment.

"Well, it's not as though the punters complain," he said, and the other men winced.

"Point made," Ryan said. "How about that report?"

"Ah, yes," Pinter said, and spun around in his desk chair to bring up the report on his desktop computer. "I'm afraid I couldn't remember the details, off-hand. I see quite a few like this one, unfortunately."

"I read through the main report in the cold case file," Ryan said. "It seems the woman was found in July of 2011?"

"That's right," Pinter nodded. "She'd been dead for around a month, by that point. A hiker found her in a shallow grave, up at Bolam Lake."

"You're sure it was around a month?"

It mattered, Ryan thought, because it could mean the difference between Esme O'Neill having died around the time Samantha said she did, or sometime later.

"We're as sure as we can be," Pinter replied. "In addition to my own clinical assessment of the skeleton, soil samples were taken from the scene and were found to contain high levels of lipid phosphorus. When a body is buried in the undergrowth like that, there's a fairly well documented biochemical cycle that affects the soil around it. We call it the 'decomposition island'," he added.

"Sounds lovely," Phillips remarked.

"How about cause of death?" Ryan pressed on. "I read in your report that you hypothesized death by ligature strangulation. Why not manual?"

"It's a judgment call," Pinter acknowledged. "When you no longer have much in the way of soft tissue to examine, it comes down to looking at what remains and drawing conclusions. In my opinion, the damage to the trachea was significant, and the force was suggestive of either extreme manual force or, most likely, a ligature aid of some kind."

"Weren't the bones all…you know, broken up, by the time the body was found?" Phillips found himself asking.

"The skin was black and hardened around the bones in the neck," Pinter explained. "It was still holding the skeleton together, although if she'd been in the ground much longer it would have been a question of referring the bones to a specialist."

Ryan nodded.

"Any other interesting markers?"

"Well, as I say, it's hard to draw meaningful conclusions as to the lady's lifestyle or occupation, except that the size, shape and analysis of the bones suggested a woman in the age range of eighteen to thirty. She'd enjoyed a reasonably healthy diet and had probably carried a baby, at some point."

"You can tell that, from a skeleton?"

Pinter nodded.

"You'd be amazed what a body can tell you."

"It's a silent witness," Ryan murmured, and looked over at the images taken of Esme O'Neill's remains. By now, he'd seen a picture of how she'd looked in life, and the contrast was stark.

"She was found clothed, but with no other personal effects aside from the jewellery she'd been wearing when she died."

"Wedding ring?" Ryan asked, but Pinter shook his head.

"No rings—but a twenty-four carat, yellow-gold charm bracelet was recovered," he said.

"Interesting that there was no wedding ring," Ryan said. "Anything else?"

"The clothes had been subject to fire damage—"

"Burned?" Ryan enquired.

Pinter nodded.

"Once again, judging from portions of charred bone, I would hypothesize that the victim was partially incinerated *in situ*. Often, killers find that fire does a disappointing job of removing all traces—so they layered the soil on top.

"They wanted her wiped out," Phillips said. "Most people would leave it at one or the other, unless it was a professional job."

Pinter nodded.

"To transport the body, drag it through the wooded area to a secluded spot, presumably at night, would take a certain level of strength," he said. "Or, perhaps, more than one person, to help."

Food for thought.

"Alright," Ryan said. "If you have no objections, I'd like to refer all the samples back to Faulkner for re-testing. He has a lot more science at his disposal now than he did eight years ago, so it might throw something up."

"I certainly have no objection," Pinter said. "I heard that it was the daughter who came to you with the new information?"

Ryan nodded.

"Terrible business," the pathologist said. "Anything I can do, just let me know."

Phillips had never particularly liked the man, but now he laid a grateful hand on his shoulder.

"She'd thank you, if she could."

* * *

When Ryan and Phillips emerged from the basement, they took a moment to breathe deeply of the fresh morning air. Mist had rolled in from the sea overnight and the air around them was damp, leaving a thin layer of moisture on the surface of their skin.

"Pinter couldn't really tell us anything new," Phillips remarked, as they stood beneath the plastic canopy outside the service entrance to the mortuary. "Just confirmed what we already knew, I s'pose."

"Not entirely," Ryan said, leaning back against the wall of the hospital. "He told us the body had been burned, and that jewellery had been recovered. That's interesting, because it means Esme's killer was intelligent. They could have dumped her in a ditch, but instead they took her to somewhere unconnected with the circus and used two methods to try to conceal her body. That could also signify a desire to obliterate her, from a psychological perspective—"

"That's reaching a bit far," Phillips said, and Ryan nodded.

"Maybe. But the most interesting fact is that Esme hadn't been wearing her wedding ring when she died. Somebody might have removed it, or…"

"She'd been intending to leave her husband, after all?" Phillips finished for him.

"Exactly, which brings him right back into the frame."

CHAPTER 18

As it happened, the task of identifying the body found in the dumpster at St Peter's Wharf was not so very hard, after all. Dan "The Demon" Hepple had been well-known to the police, with an extensive criminal record including pops for drug dealing and possession, aggravated assault and other violent crimes.

"I just got off the phone with the Drugs Squad," Lowerson said, as soon as Yates walked into the office. "It looks like our DB was already on the books. He's Daniel Hepple, resident of Whitley Bay, aged forty-one."

"And, 'good morning' to you, too, Jack," she muttered, dumping her handbag on the floor.

"That tip has saved us a lot of time," he continued, as if he hadn't heard. "We're still waiting for the DNA analysis to come back but, in the meantime, all the Drugs Squad had to do was chat to one of their informants. Pity we don't have somebody similar we could turn to."

"We do have informants," she said. "But they're old and past their sell-by date because there's a constant turnover amongst the ruling gangs. We could use some new blood, people who have something useful to tell us."

Lowerson looked at her in surprise.

"How do you know about it?"

"Common knowledge," she said, breezily.

"Right. Well, I think we should head down to Hepple's place in Whitley Bay and see what we find."

"Whatever you say, Guv."

* * *

While Lowerson and Yates made their way to the coast, Ryan went about the business of setting up a Major Incident Room. Esme O'Neill's murder was an active investigation now, and had been assigned the dubious code name, 'OPERATION SHOWSTOPPER'. A whiteboard lined one wall of the conference room and he'd spent some time tacking up images of Esme as she'd been in life, as well as candid stills of how she'd been found after a violent death. Beneath that, he'd drawn a timeline and listed any pertinent dates, including when Charlie O'Neill claimed his wife had gone missing, as well as the date she'd been found, a month later. He'd also tacked up pictures of those who formed part of the victim's inner circle: her daughter, Samantha; her husband, Charlie; and, his brother, Duke. It was already known that her mother had died following a battle with cancer and her father was living in Canada. He'd emigrated just after Esme's eighteenth birthday, leaving her in the care of the circus, where Charlie's father had employed her to look after the horses before he'd had a stroke and passed on the running of it to his eldest son.

When Phillips joined him with a steaming mug of coffee in each hand, a few minutes later, Ryan cast his eyes around the empty room.

"Where the hell is everybody? Didn't they get the message?"

"Aye, but MacKenzie's with Samantha, who's giving another statement in the Family Room, downstairs," Phillips said, and set the cups on one of the laminated tables which formed a semi-circle around the whiteboard area. He saw that each place had been set, with a small pack of printed summaries and materials on each chair. "Lowerson's Acting SIO on this Bin Body case—"

"Acting SIO?"

Phillips paused.

"That's alright, isn't it?"

"It's great," Ryan said, and smiled. In fact, it was the best news that week. For a long time, they'd worried Jack Lowerson wouldn't come back to work at all, so to hear that he'd taken the opportunity to better himself was music to his ears.

"Well, he's got Yates with him and they've headed off to look over the victim's last known address. One of the crime analysts said they'd pop upstairs later to see if you needed anything but they're under the cosh, themselves, with an influx of gang murders lately. The rest of the rabble are either off on holiday or dealing with their own caseload."

Ryan set his hands on his hips and puffed out a frustrated breath.

"Well, looks like it's you and me, Old Man."

"Less of the 'old'," Phillips replied, and took his pick from the row of empty seats before giving Ryan a gesture to continue.

"Fire away."

Ryan opened his mouth and then shut it again, feeling like a lemon.

"You already know everything I'm about to tell you," he said, hitching a hip onto the edge of the desk at the front. "The upshot is, we need to establish who else was around at the time of Esme's murder; who would have had motive, means and opportunity."

There was an awkward pause.

"Shall we just head back to the circus and get on with questioning the rest of the crew?" Ryan offered.

Phillips took a long slurp of milky coffee, then pursed his lips.

"Aye, let's just do that."

Ryan snapped his folder shut and thought that would go down as the shortest briefing in living memory. Not that he minded; both men preferred field work to being shut inside a stuffy office, especially at this time of year.

"Your car, or mine?"

"Well, that depends whether you want to enjoy the journey at a leisurely pace—"

"We'll take my car," Ryan decided.

* * *

In the Family Room, Samantha closed her eyes and ordered herself to remember.

Come on!

Think!

But there was nothing in her mind's eye; nothing except the images she had already relayed.

"I'm sorry," she said, unhappily. "I can't remember anything else."

MacKenzie set her notepad aside and the representative from Social Services did the same.

"Don't worry, you've done more than enough for one day," she said, and gave the girl a reassuring smile. "Why don't you put it out of your head, for now?"

"I don't know if I can," she replied. "I keep seeing my mum's face and hearing that music…"

MacKenzie had an idea.

"I know what we'll do," she said brightly. "Why don't we go to the seaside?"

Samantha's face broke into a smile.

"Really?"

"Really. We're going to make a quick pit-stop on the way," MacKenzie added, casting her eye over the girl's well-worn clothes. She'd brought a change of underwear and a t-shirt in her backpack, but not much else. "We'll go shopping."

Samantha had never been shopping; not like other girls her age did, with their friends or with their mums. She was given new clothes as an afterthought; not because her father couldn't afford it, but because he simply didn't care enough to notice when her legs had grown too long for her jeans.

"Can I pick the colours?" she asked, excitedly.

MacKenzie ushered her outside a few moments later, leaving Mrs Carter to collect her things at a slower pace. She thought of the burgeoning affection she'd seen developing between the little girl and the police detective, then shook her head sadly.

Pity, she thought.

It would all come to nothing.

* * *

Whitley Bay was a seaside town situated on the coastline to the northeast of Newcastle. It had a long history, having survived the Crusades and the Dissolution of the Monasteries, before coming into the hands of the Dukes of Northumberland—who had retained it over the centuries so that the present Duke remained the principal landowner. To the ordinary residents, it was a family destination, with an attractive seafront where they could stroll across the tidal causeway to St Mary's Lighthouse or pop into the 'Spanish City', a white-painted, former concert hall and tearoom, overlooking the sea. It had been erected in the early part of the twentieth century and enjoyed many years as the premier place for courting couples to dine or watch a show, before it was reimagined as a children's funfair for most of Lowerson and Yates' formative years. Thanks to a recent regeneration effort, its freshly painted towers were once again home to an impressive restaurant complex where locals could enjoy afternoon tea with a view.

"Have you been inside, since they changed it all back?" Yates asked, as they drove past.

Lowerson glanced at the elegant white curves of the building and shook his head.

"Haven't had time," he said, dismissively. *Or anyone to go with,* he added silently.

She opened her mouth to ask whether he'd like to try it out, sometime, but the words died on her tongue. A girl could only stomach so much rejection.

"It's the next street on the left," she said.

Dan Hepple had lived in a smart, semi-detached, red-brick house that had been built at the turn of the last century. It was one of the largest on the street and less than a minute's walk from the sea, where, as they would learn, he'd enjoyed a jog along the promenade each morning. Lowerson slowed the car to a crawl and, after a short battle to find a parking space, eventually performed a lengthy parallel park into a slot at the other end of the road.

"If those other cars hadn't parked over the lines, that would have been a lot easier," he said, feeling a bit hot under the collar.

"Mm-hmm," Yates said. "I don't like parallel parking either."

"Women are notoriously bad at parking," he agreed, without any irony whatsoever, and then sauntered off towards Hepple's residence. Yates' eyes narrowed at his retreating figure and she took a couple of deep breaths, telling herself she'd give him a firm piece of her mind, the next time he tried to suggest women were inferior drivers.

Better yet, she'd do the driving next time and perform a perfect parallel park.

One-handed. In heels.

Smiling at the thought, she caught up with him.

"What are you so happy about?" he asked, but didn't bother to wait for an answer. They had no time for small-talk; not when the scene inside Hepple's home could be deteriorating with every passing minute.

"Are you sure this is the place?" Yates asked, taking in the smart front door with its potted plants and stained-glass panels. "Doesn't seem to suit the man we found in the dumpster."

"We don't know who he was, except that he liked to earn money by selling drugs, and that he was killed violently. Probably because of his choice of profession," Lowerson said. "Who's to say what he was really like? He might have been a fan of musical theatre, for all we know."

"Every drugs-pusher I've ever dealt with lived in a poky flat lined with thousands' worth of electronics and branded clothing," she said. "They usually had a fancy car, too."

"Maybe this one was a bit higher up the ladder than your average," Lowerson mused, and walked up to the front door.

"No sign of forced entry," Yates breathed, almost making him jump when he realised how close she was standing.

He was mortified to learn that the simple effect of having her warm breath on his neck was enough to…

To…

To play *havoc* with his body, that's what.

The embarrassing knowledge had a flush spreading across his face.

"I'll check around the back," he muttered, almost stumbling in his haste to put a safe distance between them. "You stay here."

"Why?"

Why? Because he needed to recover himself, that's why.

"Ah, in case anybody comes along."

Yates looked up and down at the empty street, unconvinced.

"I don't think—"

"Back in a sec," he told her, hurrying around the side of the house.

As soon as he did, she smiled. If she made him just a teensy bit uncomfortable, maybe there was hope, yet.

CHAPTER 19

Ryan and Phillips arrived at *O'Neill's Circus* just before eleven, to find it closed. Sweet wrappers moved lightly on the breeze, left by the people who had trampled over the moorland the previous day, and a couple of circus hands wandered around making a half-hearted attempt to clear them up.

"Help yer?" one called out.

"We're here to see Charlie," Phillips bellowed, sending a flock of nearby birds flapping into the sky.

"He's not here," they replied. "Him and Duke have gone off for a meetin' or somethin'."

Ryan filed away that nugget of information.

"Marco can pass a message on, if y' like," the man offered. "He's in his caravan. It's the black one, over there."

The one he'd admired, Phillips thought, with some excitement.

"Thanks," Ryan called out, and paused for another minute or two to take down their names and any other information they were willing to give, which didn't turn out to be much. There was a culture of silence amongst those who worked for *O'Neill's*, and it was not easily broken.

"They say they didn't know Esme," Ryan confirmed, as they walked across the uneven ground towards the caravan park. "They only started working for the circus a couple of years ago, and they'd heard the 'Big Man' had a wife who left him, but it's never spoken of."

Phillips grunted.

"He wields a lot of respect," he said. "I have to ask myself, what did he do to earn it?"

"Perhaps it isn't respect he commands, but *fear*," Ryan murmured. "And the question therefore becomes, what did he do to earn *that*?"

They were approaching the caravan park now and decided to put their conversation on hold, since there were several people sitting on camp chairs and sun loungers, enjoying the intermittent shafts of sunlight that occasionally burst through the clouds. Their chatter died as they spotted the two police officers, and they stared openly in a manner Ryan found vaguely unnerving. It was mostly women and children milling around and he wondered where all the men had gone.

"This is the one they said belonged to Marco," Phillips said, as they approached a large, polished black motorhome.

Ryan scanned its metal edges for the door, then tapped on it.

When there was no answer, they were drawn to the sound of laughter coming from the other side, where a gazebo attachment had been set up. Beneath it, a small group of people had gathered and were enjoying cups of tea and an animated discussion.

"I'd watch Huge Jackman in anything," one woman declared.

"You mean, *Hugh* Jackman," a male voice replied, and there came the sound of laughter in response.

As Ryan and Phillips rounded the corner, they could see that the group consisted of three people—a man and two women—one of whom stood up to confront the new arrivals.

"Can I help you?" she asked, looking between them with suspicion etched all over her face.

"Maybe," Ryan said, in what he hoped was an unthreatening tone. "We were looking for Marco?"

"You've found him," the man said, rising from his chair.

He was tall, probably on a par with Ryan at a couple of inches over six feet, and spoke with a continental accent heavily imbued with a hotchpotch of regional dialects taken from his travels all around the UK.

"Who're you?"

They produced their warrant cards.

"We're from CID," Ryan added. "You may have already heard; we're investigating the murder of Esme O'Neill."

They looked amongst themselves.

So, it was true.

"I still can't believe that," the first woman said, sticking a cigarette between her bold red lips. "Got a light?"

They might have been police, but the taller one was a knock-out and she wasn't about to let a good opportunity go to waste.

"Sorry, we don't smoke," Ryan said, before Phillips could fall off the wagon.

She shrugged, and feigned surprise when she pulled a lighter out of her bra.

"It's awful," the other woman whispered, brushing a short, honey-blonde bob away from her face. "I thought Esme had cheated on Charlie, and we all thought the worst of her. I never imagined she'd been killed. I feel terrible—"

Her face started to crumple, and Marco hurried back to crouch in front of her chair and take her hands.

"Shh, don't get yourself all upset," he said. "Stress isn't good for the baby."

On closer inspection, they realised she was carrying a basketball-sized parcel beneath the loose green top she wore.

"I know, I'll be careful," she said, giving his hand a quick squeeze. "It just makes me sad to think about it."

"We were hoping you might be able to tell us when Mr O'Neill is due back," Ryan interjected, and the three looked amongst themselves again.

"He's bound to be back before the show starts," Marco said, evasively. "We can take a message, if you want."

"That's okay," Ryan said, and decided to use the cosy little setting to his advantage. "Mind if we sit and chat to you about Esme, for a minute?"

He settled himself on the bottom step of one of the doors to the motorhome, facing the others. Phillips leaned comfortably against the side, and was tempted to stroke its smooth paint finish, but stopped himself just in time.

"Lovely vehicle, you've got here," he said, falling into an easy, personable rhythm that helped to draw people out. "Circus business must be good."

Again, they paused before laughing awkwardly.

"Uh, yeah, it is. People keep coming to see us, anyway," the first woman said.

"Do you mind introducing yourselves?" Ryan asked. "And maybe you could tell us a bit about how you knew Esme?"

The first woman looked uncomfortable.

"I'm Sabina," she said. "My stage name is 'Psychic Sabina'. You might have heard of me?"

They smiled politely.

"Oh, yes, now you mention it, I think your name does ring a bell," Phillips replied.

It was not a lie, since they'd seen her name written on one of the tents.

"I'll read your palm, sometime, if you like," she said, and Phillips was about to protest when he realised the offer had been aimed at his good-looking friend.

Typical.

"Ah, that's kind," Ryan managed. "But I already had a palm-reading, just the other day."

"Oh?" Her dark brown brows drew together as she imagined professional competition, and he wondered how widespread the world of palmistry and tarot reading could be. "Someone I'd have heard of?"

"I doubt it," he said. "My wife doesn't tend to do it for a living."

Anna didn't read palms at all, and would probably laugh at the very idea, but it was a neat way to forestall any further offers.

He turned to the other woman in the party, who was sitting with her hands linked beneath her bump. She looked exhausted but happy, a look that seemed universal to most mothers he'd come across.

"I'm Leonie," she told him. "Marco's wife."

"Much more than that," he chipped in, reaching across to pat her belly. "Until this little bundle took over, you were my flying partner."

Phillips realised they meant acrobatics.

"Like a husband and wife duo?" he asked, and Leonie nodded.

"I met Marcus at another circus when I was sixteen and then we joined *O'Neill's* together. We just hit it off, didn't we?"

"It's sickening," Sabina said. "The two of them mooch about like a couple of sex-starved teenagers."

"You don't see what it's like behind closed doors," Leonie joked. "He's always leaving the toilet seat up, never makes the bed…"

"And she's always nagging," Marco said, kissing the back of her hand.

"How long did you all know Esme O'Neill?"

"I knew her before she married Charlie," Sabina replied, taking a deep drag of her cigarette. "He totally changed when he met her, by the way. He used to be strong—like he is now. But when he first met Esme…it was like seeing a lion having its balls cut off."

"Sabby!" Leonie was upset. "You shouldn't say that. Charlie loved her."

"He was infatuated," Sabina snorted. "That's different."

Leonie sighed, the action becoming an effort with the burden she carried.

"How about you, Marco?" Ryan asked. "Did you know Esme?"

Marco looked up from where he'd been playing with the blades of grass at his feet.

"Yes, of course. She was nice enough, if a bit dull, you know? Never had anything interesting to say. I was surprised when I heard she'd run off with another man—frankly, I didn't think she had it in her."

"It's always the quiet ones," Sabina said, with a touch of malice.

"Well, she was already engaged to Charlie, by the time we joined the circus," he said. "Back in 2007. I think they got married in 2008, so I guess that's about right."

"We all went to the wedding," Leonie said, with a sad smile. "She looked beautiful."

Sabina flicked her cigarette away with an angry little gesture.

"When someone dies, everybody always feels like they have to say nice things about them. But Esme was always an attention-seeker," she said, warming up to the topic. "She got her eye on Charlie as soon as he took over the circus, and once her claws were in…"

She stopped, abruptly.

"Anyway, we weren't best friends, if that's what you want to know."

Ryan gave her a searching look.

"When was the last time you saw her?"

She gave a light shrug.

"I really can't remember. Probably the day before she left—"

"*If* she left," Phillips cut in, and her mouth flattened.

"Whatever. It's not like we lived in each other's pockets. She spent most of her time swanning around showing off the baby or looking after her beloved horses. We were totally different people."

With that, she stood up again and brushed a hand over the floaty skirt she wore. It was a deep jade green embroidered with a pattern of moons and stars. On her wrists, charms and bangles of all sizes clinked together as she moved.

"I have to go and get ready," she said, turning away.

"We'll be asking everyone to give us a formal statement of their whereabouts on Friday 3rd June 2011," Ryan said, his quiet voice stopping her from beating a hasty retreat. "In particular, we'd like to know the last time you saw Esme O'Neill alive."

She sent him a fulminating glare.

"How the hell can I remember what I was doing eight years ago?" she said. "It's not like I keep a diary."

"Try," he said, evenly. "We'll be in touch."

"Don't mind her," Marco said, as she moved off in the direction of her own caravan. "She's been Charlie's…ah, unofficial girlfriend, for the last few months. Esme is probably the last person she wants to think about, right now."

"It's obvious they didn't get on," Ryan said.

"Being a part of the circus is like living with your family," Leonie explained. "You love them, but you hate them sometimes, too."

Phillips gave her a sideways glance, wondering which of them she hated.

CHAPTER 20

Yates decided her partner had enjoyed enough 'recovery time' and made her way around the back of Daniel Hepple's Victorian semi. She found Lowerson standing beside the back door, drawing on a pair of nitrile gloves.

"Find anything?" she asked.

"Hmm? Yeah, somebody left the door ajar and there's blood spatter just inside," he said. "Keep to the edges and put some shoe coverings on, in case the CSIs find anything on the paving."

"Do you want me to call them?" she offered.

"Already done," he said. "Faulkner's sending a team down to go over the house. He'd have come himself, but he's just been called out to another murder scene, over in Stocksfield."

Yates thought of the upmarket village in Northumberland, situated to the west of the city of Newcastle and close to the River Tyne, as it wound its way through the valley.

"Oh yeah? Did a fight break out after somebody's Land Rover went into the back of a Ferrari?"

He laughed at that.

"Nope, not this time. Apparently, it's another man, this time found near the edge of the railway track. There haven't been any collisions or accidents reported, so it's looking like he was dumped there."

"Who's the SIO?" Yates asked, out of curiosity.

Lowerson named one of their colleagues, outside of Ryan's division.

"Is it just me, or have there been quite a few bodies, lately?" she said, as she tucked her feet into a pair of bright blue plastic shoe covers.

In the last few days, there had been three or four deaths, all male.

"I'll request a copy of the reports, when we get back to HQ," Lowerson said. "Maybe there's a connection. Ready?"

At her nod, he stepped inside.

* * *

After what turned out to be a lengthy pit-stop in the childrenswear department to stock up on essentials, MacKenzie had taken Samantha off to the seaside, as promised. They were fortunate to have several beaches in the area but, as it was growing late in the day, she chose to take the little girl to Tynemouth as it was one of the nearest. It was a quaint seaside village boasting two sandy beaches, a ruined priory, and more ice-cream vendors than Samantha could shake a stick at—all located a couple of miles along the coastline from where Lowerson and Yates picked their way across Hepple's blood-stained floor in Whitley Bay.

"Ooh, do you think we could stop for an ice-cream?"

MacKenzie laughed as they walked along the larger of the two beaches, known as 'Longsands'.

"Sam, you've just eaten the most enormous plate of scampi 'n' chips I've ever seen. How can you be thinking about food?"

"I must be having a growth spurt," she replied. "Besides, I burned off most of the energy when we were playing 'tag', earlier."

MacKenzie pursed her lips, then sighed.

"Go on, then," she said, fishing out a couple of coins. "But that's the last one, mind."

She stayed with Samantha while they went to the van and selected something called a 'Towering Inferno', never more conscious that she was responsible for the child's welfare. It was an odd sensation, MacKenzie thought, to have somebody so reliant upon the decisions you made. She had a brother back in Ireland, who had children she saw irregularly and to whom she was 'cool' Auntie Denise, but that was the extent of her knowledge when it came to child-rearing.

Already, she was feeling a renewed respect for those who managed it every day, because there had been several occasions during the past few hours when she'd wondered if it was right to let Samantha go into the ladies' toilet alone; whether she ought to buy the girl her first soft bra, although it was clear there was no need for one, just yet; and, how to *avoid* telling her what a 'booty call' meant, after she'd overheard a conversation between two teenagers in the changing rooms.

In short, the whole thing was fraught.

And yet, it was also simple.

Despite all the clothes and ice-creams, Samantha had been overjoyed and enraptured by the sand and the sea, and MacKenzie suspected she needed little else than a bit of time, care and affection.

"Mac?"

Samantha had heard the shortened version of her name bandied around Police Headquarters and seemed to like using it, and Denise had no objection.

"Mm-hmm?"

"What's Ryan's first name?"

MacKenzie's eyebrows shot up.

"Oh, ah, it's Maxwell. Max, for short."

"Why doesn't he use it?"

The kid had a talent for asking all the difficult questions, she thought, taking a slurp of her own melting ice-cream.

"You'd have to ask him," MacKenzie began to say, then realised she'd never really asked the question, herself. "I think he prefers 'Ryan' because it represents who he's worked hard to become. When people used to call him 'Max' or 'Maxwell', he wasn't as happy as he is now, so it holds a negative association."

To her surprise, the girl understood perfectly.

"That's like when people call me 'Sammy'," she said. "It makes me think of my mum, but not in a good way. It makes me remember she's gone."

Without a word, MacKenzie ran a gentle hand over the girl's hair, in sympathy.

"I'll be careful not to use it," she promised. "Why don't you tell me a bit about your dad?"

She tried to sound nonchalant, but Samantha saw straight through the subterfuge.

"He's one of your prime suspects, isn't he?"

When no answer was forthcoming, she continued.

"He's—he can be scary, sometimes," she said, and MacKenzie's heart thudded as she anticipated some terrible disclosure was about to be made.

"He never touches me, ever," she continued, unconsciously allaying MacKenzie's worst fears whilst simultaneously sparking fresh sympathy. "He never even gives me a hug or reads any stories."

"Maybe he's just a bit busy, running the circus," she felt obliged to say, having acquitted him of the worst.

"He's always been like that," Samantha continued, smearing rainbow-coloured syrup from her ice-lolly halfway across her cheek. "It's not just me that's scared of him, either. It's the whole circus, I think. One time, somebody told him to f—Um, they said a naughty word," she corrected herself quickly. "The next day, he had this gigantic bruise across his face, and everybody said my dad had taught him some manners, but I think he punched him."

"I see," MacKenzie said, swallowing the last of her wafer with difficulty.

"A couple of times he's given me a smack, but that's when I was bad," Samantha continued.

"What was so bad?" MacKenzie asked, in a very low voice.

What could be so bad as to justify striking a child?

"Well, I went into his cupboard without asking and then, another time, I took some money out of his wallet. I needed it, to buy some stuff," she muttered.

She'd needed a haircut, and a new toothbrush.

MacKenzie dropped the last of her ice-cream into a passing bin, having lost her remaining appetite. Behind them, the waves lapped gently against the shoreline and sunlight rippled against the swell, glittering like diamonds. She watched it for a couple of seconds, pretending it was that which was making her eyes water, then turned back to the little girl at her side.

She leaned down on her bad leg, but hardly felt it.

"Listen to me, Samantha," she said quietly, and the girl nodded, enjoying the lyrical sound of the Irish accent and the soft feel of MacKenzie's hand as it took her own. "No matter what you did, no matter what you took, violence is not the answer. I want you to know—" Her voice shook, and she tried again. "I want you to *know*, there's another way. There are people who don't smack. They don't hit or lash out when they can't find the words to say what they want to say. Not everybody is angry, although, sometimes, anger can be healthy. There are ways to deal with it that don't involve hurting other people."

"You mean like the way somebody hurt my mum?" Samantha whispered.

"Yes."

"Mac?"

"Yes, sweetheart?"

"I'm a bit scared that the one who hurt my mum might come back and do the same thing to me."

MacKenzie looked her in the eye.

"They'd have to get through me, first, and I don't mind telling you, there isn't much that can."

Samantha grinned, then asked the question that ran around her mind on a constant loop, demanding to be answered.

"Do you think my dad killed my mum?"

"Do you?" MacKenzie asked.

"I think he could have," the girl whispered. "Sometimes, when he gets angry, it's like he's somebody else. Like a monster."

MacKenzie told herself to remain clear-headed but, God, it was hard.

"And what if we find out he's the one?"

Samantha thought of a young woman with long red hair and a big, bright smile.

"Then he needs to go to jail, so he can't hurt anyone else," she said. "He needs to pay for it."

MacKenzie straightened up again and, as they made their way across the sand towards the stairs leading back up to the promenade, Samantha slipped her hand into hers.

CHAPTER 21

Emi-Lee Rundle slammed her way out of the little salon where, until five minutes ago, she'd been employed as one of their beauticians. Her flip-flops slapped against the paving stones as she hurried back to her car, red-faced in a combination of humiliation and righteous anger.

So what, if she'd been borrowing a few quid from the till? she fumed.

It was only until pay day, to tide her over. There was a new bar opening that weekend and she needed something new to wear, on top of her usual spend on hairdressers, getting her lashes done, and having her hoo-ha waxed—well, you never knew, did you? It all took money, especially with the new circle she'd started hanging around with. Her old dresses looked cheap in comparison with the other girls' silk and leather numbers, and she wanted to look just like them.

She wanted to be admired.

To be wanted.

And, most of all, she wanted to be accepted.

It would have been *fine*. She'd have paid the money back at the end of the month and nobody would have been any the wiser. Except, now, *Zara* had grassed her up. Bloody big gob.

Bitch.

She was only jealous. They all were, really, because they knew she was only biding her time working in the salon until she was discovered. It happened all the time; girls much less pretty than her would be down at McDonald's, or at the cinema, and a model scout would spot them. That's what happened to Kate Moss, when she was at the airport, and Emi-Lee knew she was meant for that kind of glamorous life too. She didn't want to spend her days painting the ugly toenails of old women, filing their calloused feet while they told her boring stories about their grandchildren. She was meant for better things.

As for the rest of them, the salon was their lot in life.

She sniffed, worrying for a moment about how she'd pay her bills. The rent was due soon, and there would be the electric to pay…

There was a *whooshing* sound—as if something was approaching at speed—until the body landed with a sickening crunch on the pavement in front of her. It missed her by less than a metre, and there was no time to react before the hot splatter of blood and brains drenched her face and bare legs.

There was a second's delay, and then she was screaming.

And the dead man's eyes watched her, from where they'd fallen from his skull.

* * *

Phillips' teeth *crunched* into a toffee apple as he and Ryan made their way to the next stop on their list.

"I still can't believe you managed to wangle a toffee apple," Ryan muttered. "The stalls aren't even open yet."

"I've gnt vu gnt ov da gb," Phillips replied, between chews.

"What?"

He swallowed.

"I said, 'I've got the gift of the gab'," Phillips repeated, with some dignity. "Besides, you can't come to the Town Moor and leave without having something sweet."

Ryan would rather have a pulled pork sandwich, and began to wonder whether his sergeant could unleash his interpersonal skills on the bloke who ran the burger van.

As he was rolling the idea around his mind, they came to a large, impressive-looking caravan. It stood at the end of a row and a small fence separated it from the ticket office adjacent to the Big Top.

"Doesn't look like he's home," Phillips remarked, gesturing towards the empty spot where a car should have been.

They stood in front of the caravan, shoulder to shoulder, arms folded.

"We can't go inside without his permission, or a warrant," Ryan said, needlessly.

"O' course," Phillips said.

There was a pause, then Ryan cleared his throat.

"Wouldn't hurt to peep through the windows, though—would it?"

"No crime in peeping, unless your name's Tom," Phillips agreed, and they moved forward to look through the thick, Perspex windows of the O'Neill residence.

"Neat as a pin," Ryan remarked.

"What the hell d'you think you're playing at?"

Both men turned at the sound of O'Neill's belligerent voice, to find Charlie and his brother standing behind them with angry faces, their feet planted as if they expected trouble.

"I've heard you've been harassing my employees," he continued, jabbing a broad finger in the air short of Ryan's face. "There are laws against that. You should know."

"We've harassed nobody," Ryan replied, very calmly. "We've asked routine questions of all the people on-site, today."

"Oh, aye—and you wait until I'm not here, to do it," O'Neill sneered. "Bloody cowards."

Ryan took a single step forward.

"Care to test that theory?"

"And have you strap me with some bullshit about assaulting an officer? I'm not that stupid."

"Good, because I don't need the extra paperwork," Ryan shot back. "We're here because we want to find out what happened to your wife; the mother of your daughter. You can either be obstructive, or you can try to help us and eliminate yourself from our enquiries. Which'll it be?"

"I've got nowt to hide," O'Neill said.

"In that case, would you be willing to let us see inside your caravan?" Phillips asked.

Duke tensed and shot his brother a quick look, which Ryan caught.

"Help yourself." O'Neill decided to brazen it out, elbowing them aside to slot his key into the lock. "But wipe your feet, first."

* * *

The atmosphere was uncomfortable as the four men stepped inside Charlie O'Neill's caravan. For one thing, it was exactly as Samantha had described; from its white, PVC-leather bench and sofa, to the little kitchen to the right of the front door, where her mother had once stood listening to the radio. There was a fluffy, faux-fur rug in the centre of the living area, with a glass coffee table on top, and a mounted television on one of the walls overlooking the sofa.

There was an area of floor space where a play pen or a cot might have stood, which overlooked the kitchen area and the door beside it.

Now, it housed a large, artificial fern.

"Do you want to look inside my drawers, now?" O'Neill jeered. "Whatever turns you on, mate."

He led the way along a narrow corridor, off which there was a small bathroom and a broom cupboard, until he reached the door at the end. He threw it open with a sarcastic bow.

"After you."

Ryan said nothing but stepped around O'Neill into the largest of the bedrooms. Its main feature was a giant sleigh bed with a matching white PVC-leather headboard and a faux-fur throw, similar to the one gracing the floor of the living space.

Phillips thought he might have seen one of the characters wearing it on *Game of Thrones.*

"Was this the room you shared with Esme?" Ryan asked.

"Husbands usually share a bed with their wives, don't they?"

"Did you?" Ryan persisted. He hadn't forgotten that the body had been found without a wedding ring.

"You're a cheeky bugger, I'll give you that," O'Neill said, swiping the back of his hand across the stubble on his chin. "Alright, as it happened, I was using the spare room when she—when she died."

He looked away, seeming to cast his mind back.

"The baby hadn't been sleeping well," he said. "Esme thought I'd get more rest if I used the spare room."

"Where did you keep the baby's cot?"

If O'Neill was confused by the line of questioning, he said nothing.

"We kept her cot in the main bedroom here, by Esme's side of the bed," he said quietly, and jutted his chin towards the spot. "There was a play pen in the lounge, too."

"What kind?" Phillips chipped in.

"Eh? It was one of those white plastic ones with the bars, for when kids are toddling about. Why d'you ask?"

"Where's Samantha's room?" Ryan asked, ignoring the question.

At the mention of her name, O'Neill's face hardened.

"It's through here," he said, darkly.

It turned out that the space Ryan had thought was a cupboard was, in fact, a little girl's bedroom. It was plain, with white walls and a simple cabin bed, and just as neat as the rest of the caravan. A bit sparse on *things,* he thought suddenly. There was little in the way of trinkets or the kind of mementos that kids usually collected from their trips or days away.

That was probably because she didn't have any.

There was a bear sitting on the window-ledge, and Phillips reached out to touch it. He didn't know what he intended to do; maybe take it home and give it to Samantha, in case she'd forgotten it.

"Get your hands off my property," O'Neill snapped, and snatched the toy away before hurling it across the room, where it landed in the corner. "And you can tell her from me, that if she wants any of her things, she'll have to come home and get them."

"If you want to see her, you can always apply for a court order," Ryan told him, although he suspected the man already knew his rights. "You could see her, if you really wanted to."

O'Neill turned away, unable to look him in the eye, because the truth of it was...maybe he didn't want to see her. He didn't want to see the girl who looked just like her mother, who looked at him as if she expected better of him.

As if he should expect better of himself.

"Get out," he muttered. "You've seen what you wanted to see."

"We're grateful you've shown us where Esme lived," Ryan said, with rigid politeness. "But we still need to take a formal statement from you, about the night she went missing."

"I've already told you what happened," O'Neill argued. "I've got nothing more to say."

"I'd have thought you'd want to find out what happened to her," Phillips said. "She was murdered. Don't you care enough to help us discover who did it?"

O'Neill's eyes flashed dangerously.

"Don't start telling me what to think, or what to feel—"

"I'm not," Phillips said, with a negligent shrug. "But it doesn't look good, does it, if a husband won't even make a statement to help the police investigate his wife's murder? That's the kind of thing that sets tongues wagging."

O'Neill almost laughed because, in other circumstances, he might have liked the little sergeant with his sharp eyes and even sharper tongue.

Ryan, on the other hand, was a different kettle of fish.

"What my sergeant's trying to say is, you can either come down to the station of your own accord and make a statement to assist our investigation, or we can arrest you and slap on a pair of handcuffs, which won't look good to your friends in the circus, will it?"

"I can phone the solicitor, Charlie," Duke said, piping up for the first time since they'd been in the caravan. "I'll meet you down there."

"You can give a statement, too," Ryan interjected, half surprised to find him still lurking in the hallway.

Afterwards, he was struck forcibly by the impression that, if Duke didn't want to be seen or heard, he was the kind of man who knew how to make himself invisible. It was a skill that he'd developed, something that took time and care.

He wondered what he might have seen, from the shadows where he hid.

CHAPTER 22

The late Daniel Hepple had enjoyed a flashy lifestyle, if his home in Whitley Bay was anything to go by. Every floor was covered in expensive natural stone or thick-pile carpet; every wall was covered in marble or papered in expensive wall coverings that retailed for more than Melanie Yates spent on her annual summer holiday. The colour scheme was a combination of muted greys, navy and white which, although generally thought to be a masculine palette, seemed to resonate with femininity.

Plus, she'd spotted scatter cushions.

"Was he married?" she asked, to the room at large.

Lowerson looked across from where he stood beside one of the CSIs, who was snapping a series of photographs of the back door from all angles.

"Not that I know of," he said. "Why? Did you find a photograph or something?"

Yates shook her head.

"No, it's more of a...a feeling," she said, and Lowerson gave her a look she didn't much care for.

"We need *evidence*, Mel," he started to say. "We can't rely on feelings, that won't help us to build a case. You see—"

"Ah, Jack? Can I have a word, please?" she interrupted him, and moved swiftly into the next room, which was empty of forensic staff.

"Wha—?"

He didn't have time to finish his sentence, before she rounded on him.

"Now, listen to me," she said, in a voice that trembled with anger. "I know you're *Acting* SIO on this, but that doesn't make you some kind of big shot. You might be above me in the pecking order, but don't you dare undermine me in front of my colleagues like that, ever again. I know fine well that we need evidence to build a case, but if you think lowly things like *feelings* are irrelevant, then you're not half the man Ryan is."

That struck a nerve, as she knew it would.

"Now, just wait a minute—"

"I asked if Hepple had a wife because the whole house looks like somebody with an eye for colours and shapes has helped him to decorate," she blazed on. "I could be wrong; not all women like to decorate, and some men do have an eye for what goes together. Our gangland drugs-pusher *might* have had a subscription for *Interior Design Monthly*, or he could have hired someone to help him. Or, maybe—just maybe—he had the help of whichever woman *these* belong to."

To his surprise, she held up a pair of slinky women's knickers in her gloved hand.

"Where did you find those?" he asked, meekly.

"Upstairs, under his bed," she muttered. "While you were wind-bagging about the correct way to approach a crime scene, I went upstairs to have a root around. I found these, and what looks like a burner mobile that's password protected."

"Let's have a look," he said, but she held it just out of reach.

"I mean it, Jack," she said carefully. "I've always liked you. You've been my friend and, after what happened last year, I was prepared to cut you a lot of slack. But your free pass to be rude and misogynist has just expired. Speak to me like that again and I'll slap a complaint on you, and request a transfer."

She slammed the phone into his outstretched palm and turned to leave, before he saw how much the confrontation had affected her.

"Mel, wait a minute."

She paused in the doorway, sighed, then turned around again.

"Well?"

"I'm sorry," he said. "Everything you said was right, and I'm sorry. I think—I think you unsettle me, and I'm already nervous in case I'm not doing things right. That's not an excuse, it's just an explanation. The point is, none of that is your fault but I've been taking it out on you. You have my word; it'll never happen again."

She was silent for a long moment, thinking it was hard to stay mad at him when he was looking at her with those sweet, puppy-brown eyes.

"Good," she said. "I don't want to have to set MacKenzie on you."

She took a wicked pleasure from watching naked fear flash across his face, then she took a deep breath before saying one final thing.

"You know, I'm not Jennifer Lucas. Just remember that."

She left him to think it over.

* * *

Just before the clock struck two, Ryan and Phillips entered Interview Room C, one of the smaller rooms of the interview suite at Police Headquarters. They hadn't left Charlie O'Neill to stew for long, being of the correct opinion that it would prove to be counter-productive to their cause. However, his brother was a very different matter, so they'd left Duke waiting in another interview room with a cup of tea and one of the constables on duty. It served the dual purpose of preventing the brothers from conferring over the details of their statements, as well as placing Duke under a slightly elevated level of stress as he waited impatiently for his turn.

As Ryan had often found, people said very revealing things when they were under pressure.

He smiled genially as they entered the room, where Charlie was seated at a small metal table beside a man they assumed to be his solicitor, although they didn't recognise him. In their line of work, they came to know the names and faces of criminal solicitors and barristers in the region, both for the prosecution and defence, as well as a fair number from further afield.

Ryan checked the name that had been scrawled on his notepad: *George Kingley, of Kingley and Co., Solicitors*, and then recited the date, time and names of those present for the recording.

"Mr O'Neill, Mr Kingley—are you happy to begin?"

"My client is willing to cooperate fully in providing a statement," Kingley said, in a nasal voice that grated on Phillips' nerves. "But, first, he would like to discuss the plans for bringing his daughter home—"

"As Mr O'Neill is already aware, there are no plans for Samantha O'Neill to return to the family home until after the investigation is concluded," Ryan said. "Samantha herself has refused and has raised credible allegations surrounding the danger if she were to remain at the circus. She has been taken into the care of Social Services—"

"Who only went and bloody lost her!" O'Neill burst out.

"—who are keeping a close eye on her welfare and whereabouts, after she ran away from home," Ryan finished, while Phillips took a sudden, keen interest in his notepad.

"My client affirms that his daughter has a habit of absconding from the family caravan," Kingley said. "Therefore, this behaviour should not be given undue weight—"

"And is she often in the habit of making a police report, each time she runs away?" Ryan cut in.

There was no reasonable answer to that, so he continued.

"Social Services have kept Mr O'Neill abreast of all his rights in relation to his daughter, as have we," Ryan continued, linking his hands together atop the small folder he'd brought into the room. "Mr O'Neill is entitled to apply to a judge for a court order, if he wishes to maintain contact with Samantha."

"Bugger that," Charlie muttered. "She'll come crawling back, soon enough."

Phillips opened his mouth to defend her, but a mild look from Ryan stopped him. It would not help Samantha for anybody to work out where she might be staying.

"Moving on, I'd like to focus on the events leading up to and surrounding Friday 3rd June 2011."

"As you can imagine, my client's recollection is patchy, considering the passage of time."

"Duly noted," Ryan said, and leaned forward to create a sense of confidence. "Now, Mr O'Neill, perhaps you could tell us how you came to meet Esme?"

It was like prising open a locked box, Charlie thought. An old chest he'd nailed shut and shoved in the attic, so he could forget about it—but now he was being forced to look inside again, at memories he'd rather not have.

"She joined the circus when she was sixteen, as a stable hand," he said, in a tight voice. "I hardly noticed her, at first. She was always scruffy, never took any time with herself…"

He shrugged, unapologetically. As the son of the circus owner, he'd had his pick of the girls and still did. He hadn't needed to go slumming amongst the horses.

"But then, she started learning how to do the tricks—"

"Tricks?" Phillips asked.

"Aye, like handstands on the back of the horse, flips, all kinds as they're running around the ring."

Phillips nodded, imagining.

"She was stunning," Charlie admitted, swallowing hard. "Really something."

He could see her, even now, all decked out in a sparkling leotard, her hair shining beneath the lights as the crowd cheered.

"How soon were you two an item?"

Charlie snapped back to reality, as the memory faded.

"She held me off, for years," he said, remembering his old frustration. "Said I had a bad rep."

He ran a hand over his neck, and half laughed.

"I s'pose she was right. Anyhow, things didn't really get going between us until, maybe, sometime in 2007? Must've been around Christmas," he said. "It felt like something changed and she was looking at me differently."

"What changed?" Ryan asked.

O'Neill's face became ominous again.

"It's true my dad signed the circus over to me around then, and there were some who held it against her; said she only started showing any interest in me after I took it over. Esme was many things, but she wasn't a money-grabber," he said.

Ryan listened, watching the man's face closely, and realised something important.

Charlie O'Neill had loved his wife.

It had been by no means clear, until then—and it wasn't necessarily a point in his favour. There was a safety in being ambivalent, whereas, in his long experience, fools in love were much more likely to behave irrationally in the heat of passion. More likely to make mistakes—for love, or through jealousy.

More likely to kill.

"And so, you were married in June of 2008?" he prompted.

Charlie nodded.

"14th June," he said quietly. "We just decided to go for it. No sense in waiting, is there? Besides, she was old-fashioned, like that."

"Old-fashioned?"

"She'd been brought up religious," Charlie explained. "That's why it came as such a shock, thinking she'd gone off—"

He folded his arms, cupping the elbows in a gesture of self-comfort.

"What's the use in going over all this, now? She's dead, isn't she?"

"Yes, she is," Ryan murmured. "And she isn't here to defend herself. That's why we need to build up an accurate picture of her life; to try to understand what happened."

He nodded, then reached for a glass of water, which he downed in one gulp.

"How was married life?"

"Fine," he said. "Good, I s'pose."

When he thought of it, he realised how lucky he had been. He'd had a beautiful young wife at home, one who tended to his every need, scrubbed his floors and cooked his meals. He was the one who'd always demanded more, who'd made her feel unattractive after the baby had been born.

He pinched the bridge of his nose, willing the memory to pass.

"You were happy?"

"Yes. No. Look, we were just young. The baby came along too quick; we hardly had any time just as a couple, you know? I wasn't ready to deal with her crying and feeding all the time. I was sick of her being *too tired*."

Phillips thought, once again, that the man was a real prince.

"That must have been very trying for you," he said, with thinly-veiled sarcasm. "Weren't you happy, when Samantha was born?"

Charlie thought back to that day, in the hospital. Esme had wanted a home birth, with candles and whatnot, but the baby had other ideas. He'd never forget the fear he'd felt driving them both to the Accident & Emergency department.

He'd never forget the tiny little bundle they'd placed into his arms, and how he'd felt. The beginning of something, maybe love, had tugged around his heart.

And then she'd started to cry, her tiny face screwed up tight until she was back in her mother's arms. He'd watched them both and felt resentful, knowing from that moment onwards that he was no longer at the top of Esme's list of priorities.

And knowing something else, too.

Esme had never, ever, looked at him the way she was looking at Samantha.

"Mr O'Neill?" Ryan's voice brought him back to the present.

"I was glad there was nowt wrong with her," he snapped.

Phillips shifted in his chair, working hard to remain calm in the face of such a lack of feeling.

"I'm sorry I have to ask, but it's a standard question in cases such as these," Ryan continued. "Did you have any reason to believe Esme was having an affair?"

Charlie almost laughed.

He'd asked himself that question time and time again, coming up with the same answer every time.

He hadn't known a thing.

"No," he muttered. "She was the perfect little wife. If she had someone on the side, I never knew about it, and nobody else did, either."

"How can you be so sure?" Phillips asked.

"Because the whole bloody circus was in shock," Charlie replied, in a tired voice. "Nobody saw it coming."

Ryan decided to change tack.

"We already know Esme didn't have much in the way of family," Ryan said. "Why don't you tell us about her friends?"

"She was always close with Sabby and then, when Leonie joined, they hit it off as well," Charlie replied. "Leonie was Maid of Honour at our wedding, and Sabby was a bridesmaid."

"You mean, Sabina?"

If Ryan was surprised that Sabina and Esme had once been close, nothing of it showed on his face.

"Aye, Sabina Egerton and Leonie D'Angelo. The three of them were of an age, although Leonie's the eldest."

"And I understand Leonie is married to her fellow acrobat, Marco D'Angelo?"

"Yeah, they've been together since they were kids."

"I see—and when did you first strike up a relationship with Ms Egerton?"

Charlie didn't bother to act surprised. It was no secret, anyway.

"When we were kids, just teenagers, we used to bounce around a bit," he said. "And she kept me company a few nights a week, when I wasn't getting anywhere with Esme. But I never touched her while I was married," he said, firmly. "After Esme left, I guess Sabby was just *there*."

He rolled his shoulders, wishing for a cigarette.

"Were you the reason Esme's friendship with Sabina began to deteriorate?"

He ran his tongue around his teeth, wondering how much to say.

"Look, I don't know what goes on in women's minds," he muttered. "But Sabina was making a nuisance of herself, turning up at all hours, hanging around the house like a third wheel. I had to speak to her about it."

And she'd put up a fight, he remembered, with a trace of admiration. After all, he was a desirable man, especially in his own eyes.

"How would you describe your relationship with Esme, leading up to her disappearance on 3rd June 2011?"

"It was…fine," he said. *No sex. Arguments every day.* "Things were good between us."

Ryan cocked his head.

"Was she ever in the habit of removing her wedding ring? While she was cleaning, for example?"

"No, she kept it on and wore rubber gloves," he recalled, then grew suspicious. "Why?"

"It helps us to build up a picture," Ryan repeated. "Talk us through what happened, on the day she disappeared."

Charlie leaned back in his chair, and prepared to dive down the rabbit hole one more time.

CHAPTER 23

While Ryan and Phillips picked apart the last known movements of Esme O'Neill, Lowerson and Yates made their way back to Police Headquarters. The CSI team remained at Daniel Hepple's home, looking through the minutiae of his life for clues about his death, but they had already taken several useful swabs and fingerprint samples. They would be sent to the tech team who, they hoped, might be able to unlock the cheap, burner mobile phone they had found. It would also serve the useful purpose of identifying which set of prints belonged to the dead man, so they could focus on the remaining sets, one of which might belong to his killer.

Since Yates had given Lowerson a piece of her mind, the air had cleared a bit and they were enjoying a spot of early-nineties dance music on the car radio when her phone began to ring. She turned the music down and answered the call, which turned out to be from the Control Room.

"Any other details?" she asked, after a minute. "Alright, tell them to cordon it off and keep the crowd back. We're on our way."

She turned to her partner.

"Another male," she said. "Fell from the top floor of the multi-storey car park, on Dean Street."

Lowerson executed a slow U-turn, eliciting a couple of angry toots from commuter traffic on the road, and then moved off towards the centre of town.

"Fell—or was pushed?" he asked.

"That's what we need to find out. We need to determine whether it's a jumper or something for CID."

"We get all the best jobs," he murmured, with a smile.

"Nobody said it would be glamorous," she said, tucking her tongue into her cheek.

He shook his head, secretly glad that she had forgiven him sufficiently to tease him.

"A wise man must've said that."

"Nah, it was just some muppet," she said, and he laughed appreciatively.

"Have we heard anything back from the maintenance team at St Peter's Wharf? I was hoping they'd have sent through the CCTV footage from the apartment building, by now."

"It came through just as we were getting in the car," she said, dragging her mind back to business. "I've asked one of the analysts to start going through it."

Lowerson tried not to feel put out by her obvious talent for leadership, telling himself he was lucky to have such a great partner.

"Any word from the pathologist?"

Yates nodded.

"He's been delayed because of a big road traffic incident the other day, but he'll have a preliminary report ready for us by the end of today. Hopefully, we'll be able to stop into the mortuary first thing tomorrow."

"Right after breakfast," Lowerson said. "Here's hoping."

She chuckled.

"I never realised you were such a wuss around dead bodies."

He didn't bother to deny it.

"I've managed to camouflage it for some years, now," he said. "Until you came along and exposed me as a fraud."

"You're as bad as Phillips," she grinned. "How have you managed to hide it so well?"

He lifted a shoulder.

"I learned from Ryan," he said, because it was true. "I don't know anybody better at being able to shut it all down, to pack away his emotions. It's frightening, how well he can do it."

As they turned off the main roundabout leading into the centre of Newcastle from the west, they fought their way through the early evening traffic along Neville Street and then took the first left along Dean Street, which was the road leading down towards the Quayside from that part of town. Halfway down the road, there was a large multi-storey car park which served the working population as well as tourists and daytime visitors who didn't want to walk too far to the main shopping district or to the river.

Now, its access road was closed to the general public and was being manned by a small army of local police who were, by the looks of it, having a difficult time holding off angry motorists who wanted to retrieve their vehicles from within the multi-storey. Unfortunately, the body had fallen almost directly in front of the pedestrian access route, judging from the position of the forensic tent that Faulkner was in the process of erecting.

Lowerson parked on the kerb and they made their way through the crowd.

"What's the problem, here?" he said, in what he hoped was a commanding tone. "Stand back from the police cordon, please."

"Are you the one in charge?" somebody demanded. "Can you tell your minions to let me get my car? I need to go home and he's blocking the way."

"Detective Constable Lowerson," Jack said, flashing his warrant card the way he'd seen Ryan do it. "Unfortunately, a person has died, and there are certain procedures we have to follow to ensure their body is properly taken care of. Now, if you'll be patient for a short while longer, we'll see about creating a one-way system using the other set of barriers and everybody can be on their way."

To his surprise, that seemed to do the trick.

"Ever thought about running for office?" Yates joked. "With charm like that, the voting public would be putty in your hands."

As she slipped under the barrier to speak to the first responders, he found himself wondering whether he might be able to apply that so-called charm to other areas of his life.

Then again, he couldn't work miracles.

* * *

Neither, it seemed, could MacKenzie.

No matter how hard she tried, she couldn't figure out how to set up the parental controls on the new television Phillips had bought, after experiencing a rush of blood to the head on what should have been a routine trip to the nearby supermarket.

"I can help, if you like," Samantha offered, taking pity on the elderly.

"No, no, it'll just take me a minute—" MacKenzie muttered, pressing buttons at random on the remote control, which itself looked like something from the space age.

"You do it like this," Samantha said, plucking it from MacKenzie's hands. "What password do you want to use?"

MacKenzie opened her mouth to say something, then waggled her finger.

"Nice try," she said.

"You know, I'm not really interested in the telly," Samantha continued, as MacKenzie went about the laborious task of entering a password, letter by letter, using the remote control, while she looked away.

She would bet anything that she'd chosen 'FRANK' as the password.

"I don't really watch it, very much," she continued. "I'm too busy with the horses."

"Who taught you how to look after them?" MacKenzie asked, once she'd discarded the remote. "Your dad?"

"I sort of remember my mum liking horses," the girl said, playing with the zip on her new red hoodie. "But I was too young to remember. My uncle, Duke, showed me how to brush them down, how to muck out and all that. He helps out when he's not performing."

"What does he perform?"

"Oh, he's the clown," she said, with a smile.

"It sounds as though you like your uncle."

Samantha's lips twisted.

"He'd be okay if he wasn't trying to impress my dad, all the time. He never stands up for himself, and it gets on my nerves. One time, he saw…well, he saw my dad giving me a smack, and he didn't say anything. He just watched, then looked away."

She gave a sad little shrug.

"He'd probably jump straight off the Tyne Bridge, if my dad asked him to. Some people are strong, and some people are weak, I guess."

MacKenzie nodded, because it was only the truth.

"I think you're very strong, Samantha," she said. "It can't have been easy to walk away from your family."

Samantha had worried about it, as they'd strolled along the beach earlier in the day. Every time she'd started to feel happy, she'd worried her dad would appear out of the blue, ready to drag her home.

At first, she'd thought the police would find her mother's killer and then she'd go home, and things would go back to normal. But she was starting to understand that there were very different kinds of 'normal' and, now that she'd seen another kind, she wasn't sure if she could ever go back.

"Tell me about some of the other people at the circus," MacKenzie asked, in the comfortable silence. "Who do you like?"

"Leonie and Marco are nice," she said. "Leonie gives me chocolate, sometimes, and Marco showed me how to do a backward flip on the grass."

"Really?"

"Yeah, they're both acrobats, except Leonie's pregnant now, so she can't do her normal show at the moment. She still helps to set up and she trained the girl who's replacing her, until she's had the baby."

"Have they been with the circus a long time?"

"Yeah, for years. They used to know my mum, before she died," Samantha said, and realised it was becoming easier to admit that her mother was dead. "My dad doesn't let me keep any pictures of her in the caravan, and he got really mad when I found some old ones of him and my mum in a box."

He'd thrown them away, in a fit of anger, and she'd cried long into the night.

"But Leonie and Marco had some of her from before she had me, and one from the wedding to my dad."

"Where are they now?"

Samantha hesitated, then jumped off the sofa. A moment later, MacKenzie heard her small feet stomping up the stairs and back down again.

"I brought them with me," she said. "I gave one to Ryan to borrow, in case he needed it, but I kept the rest."

MacKenzie couldn't have said why she felt so nervous accepting the old prints, but it might have had something to do with the fact she had been entrusted with the safe-keeping of this woman's daughter. If Esme O'Neill was looking down and watching the pair of them, she hoped she would approve of what she saw.

"Your mum was very lovely," she said, holding the photographs in careful hands.

And so young, MacKenzie thought.

She saw a slim woman with gleaming red hair and a wide smile, dressed in skinny blue jeans and a casual shirt, tied at her waist. She was captured standing in a crowd of people roughly her own age, and MacKenzie pointed to the first one.

"Who's this?"

"Oh, that's Psychic Sabina," the girl replied, without enthusiasm. "She fancies my dad."

MacKenzie blinked at the candour, then remembered that children saw everything, whether you wanted them to, or not.

"Marco and Leonie are the ones standing on either side of my mum," Samantha said. "My dad's next to Leonie, and then that's Ginger, who used to work for the circus, but he got a new job working for a call centre, apparently. The one on the end is my uncle, Duke."

It was a motley crew, MacKenzie thought, and the O'Neill brothers appeared to be like chalk and cheese. Where Charlie was standing confidently, chest puffed out and tattoos on show, his brother stood awkwardly at the end of the line. Taller, ganglier, and pale as pasteurised milk, as he looked not at the camera, but at someone else in the group.

Maybe even at Esme.

CHAPTER 24

Ryan and Phillips spent over an hour with Charlie O'Neill, recording his version of the events of Friday, 3rd June 2011. Having discharged him from the station, they stood in the small viewing room overlooking Interview Room A, where his brother, Duke, had been waiting for some time. He was talking to their family solicitor, George Kingley, who was now providing his counsel to the younger O'Neill.

"What d'you make of Charlie's statement?" Phillips asked, keeping his voice low.

The rooms were supposed to be soundproof, but discretion was a habit that was hard to break.

"I think his statement is very difficult to disprove without evidence," Ryan said. "Unless an eyewitness comes forward and tells us they saw somebody enter and leave the caravan dragging Esme's body behind them, we'll have to piece the timeline together like a jigsaw."

His eyes never moved from Duke's face, which displayed the signs of severe stress.

"This O'Neill brother seems disproportionately worried, for someone who's been asked to come in and make a routine statement about his sister-in-law," he added.

Phillips agreed.

"He's the nervy type, that's for sure. Wonder if he's like that all the time, or whether it's only around the fuzz."

"We'll find out, in a minute," Ryan said, and stuck his hands inside his pockets. "Charlie says he left the caravan around seven in the morning on the day Esme disappeared, and that everything was fine when he left. He confirms she was wearing blue jeans and a pink t-shirt, just as Samantha said, and that Esme was feeding the baby her breakfast the last time he saw her."

He paused, thinking of what might have happened in between.

"Charlie says it was his brother who ran to him to tell him Esme was missing, after people had been complaining about the baby crying for a long time," he said. "He seems to think this was sometime during the early afternoon. He went into the caravan to find some of her things missing and a note waiting for him."

"Let's see if their stories match," Phillips said, nodding towards the man on the other side of the toughened glass wall. "Although, God knows, they've had plenty time to come up with a cover story, if they needed one."

Ryan's jaw hardened.

"Esme's murderer—*or murderers*—did their best to destroy all traces of her. After all this time, they probably hoped she'd never be found. But she was. We have the evidence, we have the manpower, and we have the skills to crack this, Frank. We just need time."

"And a bit of good luck," Phillips muttered.

* * *

Duke O'Neill was sweating like a pig on market day, as Phillips' old grandma used to say.

After Ryan had completed the preliminaries for the record, he reached across to pour the man some water. He would prefer that a suspect passed out thanks to his robust questioning techniques, rather than simple dehydration.

"So, Mr O'Neill," he said, with a welcoming smile. "Thank you for taking the trouble to come in and give a statement."

"Has Charlie finished his, now?"

Ryan smiled.

"Yes, your brother's gone home now," he replied, and noticed the casual hurt flicker across Duke's face, because Charlie had not bothered to wait around as he might have done.

"How will I get back to the circus?"

"We'll have one of the squad cars drop you off," Ryan assured him, and thought that, if he hadn't known Duke was the same age as himself, he might have pegged him for a much younger man. "I wonder if you could tell me the first time you met Esme O'Neill?"

"She wasn't an 'O'Neill' when I first met her," Duke replied, and took another long gulp of water. "She was just Esme."

"And when was that?"

Duke couldn't meet his eyes.

"Must've been around 2003," he said softly. "She had just joined the circus, to help look after the horses. We were doing this stint in Leicester, and she rocked up one day asking if she could come along with us."

"Did you like her?"

Duke swallowed painfully.

Like her? He'd loved her: painfully, enduringly—unrequitedly.

"She was nice," he said awkwardly. "She was kind to the horses." *And to me.*

"You got along, then?"

"Yes, we were friends."

Ryan leaned forward, so that Duke could try to fool himself that they were just two blokes, sharing a story.

"And, since she was your friend, I guess she must have told you things about her life?"

Duke shrugged.

"Esme was a private person," he said. "If she told anyone anything, it would have been Sabina or Leonie. They were the closest, the three of them."

"How about your brother?" Phillips asked. "Wouldn't you say she was close to him, too?"

"Well, yes, of course—" he stammered, conscious of having said the wrong thing. "But, for a long time, she avoided him. He wasn't her type."

"What was her type?" Ryan asked, gently. "Someone…quieter?"

"Is that a relevant question, chief inspector?" Kingley asked. "It has no bearing on the events of 3rd June 2011."

"That's debatable," Ryan said, watching Duke twirl his water glass. "But we'll move on, for now. Mr O'Neill, can you tell us what happened, to the best of your recollection, on the day that Esme disappeared?"

He ran both hands through his hair, stretching the skin back on his forehead.

"Ah, yeah. Yeah, sure. Um, I was helping Charlie to get the rigging up in the morning, and I'd planned to head over and help muck out the stable tent before the afternoon show. Esme usually took the baby over to see the horses after lunch and Samantha would nap while she did the grooming. Anyway, when I got there, the horses hadn't been touched. Nobody had fed them, either, which was strange."

"What time was this?"

"Must've been sometime after one," he said. "Usually, it took a couple of hours to wash the horses down, clean them up, and get them ready for a show. Since the baby came along, Esme hadn't been able to do it all alone, so I was helping out again."

"So, what did you do, after you found she wasn't there?"

"Well, I fed the horses and gave them a bit of water, cleaned up the worst of it, then I started to worry in case something was wrong. It was so unusual for her to forget them," he explained. "So I decided to stop by the caravan and check she was okay."

"Around what time did you reach the caravan?" Phillips asked.

"Maybe around two?" Duke said, then scraped his hair back again, his eyes suddenly wild. "I just keep thinking—if I hadn't stopped to muck out the bloody horses, if I'd got there a bit sooner, maybe I'd have been able to help, to—to stop whatever happened to her."

"You're doing the right thing now, in coming forward to help," Ryan said.

"I wish I could tell you more," Duke said, and his malleable face fell into long, sad lines again. "But when I got there, all I heard was the baby crying. The front door was closed—"

"Was it locked?" Phillips asked, but Duke shook his head.

"Nobody locks their doors, except at night," he continued. "As I said, I heard Samantha crying. It sounded pretty bad, so I just went inside."

"What did you see?"

"See?" he repeated, blankly. "Just the baby—I went straight to her. The play pen sort of faced the door, and she was standing up and bawling her eyes out, pointing towards something and saying 'mama' over and over."

"What was she pointing at?"

"I dunno—it just looked like she was reaching for the floor."

Phillips thought back to Samantha's memory of her mother's murder and imagined the horror of being unable to put it into words.

"Think back to the caravan, Duke. Did you see anything else?"

"I went inside…I nearly tripped over the coffee table because somebody had shifted it out of its usual spot, and then I snatched up Samantha to give her a cuddle. She was in a state, and it was really loud because the radio was blasting. I turned it off, then called out for Esme and went to look in each of the rooms, but she wasn't there."

"Did you see a note?" Ryan threw in.

Duke looked confused.

"What?"

"The note she left for Charlie," Ryan repeated. "Was it there?"

"I—yes, I think so."

He snatched up the water again, draining the glass this time.

"Is—is there anything else? I'll be late for the show starting."

"Just a couple more questions," Ryan said. "We appreciate you being so co-operative."

"It's just, I don't know what else to tell you."

"You could start by telling us whether you believed that Esme had gone off with another man?"

Duke shook his head, vehemently.

"Esme wasn't like that," he said. "I know that's what Charlie thought and since he found that note…I know it looked bad. But when you came to the circus that day and told us she'd been killed, it all seemed to make sense. It must have been some crazy person, who snatched her. Or maybe she went off to get something, really quickly, and they kidnapped her from the road—"

"They're good suggestions, and we'll bear them in mind," Phillips said, in a fatherly manner. "Is there anything more you can tell us about the caravan? For example, was anything overturned, or messed up? Anything out of place?"

"Not really, although the coffee table was in the wrong place, and I think the fridge had been left open because there was a stale smell. That could have been Samantha's nappy," he reasoned.

"One final thing, for now, Duke. What was Esme's relationship like, with your brother? Was she happy?"

His shoulders slumped as he was torn between family loyalty and the truth.

"She never said anything to me, but I—I see things," he said. "I don't think Charlie was ready to be married. He was no good at it; always shouting at her, saying she wasn't doing things right. He was struggling to be a father, too. You never met ours," he said, meaningfully. "He wasn't exactly the touchy-feely type."

They nodded their understanding.

"All the same, Esme would never have gone off and left Samantha. She adored that baby."

And, not for the first time, he thought of everything he had failed to do for her; everything he had failed to be.

But then, as she had observed, there were some who were born with strength and others who weren't.

CHAPTER 25

After marking out a route to allow people to access their cars—under police supervision—and exit the multi-storey car park on Dean Street, Lowerson and Yates dipped inside the protective tent Tom Faulkner had set up around the remains of the man lying splattered on the pavement at their feet. As they entered, he looked up from his grisly task.

"Jack, Mel," he said, his voice muffled behind the mask. "This is becoming a daily habit."

Lowerson chewed furiously on a stick of menthol gum, which Yates had offered him as they'd approached the tent. It didn't quite cover the stench of blood, but it helped, most of all, to distract him.

He sent her a grateful look, and she smiled, chewing her own gum.

"I heard you had another one to deal with, earlier today," Lowerson said. "The body up on the tracks at Stocksfield?"

"Yeah, that's looking like a professional hit," Faulkner said, moving across to where they stood. "In fact, if I hadn't got your call to come down here, I was going to ring you, myself."

"Oh?"

"There are certain similarities between the body I saw this morning and the one you picked up from St Peter's Wharf. In both cases, their fingertips had been removed, there were contusions all over the torso, and their faces had been beaten to shreds."

"Could be a serial," Yates suggested, and felt immediately guilty for the excitement that followed.

"Or, more likely, it could be a professional hitman with his own style," Lowerson said, with a note of apology. He liked the big cases as much as the next murder detective, but you couldn't imagine serial killers around every corner.

Besides, that was Ryan's specialist subject.

"What about this one?" Yates asked, nodding towards the mess on the floor. "Any similarities?"

"I'd say almost certainly. I can't tell you much about his torso, or even draw conclusions about whether his face was beaten—for obvious reasons. But I can tell you his fingertips are missing, so it's almost certain that he died elsewhere, before being brought here and dropped from a height."

"It seems strange," Yates remarked. "Why would anyone in the gangs want to draw attention to themselves like this?"

"It's sending a message," Lowerson replied, feeling his stomach jitter again. "If we're right and there's a connection between these victims, that would make three in as many days. It's short, swift retribution from a ruling gang lord for some kind of crime—which is ironic, when you think about it."

He turned back to Faulkner.

"Anything else you can tell us?"

Faulkner turned to face the body, his suit rustling as he went.

"Ordinarily, I'd try to draw conclusions from the position of the body but, to be honest, the usual principles go out of the window if it's the case that he was already dead when he fell. In those circumstances, he was probably rolled off the edge of the building, which is why he landed sideways."

From where they were standing, it was hard to tell.

"Thanks, Tom. Let us know if you find anything else."

"I'm backed up with work at the moment, so I'll get onto it as soon as I can but, if you see Ryan, let him know I'm looking at those old samples he sent through and I hope to have some results by tomorrow or the day after, at the latest."

He paused, sniffing the air.

"Is that menthol chewing gum?"

* * *

When Charlie returned to the circus, he found Sabina waiting for him.

"For God's sake, why aren't you over in the tent?"

The stalls had been open for well over an hour, and she was losing business.

His business.

"I missed you," she purred, and laid her head on the pillow of his bed. "How did it go at the police station?"

All he could think was that her head was resting on the same side where Esme had once lain, as he'd shown the police that very morning.

"Move your head away from there," he muttered.

"What?"

"Are you deaf, as well as stupid?" he roared. "I said, *move your head away from there!*"

Close to tears, she scrambled off the bed and hurried to pick up her clothes, which she'd discarded on the floor. She'd hoped to give him a little 'welcome home' present and then talk about what happened down at the station, but it would have to wait.

There was no talking to him, when he was in a mood like this.

"Be careful, Charlie," she said softly. "With a temper like that, people might start to think you killed her."

His skin went hot, and then very cold.

"Or maybe, with you sniffing around here all the time, they'll start to think it was you."

She laughed a strange, tinkling laugh, then trailed a finger down his chest.

"You'd like that, wouldn't you?"

Hating her, hating himself, he turned to her. Hard, angry and without feeling, he drove out his demons there on the big sleigh bed.

* * *

With Yates at the wheel, she and Lowerson managed to make it back to Police Headquarters ahead of the five-thirty shift change, when many of their colleagues tended to spill from the building craving corned beef pasties. As they waited in line at the Pie Van, a familiar voice called out to them.

"Fancy meeting you here!"

Phillips and Ryan crossed the forecourt to join them in the queue.

"Long day?" Ryan asked. "I heard you caught another one, this afternoon."

He might not be the SIO, but he was their Chief Inspector, and remained responsible for all murder investigations across his division.

"Yeah, it's looking as though they might be connected," Yates said, while Lowerson stepped up to order something that sounded suspiciously like quinoa. "And there's a third one that we need to look into."

"All gang-related?" Ryan asked, with a slight frown. "Even for us, that's a high volume in just a couple of days. Have you set up the MIR?"

Lowerson turned, balancing a couple of eco-friendly cartons beneath his chin.

"About to do it now," he said. "Except, all the conference rooms are taken."

"Share ours," Ryan offered, and thought it was also a neat way to keep an eye on things. It was Lowerson's first case as SIO, and three bodies represented a lot of balls to juggle, even for an experienced murder detective.

They were about to turn away, when Yates remembered something.

"Oh, Faulkner had a message for you," she said. "He's received the samples from the cold case you're working on, and he says he hopes to have a report back by tomorrow, or the day after."

Ryan nodded.

"I've got a message for you, too," Phillips said, as he stepped up to the counter. "Someone calling themselves Dennis—or Dante?"

Yates shot Lowerson a look, but he appeared to be engrossed in his phone.

"Ah—"

"Anyway, he rang the office earlier and said he's sorry, but his phone is out of action. He left a new number and says you can reach him on that. I posted a note on your computer; in case it was important."

"Thanks," she said, feeling Lowerson's eyes boring into the side of her head.

"Dante?" he asked, as they walked back towards the office a moment later. "Isn't that the name of the barman, down at *The Shipbuilder*?"

"Yeah, he, um, asked me out on a date."

Lowerson pasted a blinding smile on his face.

"Right! Yes! Great. That's great. For you. I'm happy, I mean. Happy, for you."

He shouldered through the door leading to the executive suite and walked quickly up the stairs, calling himself all kinds of idiot.

He had obviously misread her signals, completely.

CHAPTER 26

Rochelle White stared fixedly at herself in the long mirror in the dressing room. It was a beautiful room, designed by herself, for herself, and funded by the man who lay sprawled on the bed next door.

"Babe! What's taking so long?"

Her whole body jerked at the sound of his voice and she was galvanised, hurrying across to one of the rails. She was again racked by indecision, her manicured hand hovering over the rows of expensive fabric.

"Everything alright?"

She spun around to find her boyfriend leaning against the doorway, already resplendent in his dark dinner suit.

"I'll—just be a minute," she said. "I can't decide what to wear."

Her skin crawled as his arms came around her midriff, then moved up to cup her breasts through the filmy bra she wore.

"Maybe we should stay in, after all," he muttered thickly, rubbing against the back of her legs.

She tasted bile, but managed to swallow it and turn to him with a teasing expression.

"You know you can't cancel, now," she said, gently nudging him away. "You're sponsoring the event tonight."

With a dramatic sigh, he reached across and selected a slinky red number that went well with her skin tone and hair.

"Wear this one," he said. "But leave the bra off."

It was not a request.

She gave him a pliant smile and unhooked her bra, feeling his eyes running all over her as she hurriedly zipped herself into the dress. She was about to slip into a pair of matching red heels, when his voice stopped her again.

"The gold ones would look better."

She smiled again, and reached for them with shaking fingers.

When she was ready, he took her chin in a firm grip, tugging her face towards him until his lips were almost touching her own.

"Never, ever push me away again," he whispered, then gave her a hard kiss. "Time to go."

"I'll—I'll meet you downstairs. I just need to use the loo."

He nodded.

"Be quick."

After he left, she sank down onto the small sofa and willed the trembling to stop.

She had to get out.

He knew.

He had to know.

If he knew, she would be next.

Just then, a phone started to vibrate. Not her ordinary phone, but the one she kept hidden away, in a compartment she'd built herself.

It couldn't be ringing.

It wasn't possible.

Her eyes flew to the door, as she scrambled to find it before Bobby came back.

* * *

"The tech team managed to unlock the phone," Lowerson said.

Yates looked up from her jacket potato, hating the formality between them, now.

"Oh, yes? Did they find anything interesting?"

"Well, it obviously wasn't Dan Hepple's main phone, because it was almost empty. However, it seems you were right about there being a woman in his life, because there was a bunch of compromising pictures and a fair number of saucy text messages."

He forced a smile.

"What's her name?" Yates asked. "Anything we can use?"

"She's just listed as 'R' in the phone, but I'm going to try calling the number and see who we find at the other end."

"Don't you want to trace it?" she asked.

Lowerson pulled a face.

"Could take days and, even then, nothing could come back."

Yates knew burners could be hard to trace; that's why they were so popular amongst a certain class of criminals and married men.

"Let's hope her husband doesn't answer," she said, as he dialled the number.

* * *

Rochelle clawed at the panel in her shoe rack until she could grasp the mobile phone hidden behind it. She only had moments before Bobby would come to look for her, if he wasn't already on his way.

She pressed the 'mute' button, and hurried into the adjoining en-suite, locking the door behind her.

The phone still vibrated in her hand.

The only person who knew this number was Dan—or so she thought.

Was this a trick?

Would she answer, only to find Bobby laughing at her on the other end of the line?

Her lip trembled, and she willed herself not to cry. It would ruin her make-up, and then he'd know something was wrong.

The phone was still ringing.

With a shaking finger, she pressed the green button.

"Hello?" she whispered.

* * *

Lowerson sat up in his chair and gave Yates the 'thumbs-up' signal.

"Oh, ah, hello. Who am I speaking to?"

At the other end of the line, Rochelle frowned.

"Is this a cold call, or something?"

"No, no. My name is Detective Constable Jack Lowerson, from Northumbria CID. We found this number listed on a phone belonging to a man named Daniel Hepple. We're hoping you can help us with some enquiries."

Rochelle fought to control her grief, willing back the tears that clogged her throat.

"He's—Daniel's really dead, then?"

"Are you Mr Hepple's next of kin?"

"I-I was…no, we weren't married," she whispered. "Look, I can't stay on the line. I have to—I have to go. Please, don't call this number again."

"Wait! What's your name?"

There was a short silence.

"Rochelle."

"Rochelle, listen to me. We're investigating Daniel's murder and it's important we find out more about his life and the people around him. Maybe you could help us with that."

How could she help? she thought, hysterically. *She couldn't even help herself.*

"I have to go. Please. He'll kill me if he finds out."

Lowerson knew he was about to lose her, maybe forever.

"Look, Rochelle. We can help you. I'll meet you anywhere you like, somewhere neutral. You name the place. Please, if you're in fear for your life, let us help you."

Across the room, the others fell silent—including Ryan and Phillips, who had returned bearing cartons of food and drink.

Rochelle thought she heard the outer bedroom door opening and, in another moment, he would be banging on the bathroom door.

"The petrol station in Corbridge," she said quickly. "Tomorrow at ten."

"I'll be there."

After the line went dead, Lowerson stared at his mobile phone for a long moment and wondered if the woman would make it to the petrol station the following morning.

"Well done, Jack."

He looked up to find Ryan standing beside his desk, holding out a fresh latte. He wrapped grateful hands around the paper cup and nodded.

"Thanks. I forgot my crisis training. It's been a while—"

"Sounded pretty good to me," Ryan argued, and clinked his paper cup against Lowerson's. "To avoiding crises."

"I'll drink to that."

* * *

While Lowerson and Yates discussed strategy ahead of their meeting with Rochelle the next day, on the other side of the room, Ryan and Phillips discussed murder.

"We've got DNA swabs from everyone at the circus who'd offer one voluntarily," Ryan said. "Which was a surprising number, when you consider they're generally predisposed to hate us."

Phillips nodded sagely.

"Anybody refuse to give one?"

"Only a couple of the circus hands, and I expect that's because they've got a sheet," Ryan said. "All the same, we'll check them out."

Phillips took a slurp of his milky tea.

"Did you see the e-mail from Faulkner? He's going to run the swabs through the system and then we'll be able to see if there's a match to any known DNA profiles," he said. "Worth a shot."

Ryan nodded, then turned to look at Esme's face looking out at them from her photo on the whiteboard.

"What did she do, Frank? What did she know? You don't just kill a person for no good reason, not with that level of planning and execution."

"How d'you mean?"

Ryan leaned back against his desk and folded his arms, while he thought.

"We've seen frenzy killings and serial murderers, as well as the kind they're dealing with," he said, bobbing his chin in the direction of Lowerson and Yates. "But Esme O'Neill? This feels simpler; old-fashioned, somehow."

Phillips followed his train of thought.

"She was set alight before she was buried, and strangled long before that. It suggests some serious commitment to the killing," he said. "It suggests some sort of deep-rooted feeling, not a contract kill."

"I agree. A professional wouldn't have left the child."

Phillips experienced a sharp, unexpected ache in his chest as he imagined Samantha having been murdered, too.

"You're right," he said quietly. "They slipped up, there. Probably thought she was far too young to remember and, since she couldn't talk properly, she couldn't tell anyone what she saw. By the time she grew old enough to be heard, they'd already planted the idea that her mum had left her, so the memory was buried."

Ryan thought of the person they hunted, trying to build a mental picture.

"It takes a very specific kind of person, not only to kill, but to maintain that level of deception for so long," he said. "They'd have seen Samantha every day, probably talked to her each day, watching out for any sign that she was remembering. She told us she had the flashback when she was looking after the horses—but what if she'd gone to someone she trusted and told them about it? She might never have lived to turn up on my doorstep."

Phillips ran a hand over his chin, feeling a sense of relief.

"Aye, I know. But it must have been one of the men in her life, at least we know that much—"

"Do we?"

Phillips stopped short.

"Eh? How else would they have managed to hulk a dead body out of the caravan, especially quickly, in broad daylight? They had to have sheer physical strength and, looking at the women in the circus, they're all slim, almost petite."

"Maybe they didn't need to do all of it, straight away. I've been thinking about what Samantha told us, Frank. She said her mother's hand was there, on the floor, and then it seemed to disappear. She doesn't remember her being taken out of the front door to the caravan."

"There might be a side door," Phillips started to say, and then shook his head. "No, there wasn't one when we were looking around it, the other day. But she can't have disappeared, just like that. Do you think they put her in a cupboard, or in one of the other rooms?"

"Had to be," Ryan said. "In which case, only one of two people could have known about it."

"Charlie or Duke," Phillips realised.

"Yes. No way Charlie wouldn't have looked around his own caravan and, no way, either, that Duke wouldn't have seen it, considering he claimed to have looked around, too."

"It's a lot easier to dispose of a body when you're not in a hurry," Phillips said.

"Duke told us he was looking after Samantha, that night. It wouldn't have stopped him helping his brother, while she was asleep."

Phillips nodded, imagining the actions of two desperate men.

"There's just one problem."

"I know," Ryan sighed. "There isn't a scrap of evidence to prove any of this. Unless Faulkner comes back with a miracle, we're pissing in the wind. Charlie, Duke, Marco, Leonie—even Sabina. Theoretically, it could have been any one of them—or more than one, acting together."

"What about hypnosis?"

Ryan raised an eyebrow.

"I'm not sure Paul McKenna or Derren Brown can help us with this one—"

"No, man," Phillips waved a hand in the air. "I was thinking for Samantha. Maybe it would help her to remember some more details, if she spoke to a child psychologist or something?"

"The problem would be convincing her to do it. She doesn't like 'quacks', remember?"

Phillips' lips twitched.

"Aye, I remember. What about if you had a word with her? Bring it up over dinner, so it doesn't feel so much like she's being cornered."

"You're a sneaky one, Frank."

"Ah, stop it, you're making me blush."

Ryan grinned.

"What about Gregory?" he said, suddenly.

"Who?"

"The guy who helped us when Denise—ah, when we were searching for Keir Edwards." Ryan didn't want to rake over bad memories, for either of them. "Alexander Gregory gave us a profile to work with, but he's a clinical psychologist, first and foremost. He'd know how to draw her out."

"Would he agree to it?" Phillips asked. "Has he worked with kids?"

"I don't know," Ryan said. "And he might be busy or overseas. But there's no harm in asking. I'll sign it off with Social Services, first, and we can take it from there, if Samantha's willing."

Phillips nodded.

"That's fair enough. And, if she doesn't want to—"

"Then, it doesn't happen," Ryan said clearly. "I don't want to hurt the kid, any more than you do, Frank. But we're clutching at straws and she came to us for answers. I'm starting to think she might have had the answers all along, buried somewhere inside.

"Maybe she just needs to speak to someone who can help her to dig them out."

CHAPTER 27

"Charlie?"

He turned to find Marco standing in the shadows, the sheen of his leotard just visible in the dim light. The early show had finished, and the arena had emptied again to allow them to turn it over in time for the next group, at seven-thirty.

"What is it? Got a problem with the harnessing?"

Marco shook his head.

"No. It's nothing like that. I just—I wanted to say how sorry I was, about Esme. I never really said it because we all thought…But now that we know—"

"You know, what? Now you know she was *murdered*, you think I need molly-coddling? You think I need some ponce in a catsuit to lend me a shoulder to cry on?"

Marco sighed.

"We've known each other a long time," he said, wearily. "I wanted to tell you, there are people who would listen, if you wanted to talk about it. That's all."

Charlie knew he meant well. He knew it was an olive branch, a gesture of goodwill, if not quite friendship. Never friendship; he neither needed it, nor invited it. But it was a form of kindness. A part of him knew that, and was grateful for it.

But the other part rejected it.

"Now, listen to me, you greaseball. The day I need your help is the day they put me six feet under. Until then, mind your own bloody business. Go and look after your wife, plan your perfect little family, alright? Leave me and mine alone."

Marco's eyes turned hard.

"At least I have some family left. There's what's left of yours," he said, and Charlie followed his line of sight to where Duke was clowning around the arena with his pet monkey, which he'd trained to do all manner of ridiculous tricks.

He turned back, ready to plant a fist in the Italian's face, but Marco had already gone.

Charlie looked quickly in either direction but saw only shadows. He laughed, a bit nervously.

"You're losing it," he warned himself, and pulled his gloves back on.

There was work to be done, before the next show.

* * *

Leonie made her way back to the caravan she shared with her husband, wishing that she'd never insisted that she wanted to continue working. She was seven months pregnant with their first child and Marco was right; she had been pushing herself far too hard, lately. Add to that all the stress around them—Esme, the police—and it was small wonder she'd been feeling more tired than usual.

The crowds were building again, ahead of the evening show and fireworks display they put on afterwards, for the children.

She smiled and rubbed a hand across the hard ball beneath the cotton top she wore, wondering whether it would be a boy or a girl. If it was a boy, she hoped it looked like Marco, with his dark hair and olive skin. If it was a girl…

She looked up to find Sabina's tent on the left.

Psychic Sabina.

It was silly, really. It was well-known that Sabina used simple techniques, like reading someone's body language, to come up with her so-called psychic readings. They had even laughed about it, after a drink or two.

All the same, she was superstitious. She'd held off buying too many things for the baby, just in case anything bad was to happen, but now it was getting so close perhaps she could afford to get a little excited.

There didn't seem to be a queue outside the tent, so she dipped beneath its folds and into the darkened interior.

"Sabina?"

The room was lit up by strings of fairy lights and what appeared to be stars against the night sky, which was actually a special material inlaid with LED lights that had been draped over each inner wall of the tent. Framed studio portraits of Sabina stood on rickety side tables and, in the centre, a large, battery-powered crystal ball sat on a round table covered in a scarred velvet tablecloth.

An empty chair stood on one side, whilst Sabina was seated on a gold-painted throne on the other, dressed in an elaborate outfit of floating skirts with a tight, corseted top.

"Leonie?" she said, looking up from her smartphone where she'd been playing Candy Crush. "Is Charlie asking for me?"

"No, I haven't seen him," she replied. "I just thought I'd pop in for a minute. If you're not busy, maybe you could read my cards."

Sabina's red lips curved into a smile.

"You know it's all bollocks," she said, in a stage whisper. "I won't really be able to tell you anything."

"I know, I know," Leonie laughed, settling into the spare seat. "And I've only got ten minutes before I need to dash back. But let's have a giggle, anyway."

Sabina shrugged and flipped a black lace veil over her face, so that only her pale skin, kohl-rimmed eyes and red lips were visible. She dipped her hands in some white talcum powder and tapped them together, to prevent friction on the crystal ball.

"If you're ready, we shall begin," she said, in a dramatic voice, which made her friend laugh.

Sabina lifted her veil to cast her a stern look.

"You have to take this seriously," she warned. "Or I'm not doing it."

"Fine. Sorry," Leonie said, folding her lips. "Please, continue."

Sabina reached for an ivory box which held a stack of cards, each with different pictures.

"You look like Solitaire, from that old Bond movie. You know, the one with Roger Moore—"

"Shh," Sabina said, and handed her the cards. "Shuffle them yourself."

They'd done this a few times before, so Leonie began to work the cards through her fingers, while they chatted.

"Had any funny ones, today?"

Sabina rolled her eyes.

"How am I supposed to concentrate, when you keep distracting me?" she complained, then leaned forward to gossip. "I had one woman come in earlier with a smoker's cough. I told her she was going to die from cancer by the time she was fifty."

"*What?*" Leonie said. "You can't go around telling people things like that!"

"It's probably true," Sabina sniffed. "She should stop chain smoking and stick to one or two a day, like me. That way, she'll avoid getting a mouth like a cat's arse, too."

Not for the first time, Leonie found herself wondering why they were friends.

Too much water under the bridge, she thought. Too much investment to back away, now.

"Okay," she said, handing the cards back. "Do you think that's long enough for the cards to have taken on my *essence*?"

Sabina shot her a warning look, and settled back in her 'throne'.

"Select three cards but do not turn them over," she said, in her dramatic voice.

Leonie shuffled in her seat, then made her selections. She felt oddly nervous, and put it down to Sabina's flair for the dramatic.

"There you go."

Sabina let her long fingers hover above the cards while she sucked in three deep breaths, letting the air out slowly.

"The energy is strong—"

Leonie snorted, then held up a hand of apology.

"Sorry," she whispered. "Sorry."

"—the energy is *strong,*" Sabina continued. "There is both great light, and great darkness."

"Any Mediterranean cruises on the horizon?"

Sabina ignored that, and flipped over the first card, which showed a woman sitting on a throne much like herself.

"The High Priestess," she murmured. "A strong card. It could signify your position, as head of your family; wife, mother, giver of life."

"General dogsbody," Leonie mused, with a smile.

"It could also signify mystery," Sabina's husky voice continued. "Things around you are not what they seem. You must use the guiding forces to find a pathway through the darkness."

"Interesting," Leonie said, playing along. "And the next one?"

Sabina's hand hovered over the second card and, when she flipped it over, her hand stilled. Her eyes strayed up, to look at Leonie's belly.

"What?" she asked, sitting up in her chair. "What is it?"

Sabina let the card fall onto the table.

"Death."

Leonie's hand flew to her stomach.

"W-what does it mean?"

Sabina licked her lips.

"It does not always mean physical death," she said, but there was concern behind her eyes. Leonie saw it. "It could mean something more symbolic, such as a change in your life."

Leonie nodded vigorously.

"Like the birth of a new child?"

Sabina hesitated for a fraction too long.

"Yes, it could mean that."

She flipped her veil back and reached out to collect the cards up.

"Wait! You didn't do the last one," Leonie said, grabbing her wrist. "At least finish the reading."

"Look, this is just a lot of hocus," Sabina said. "It's been more than ten minutes, anyway—"

"They can wait."

Sabina sighed. She knew that look on her friend's face; she'd seen it many times before.

"Fine, if it means all that much to you," she muttered, and hoped it would be something light.

But, when she flipped over the next card, her stomach fell, and she began to wonder whether the cards were Leonie's, or her own.

For there, written in bold text beneath a set of hand-drawn scales, was a single word:

JUDGMENT

CHAPTER 28

As Charlie O'Neill strode across the entrance of the circus arena and told the evening crowd to "Roll up, roll up, for the greatest show on Earth!", Phillips, MacKenzie and Samantha set up a production line in the kitchen, to clear away the dinner dishes. Phillips washed, Samantha dried and MacKenzie put them away.

"Don't you ever use the dishwasher?" Sam asked.

"Nah, it's more fun this way," Phillips replied, handing her a plate, which she dried carefully. "How was your day, today?"

"It was great!" the girl exclaimed, and made MacKenzie smile. "We went to get some clothes—do you like my new top?"

She turned, dripping soap suds on herself, and Phillips made a show of admiring the new red hoodie decorated in a pattern of small gold stars.

"Lovely!" he exclaimed. "Do you think they have one in my size?"

The little girl giggled, but MacKenzie wasn't altogether sure he was joking.

"No, you're too big. Then, we went to the beach at Tynemouth. Didn't we, Mac?"

"Mm, aye, we did," MacKenzie said, taking the plate from her before it could smash to the floor in her excitement. "We can go back another day, if you like."

Samantha grinned, but Phillips cast his wife a searching look. It was easily done, but they couldn't start making any promises they might not be able to keep.

He cleared his throat, absent-mindedly scratching the end of his nose with a wet rubber glove.

"Ah, you know, Sam, I was chatting with DCI Ryan today," he began. "We were wondering if you might feel up to having another chat about what you remember."

There was a short silence in the kitchen, which he regretted, but it was unavoidable.

"I guess you haven't found anything yet?" Samantha deduced.

Smart kid, MacKenzie thought, taking the cutlery from her.

"We've spoken to everybody, we've checked over every detail we can find about your mum when she was alive," Phillips said, gently. "The problem is, nobody is coming forward and nobody seems to have seen anything."

He decided not to mention their theory about her father, or her uncle, for the present.

"Except me," Samantha whispered.

And at least one other person, he thought.

"Do you want me to come down to the police station again and see if I can remember anything new?" she offered. "I've been trying, but I just keep seeing the same things."

"Actually, we had a bit of an idea," he said. "We know this man called Alex, who's a psychologist. He—"

"I don't want to speak to anybody like that," she said, defensively. "I'm not crazy, you know."

MacKenzie almost laughed.

"Of course, you're not," she said. "He wouldn't be thinking any such thing. What Frank is trying to tell you is, Alex has some very special skills. He knows how to hypnotise people and help them to remember things they've forgotten."

"Oh," Sam said, knowingly. "I know all about *that.* We have a magician at the circus called Mike, who does illusions and things, and he sometimes makes people think they're chickens. Or, at least, it looks like he's done it but, really, they're actors my dad's paid to come along and cluck."

Phillips laughed, long and loud.

"We're not talking about any Mike the Magician, here," he said.

"And we don't want you to start clucking, either," MacKenzie put in, to bring a smile.

"Alex just knows how to make you feel very relaxed, and he knows exactly the right questions to ask to help your mind to remember all the things it might not want to."

Samantha looked up at him.

"You promise he won't put me in an asylum?"

"Not unless you start clucking," Phillips replied.

"Fair enough," she said, and held out a hand for the next plate. "I'll try it, if you think it might help my mum."

* * *

Back at Police Headquarters, Lowerson finally logged off his computer and leaned back in his chair, stretching out his arms.

"Long day, eh?"

He looked across at Yates, who was sipping a cup of coffee that had gone cold.

"Yeah, I just keep worrying about how Rochelle sounded on the phone," he said. "I wish we knew something about her."

Yates leaned forward to clear the screensaver on her computer.

"I think her name is Rochelle White," she said. "She runs *Rochelle Interiors,* an interior design company whose annual turnover was over six million last year, according to the accounts submitted to Companies House."

Lowerson frowned.

"Firstly, great work," he said, and meant it. "But are you sure it's the same Rochelle?"

"I don't know for sure, but it seems likely," Yates replied. "She's the girlfriend of Bobby Singh, a property developer and, according to our colleagues in the Fraud Team, a man who isn't above a bit of money laundering. It wouldn't surprise me to learn he has his fingers in all kinds of pies, including drugs—especially now that Jimmy Moffa is out of the picture. There's been a turf war going on, ever since he died."

Jimmy 'The Manc' Moffa was a notorious local gangster who'd taken the city by brute force some years earlier and who had come to a gruesome end at the hands of an even more brutal character than himself.

"Anyway, when a search popped up showing Rochelle at some gala dinner with Bobby, it rang some alarm bells. I also think her accounts look a bit skewed; nobody makes that much from interior decorating, unless you're working for a Russian oligarch who's making over his mansion in Kensington."

Lowerson tended to agree.

"So, Hepple hired an interior designer, after all?" he said.

"By the looks of those photos, he didn't have to," she replied. "But, either way, Rochelle's right about one thing. If her boyfriend finds out she was playing away from home, there'll be hell to pay."

"Let's just hope we get to her first."

CHAPTER 29

Charlie raised his hands up to the sky as a crowd of eighteen-hundred strong cheered.

It had been a particularly good night, and the takings had been healthier than usual. It wasn't like the old days, when the circus was the main event in town. Now, there was more competition, and they needed to work harder to impress. Even if they sold out every night, as they often did, overheads were rising, and it was becoming more difficult for the circus to survive. They'd evolved, over the years, adding more spectacular displays, pushing their own limits until they could stand alongside the best in the world.

And still, it wasn't quite enough.

He needed to diversify, or die.

With that in mind, he walked swiftly from the arena, stopping only to throw a careless word of congratulations to those he credited with having done a good job.

"Charlie!"

He turned to see Sabina waiting for him.

"Not now," he barked, walking quickly to beat the crowds.

He left the Big Top through the main exit, which happened to be closest to the ticket office and, beyond it, his caravan. As he passed the ticket office and skirted around the edge, a security light flickered into life and he looked up at it, automatically. It was hardly going to stop anybody who was serious about breaking and entering, but the CCTV would give him a good starting point when he took a couple of the boys and went to find whatever unfortunate soul had picked the wrong mark to steal from.

He smiled a bit at the thought, peeling off his gloves and hat as he crossed the grass. A fence had been laid out to keep the punters from wandering into the caravan park and he let himself through a small gate separating the two areas. It was like switching between personas, he thought: one, where he was Charles O'Neill, fourth ringmaster of his family's circus; and the other, where he was Charlie, widower, father, and small-time criminal.

Soon to enter the big leagues, he thought, if he could only get the police off his back. One of the major prerequisites of his new side-line was *discretion*, and having half of CID darken his door each day was very bad for business.

He paused outside his caravan to look up at the sky, which was resplendent with stars. He surprised himself by standing there for a moment longer, wishing he knew what their names were, wishing he had the wherewithal or the time to learn. He wondered whether this is what the Big Man had always wanted for him; whether this was the life he was always meant to lead.

He wondered whether one of the stars was called Esme.

What would she think of the mess he had made? What would she say, if she knew he'd lost their daughter?

None of it mattered, now.

He opened the door to the caravan and stepped inside, shutting it softly behind him.

* * *

Twenty minutes later, the crowd were growing restless and cold.

"Where's Charlie? The fireworks display was supposed to start five minutes ago," Duke said, blowing balloon shapes to keep people entertained.

His brother was responsible for lighting the first firework; it was a little tradition they had, and something he never deviated from. It was unusual for him not to turn up.

"I'll go," Sabina offered.

"Or we can," Marco said. "I'm taking Leonie back to the caravan, anyway. She looks tired."

"Thanks," she muttered, good-naturedly.

He leaned down to give her a quick kiss on the nose.

"You're still beautiful, to me," he said. "But you've done too much, today."

"Okay, just tell him he needs to get down here otherwise it'll start without him," Duke said.

They left to walk around the side of the Big Top, past the main entrance and around the ticket office. As Charlie had done, they looked up as the security light popped on, then let themselves in through the same gate. Charlie's nearest neighbour, who happened to be one of the lighting technicians, passed the time of day as he made for his own front door.

"His light's on," Leonie said, yawning. "He must be home."

Marco stepped up to give three short knocks on the door, then waited for a response.

"Try again, he might be in the shower," Leonie suggested.

Marco tried again, louder this time.

Still nothing.

"Maybe he's not in."

"That's odd," she muttered. "He's quite a stickler for wasted electricity. Can you see anything through the windows?"

"Let me see—"

Marco leaned across to peer through one of the windows, straining to see all four corners of the living from.

Then gave a shout and stumbled away from the window.

"What? What is it?"

"It's Charlie," he said, tremulously. "He's lying on the floor and there's blood everywhere."

Leonie clamped a hand over her mouth, wide-eyed.

"What? *What?*"

"Look for yourself," he said, and she stood on tip-toes, peering into the living area beyond the glass.

"Oh, my God," she said, sickly.

Marco tried the handle on the front door.

"What are you doing? Don't go inside!"

Somewhere behind their heads, the fireworks display began, and Catherine wheels rose up into the sky in swirls of fiery yellow and red.

"What if he's still alive?" he argued, raising his voice above the explosions. "You go and get help, while I go inside and see if he's still breathing."

"Be careful," she told him, and then cradled his face in her hands. "Please."

"I will," he promised.

As Leonie hurried to find Charlie's neighbour, trying not to stumble over the grass in her haste, Marco took a deep breath and tried the door. He jiggled the handle, then decided to use brute force.

With a couple of hard kicks, the door flew open.

* * *

Samantha had just gone to bed, when Phillips took the call from Ryan.

"That's good timing," he said, cheerfully. "I've got a bit of good news for you; she's decided to give the hypnosis a go. She's sceptical, but that's just good sense, if y' ask me—"

"Frank."

"—and it's worth a go, even if nothing comes of it. At least we might get a bit closer to knowing whether it was her dad, and one step closer to bringing him in."

"He won't be putting up any kind of fight, now," Ryan said. "He's dead."

Whatever Phillips had been about to say died on his lips.

"Say that again?"

"He's dead, Frank. It's looking like he locked himself inside his caravan, shoved a gun in his mouth, and blew his brains out."

MacKenzie overheard the change of tone in their telephone conversation, and cast a concerned eye to the ceiling, indicating that Phillips should keep his voice down.

He nodded.

"I'll meet you there in twenty minutes."

"I'm on my way," Ryan said.

MacKenzie walked straight across the room to take Phillips' hand.

"What's happened?"

"The worst, Denise. The bloody worst. Her da's only gone and killed himself, by the looks of it. The poor kid. It was bad enough he might have been the one to kill her mother but, somehow, this is even worse."

"Maybe he killed himself because he was the one who killed Esme," MacKenzie said. "It's the most obvious explanation."

Phillips gave her a gentle kiss.

"I wish you were with us," he said, honestly. "We could use your eye on this, because it's not proving to be as easy as any of us hoped. But I don't think that wee lass could be in better hands than yours."

She smiled, and pulled him in for a better kiss.

"That's just to keep you going."

CHAPTER 30

Twenty minutes later, Ryan looked upon the wasted body of Charlie O'Neill with calm grey eyes. He stood on the extreme edge of the doorway, covered entirely in overalls, and made no attempt to enter the room. He would have liked to step inside, but to do so risked contamination, so he took his turn to view the body as a mourner might view a relative, in state.

"Has anything been moved?"

The first responding police constable shook his head.

"No, sir—not that I'm aware. The witness who discovered the body says they broke open the door to be sure the victim wasn't alive and needing medical attention, but quickly left again when it was clear nothing could be done."

Ryan nodded, continuing to scan the area.

O'Neill lay sprawled on the floor, a small amount of blood spattered in a fan around his head, which bore a fist-sized hole on the right side of the crown. He wore his costume, but he'd discarded the overcoat, hat and gloves, which were folded neatly on the edge of the sofa.

A small pistol lay on the floor beside his right hand.

In short, everything pointed to suicide.

"Where's his brother?" Ryan asked.

"Waiting in his caravan with one of the other PCs," came the reply. "He was distraught, when he heard."

Ryan took a final, sweeping glance around the room and then turned away to allow Faulkner to make the most of what could be found, putting a grateful hand on the man's padded shoulder as he passed.

"It's like a revolving door, today," the other man complained. "Why can't the dead choose to end it all between nine and five?"

Forensic humour, Ryan thought. It was a killer.

"I appreciate you putting in the overtime, Tom."

"At least we've already started work on the swabs you sent over," he replied. "Once we've swept over the caravan, here, we'll compare the findings and it should be a lot quicker than usual."

Ryan nodded, and moved across to join Phillips.

"Have any preliminary statements been taken?" he asked.

"The PCs are going around the caravans in the immediate vicinity, now. I've got a PC with Marco and Leonie, another one in with Duke and there's a community support officer in with Sabina," Phillips replied, then bobbed his head towards Charlie's caravan. "Looks pretty cut and dry, doesn't it? Short-range gunshot wound to the skull. Pretty old-fashioned, but it gets the job done."

Ryan stuck his hands inside his pockets and rocked back on his heels, thinking aloud.

"Did you notice the position of the exit wound? It looked a bit off to me, but I can't put my finger on 'why'. It'll probably come to me," he muttered. "And why the hell wouldn't he have been sitting down, when he did it?"

"Eh?" Phillips said, eloquently.

"I mean, why would a man who intended to kill himself decide to do it standing in the middle of his living room? Why wouldn't he sit down, comfortably, somewhere?"

"I'm not sure he'd be thinking straight, at the time," Phillips said. "But I take your point. It sounds like you're not convinced it was suicide."

"Probably because I'm not," Ryan said. "I won't say there's a suicidal 'type', because there isn't. But I will say that, if there was a type, he most definitely wasn't it."

A man less likely to off himself, he was yet to meet.

"Aye, but the door was locked from the inside," Phillips argued. "There's no way somebody could have picked the lock to close it, after they left. There wouldn't have been time, because anybody could have wandered by and seen them. Besides, there was no sign of a struggle, and there would have been if Charlie was taken by force."

Ryan smiled.

"That's the mystery, isn't it?"

* * *

As the clock struck quarter-to-eleven, they tapped on the door to the D'Angelo's sleek black caravan, which was answered by a tired-looking police constable they half-recognised from the Tyne and Wear Command division.

"Thanks, Constable. We'll take it from here."

Inside, they found Marco and Leonie sitting on a plush, L-shaped sofa. He, with his feet resting on the coffee table and, she, with her head resting on his lap. A blanket had been draped across her midriff and she appeared to be dozing.

"Sorry, it's been a long day," Marco said quietly, and gave her arm a gentle pat to wake her. "Love? The police are here to ask us what happened."

Leonie's eyes were bloodshot when they opened, and she rubbed at them with a tired hand.

"I can see you're tired," Ryan said. "I'll make this as fast as I can."

"Thank you," Marco said. "I think we're both a little…shell-shocked, to be honest."

"Cup of tea?" Phillips offered. "I don't mind making it."

Ryan gave him an accusing glare, knowing fine well he wanted to test-drive the facilities inside the motorhome.

"That would be lovely," Leonie said. "There's some decaf tea, for me, in the smaller jar. The normal stuff is in the bigger jar, beside the kettle."

Phillips skipped off to the kitchenette.

"I know it's been a long night for both of you," Ryan continued. "But if you could start by telling us how you came to find Charlie?"

Marco tucked an arm around his wife, who leaned against his chest in silent support.

"Well, we finished the last show just after nine o'clock," he explained. "We hung around for a few minutes afterwards, clearing up, chatting and all that, while we waited for the fireworks display to start."

"What time was it due to start?" Ryan asked, as Phillips poured water into the kettle.

"Around twenty-past," Leonie mumbled. "It gives people a chance to clear out of the arena and walk over to the open area, on the other side of the Big Top. That's where we do a display every night after the late show."

"Did Charlie go along to that?"

"No, that's just the thing. Leonie and I headed down to catch the fireworks, but they were late starting. Duke was worrying, because Charlie always likes to light the first firework of the evening and he wasn't there."

"So, you offered to go and look?"

"Well, Sabby offered, first, but by that point I was really knackered and ready for bed," Leonie said, her eyes drooping with exhaustion. "Marco said he'd walk me back to the caravan and we'd stop in by Charlie's, to give him a nudge."

"Around what time was this?" Ryan asked, as Phillips set down steaming mugs of tea.

"Must've been sometime around half-past," Marco said, looking to his wife for confirmation. "Wouldn't you say?"

"Yeah, sounds right. Actually, we went by the ticket office and there's a camera there, so you can probably check the exact time from that."

Ryan made a mental note.

"Thanks," he said, wondering who else the camera might have captured during the evening. "What happened once you reached Charlie's caravan?"

"Well, it looked like there was a light on, inside, so we knocked a few times," Marco told them. "There was no answer, so I had a look through the window and saw him lying there. Leonie had a look too—"

"It was awful," she muttered, feeling sick at the memory. "It looked like half his head was missing."

"Try not to think about it, love," Marco said, pressing a kiss to her temple.

"What happened next?"

"I went to get help," Leonie said. "Marco was trying to get inside to see if there was anything he could do."

"I had to break down the door," he said, with a note of apology. "I'm sorry, I don't know if that was the right thing to do. I just wanted to check if he was alive—"

"Don't worry about it," Ryan said. "How many strikes did it take to bust the door?"

Marco rubbed his head, trying to remember.

"Uh, maybe two? Sorry, I can't really remember."

"What did you do when the door opened?"

"I think I might have stepped inside, I don't know, I thought I could help..." Marco shook his head, suddenly overcome. "Sorry. I didn't even like the bloke, that much."

He looked stricken.

"I didn't mean to say—"

"Again, don't worry about it," Ryan said. "You're not expected to like everybody."

Marco nodded.

"Like I say, I stepped inside, but it was obvious...you know, he was dead."

"What then?"

"I went back outside and...God, I'm ashamed to say it, but I threw up. Pathetic," he muttered.

"Happens to the best of us," Phillips put in, as the voice of experience. "Who was the first to arrive?"

"I came back, with Doug. He's the new lighting technician, who lives in the caravan next door," she said. "He rang the police and then Marco went off to find Duke and let him know. He was devastated—"

"I had to hold him back," Marco said, saddened to think of it.

"How come you didn't use your mobiles to ring the police?" Ryan asked, and the pair of them looked amused.

"Well, as you can see," Marco heaved himself off the sofa to show them the leotard he still wore. "This little number leaves little to the imagination, and there's no room for pockets, or smartphones."

"I just didn't bother to bring one," Leonie said. "The only person I'd normally text would be Marco, and I was with him all evening."

"I see, thanks for clearing that up," Ryan said, ticking off his mental list. "Last thing, for now. Did either of you hear a gunshot, or see anyone fleeing the caravan?"

"No," Leonie said. "We didn't hear a thing, and it must have happened not long before we arrived. He only left the show at nine, and we were outside his caravan by half-past."

"Did Charlie seem upset, at all, today? Was he behaving in an unusual way?"

Marco didn't like to speak ill of the dead, but they needed to know.

"I had a word with him earlier, before the start of the evening show. He was angry and seemed distracted, as though his mind was elsewhere. He was even more antisocial than usual."

"Marco," Leonie whispered.

"They need to know what kind of mood he was in," her husband said. "Isn't that right?"

Ryan nodded.

"It's admirable to want to respect the memory of the dead but, in our business, we'd rather have the truth, warts and all."

She paused, seeming to wage some kind of internal battle.

"Is there something else?" Ryan prompted her.

Leonie looked at Marco with a guilty expression.

"I knew something bad was going to happen," she said, earnestly. "I went to have my cards read, with Sabina, and—"

"*Dio Mio!* Leonie, I've told you a million times before, you only upset yourself when Sabina fills your head with that nonsense."

"Not this time," she said. "One of the cards was the 'Death' card, Chief Inspector. It's like a premonition, isn't it?"

"Ah—" Ryan said.

"The police aren't interested in silly card games, and nor should you be," Marco muttered. "The last thing you need is more stress, at a time like this."

"I feel terrible," she said. "I keep thinking, I should have known something bad was going to happen. I just thought it was going to happen to *us*."

She began to cry, cradling the baby bump as she wept, and Ryan exchanged a glance with Phillips.

Time to leave.

CHAPTER 31

Duke O'Neill was a broken man.

He was seated inside his small caravan with his head in his hands, mumbling to himself, and occasionally rocking back and forth. A police constable looked up in relief as Ryan and Phillips entered, clearly unsure how to deal with such rampant grief.

"Do you need me for anything, sir?"

Ryan shook his head, and as soon as the door clicked shut, he took a seat beside Duke on an uncomfortable, pine wood cabin bench.

"We're very sorry for your loss," Phillips said, taking the lead this time. "Can we get you anything? A drink, maybe? Can we call one of your friends?"

"I don't have anyone, now," he said, between sobs that racked his gangly body. "I can't b-believe he's dead."

Duke lifted his head for the first time, swiping the back of his hand beneath his nose.

It was quite a sight, Ryan thought, to see a clown who had been crying. He happened to find clowns mildly creepy at the best of times; a fact he'd been willing to overlook for the duration of their investigation. But after an hour spent weeping into his stage make-up, this one looked more like a melted waxwork from a horror movie and it was hard not to make the comparison.

"Have a tissue," he urged, reaching for the small packet he kept in his back pocket.

"Thanks." Duke blew his nose loudly.

"We know it's hard, son, but we need to ask you a couple of questions," Phillips said. "For instance, when did you last see Charlie?"

"I saw him as he was heading out of the main doors, just after nine," Duke said. "He didn't see me, of course."

"Of course?" Ryan queried.

Duke let out a nasal laugh.

"He was preoccupied—you could see that from a distance. Besides, people tend to forget I'm there, even when I'm wearing a giant yellow suit."

Ryan couldn't argue with the truth of that.

"And, when you saw your brother in the caravan, how did you feel?"

"I-I think I just flipped out," he said, seeming to come out of a daze. "I just saw him lying there and I couldn't handle it. I can't believe he killed himself. I can't believe he would do that."

"No?" Ryan enquired. "Did he give any indication that was how he was feeling, or what he planned to do? Do you know if he'd made any other attempts?"

Duke shook his head.

"Never. Charlie was so strong, completely unshakeable. He could handle anything. I never knew that was how he was feeling, all along."

"Do you have any idea why he might have done it?" Phillips asked, and Duke looked away, unable to meet his eyes.

"He—well, he's always worried about cash flow, f-for the circus," he managed. "Bills to pay."

"Is that all?"

"Mm-hmm."

Ryan noticed the man was sweating again, and thought privately that he should never consider taking up poker.

"It's important that you tell us, if there's something that might have affected his state of mind, Duke."

"There's nothing," he said, sounding unsure. "There was Esme, of course. He never said as much, but it was playing on his mind. He wanted to find out what happened, like we all did, maybe more so."

"Do you believe it's possible your brother…knew something about what really happened to Esme?" Ryan asked, and watched closely for any further perspiration.

But Duke had himself fully in control again, and the moment was lost.

"No," he said firmly. "He knew as much as the rest of us, which is *nothing*."

Ryan raised an eyebrow at the tone, which was curiously authoritative coming from this mild-mannered man.

"Things will change now, won't they, Duke?"

"Of course," he said, sadly. "I don't know what we'll do without him."

"Well, that's easy, isn't it?" Ryan continued, in the same pleasant tone. "The circus will pass to you, now. It'll be *you* at the helm, and not Charlie."

He saw the moment the truth of it hit home for Duke, and caught the quick flash of excitement that was quickly concealed.

Yes, he thought. Everyone had a motive, if you looked hard enough.

Sometimes you hardly needed to look at all.

* * *

Their final interview of the evening was with Sabina, who had buried her grief behind a wall of anger.

"Your son will get his place at university," she was saying, as they stepped inside her small motorhome. "Good fortune rests on your horizon."

Catching sight of the new arrivals, the community support officer sent them both an apologetic look, and hastily excused himself.

"Sorry to trouble you, so late," Ryan said. "May we sit down?"

Sabina looked between the pair of them and nodded.

"Why not? I can crack open a bottle of wine," she said, in a brittle voice. "Let's get a takeaway and make an evening of it."

"It's alright to be upset," Phillips told her. "You've had a terrible shock."

"Have I? Yes, I s'pose I have. He always was a man to keep you guessing. Well, he's really taken the prize, this time. Bastard," she tagged on.

"When was the last time you saw him?" Ryan asked, shaking his head when she offered a packet of cigarettes. He kept a close watch on Phillips, who seemed to be sniffing second-hand smoke everywhere they went, lately.

"It was just after he finished the show, a couple of minutes after nine," she said. "I was waiting for him by the main entrance and I called out to him, but he said he didn't have time, or something like that, and kept walking. He was in a hurry to kill himself, apparently."

Phillips reminded himself that her acerbic remarks didn't necessarily mean anything sinister; some people laughed at funerals; others cried. People dealt with their grief in very different ways.

"You two had known each other a long time," he murmured.

Sabina leaned back against a wall, to stop herself pacing.

"Yeah. I grew up in *O'Neill's*, and he was older than me. Cool, the bad boy—you know, all that stuff."

She took a long drag of her cigarette.

"You probably know, by now, that we had something going on for years. Off, on, off and on again. That's how it went, until Esme messed up the rhythm."

"You didn't have any kind of physical relationship while they were married?" Ryan asked, because he was interested to know what made the dead man tick.

"Right at the beginning, just before they buggered off to get married, I thought things were going to turn back my way," she said, in a funny, faraway voice. "But she won. She always won."

"She was your friend, wasn't she?" Phillips asked.

Sabina looked him dead in the eye.

"I haven't got friends, sergeant. I have people who help to distract me from how shit my life is," she said. "You can call them what you like, but we don't spend time together because we've got so much in common. It's because there's nobody else."

"If you hate it so much, why not leave?" Ryan asked.

She smiled.

"Because of *him*, chief inspector. I always hung around because of *him*," she replied. "But now he's gone, so I'm free to go anywhere and be anything I want."

The cigarette burned down to the end and she stabbed the butt into a porcelain teacup on the counter near where she stood.

She turned to them both with another hard smile, and her eyes were over-bright.

"See? Good fortune rests on my horizon, too."

* * *

It was after midnight by the time Ryan and Phillips finished on the moor. It had taken some time to oversee the process of collecting statements and transferral of the body, to seize the tapes from the camera which was positioned next to a motion-activated light on the side of the ticket office, and to deal with the endless round of inane questions from the general public, which was par for the course in their job.

After a final word with Faulkner, whose team was finally packing up for the day, each man returned to his car and looked forward to the comfort of home.

Neither of them noticed a car crossing the moor shortly after, following at a safe distance. Just as they hadn't noticed it the day before, either.

Its driver was adept at blending in—driving neither too fast, nor too slow—and remained focused on finding the one person who had the ability to destroy it all.

Samantha.

There was only one place she could be.

CHAPTER 32

The nightmare was dark and all-consuming.

It made no allowances for age, nor softened the edges of its horror to protect the little girl's mind. Instead, it turned against her, ravaging her heart while she slept.

She saw her mother's face, smiling down at her. There were crinkles at the corners of her eyes. She raised her arms to be held but was too late. There was nothing but air; icy cold against her skin, and sickly, like fruit rotting in a bowl.

In the centre of the bed, Samantha shivered uncontrollably, her body tucking into a ball, her arms wrapped tightly around her knees.

This is Tyne Radio…

This is Tyne Radio…

I love you, Esme.

A man's voice, and then her father's face appeared, smiling at first and then angry.

Shut that kid up, Esme! She's nothing but a crying brat!

Sorry, Charlie, she's only a baby. Her teeth are sore.

Women's laughter, their faces peering into the play pen, one after another, and their whispers in her ear.

You would have been mine…

You should have been mine…

A man's voice now, his eyes like her own.

You're mine, he whispered.

She began to cry out, to cry for her mother. Fretful murmurs, at first, then tearful shouts that woke Phillips and MacKenzie in their room along the hall.

She saw her mother at the sink and already knew what would come next. She fought to get away, to claw her way out of the dream, but there was nowhere to run. She could not hide from what she had already seen.

The door opened.

White hands. The monster had white hands.

Smiles, at first, then anger. Hard words, hard hands.

That sound again, the choking sound of her mother dying, while she looked on, helpless to stop it.

Your turn, now.

The monster's hands, reaching down.

Samantha scuttled away, so fast her arm dislodged the lamp on her bedside table, but the noise of it breaking didn't wake her.

MacKenzie rushed into the room.

Your turn, baby. You can't live to tell anyone.

She started to scream, a long, keening wail of torment.

"Sam! Wake up, Sam!"

Mama?

"Samantha! Wake up! You're safe," a voice said. "You're safe with us."

Her eyes finally opened, and she looked at MacKenzie for long seconds—unsure, disorientated, and rendered immobile with terror.

She felt something warm pool against the sheets and began to cry.

"Oh, sweetheart," MacKenzie said, reaching out her hand. "It's okay. Don't worry about that, we'll clean it up."

Samantha crawled into MacKenzie's arms and buried her face against her shoulder, hugging her tightly in case she, too, would evaporate on the air. From the doorway, Phillips hesitated, then came to sit beside them and wrapped his arms around both of them.

Samantha's racing heart began to slow again as their arms surrounded her, and the tears eventually dried.

And in the street below, a driver looked up at the figures moving behind the window with the buttercup yellow curtains.

* * *

The departure lounge at Paris Charles de Gaulle Airport was almost empty, the last flight out of that terminal having already departed in the early hours. Cleaning staff and the occasional security guard patrolled the corridors, moving like automatons as they ploughed through the night shift, moving around the solitary man seated across two chairs beside the floor-to-ceiling window. In a couple of hours, there'd be a spectacular view of the sunrise, but for now, the windows served as a giant mirror against which depressing low-energy lighting was reflected.

Doctor Alexander Gregory rested long legs on top of a small carry-on suitcase, and re-read the e-mail from Detective Chief Inspector Ryan. It had been a little while since they'd seen one another, and the last time had been in the context of a highly-charged manhunt where his involvement had been born of police desperation rather than a genuine belief in his ability to help.

Gregory wasn't offended by that.

The police were generally predisposed to be mistrustful of outside help and, frankly, they were right to be cautious. The world of criminal profiling was riddled with charlatans; fame-hungry men and women who chased their next 'success' story like some lawyers chased ambulances. He came across them all the time, usually because he'd been drafted in to clean up the mess. As a clinical psychologist by profession, he was reticent to call himself anything other than that. His work delved into forensic psychology, since he was often required to assess people accused of a crime as to their fitness to stand trial, as well as often being required to give expert testimony in court.

But, then, there was the profiling.

Perhaps, because it had such a terrible reputation for being long on guesswork and short on science, he was reluctant to use the term or be associated with it. But there was no denying that his career had taken an interesting turn in that direction, whether he'd wanted it that way, or not.

The fact Ryan was seeking his help in a strictly clinical capacity was both surprising and appealing, especially as the client was a young girl of ten. He'd done some work with children, although mostly those who had committed early offences and for whom the state had high hopes of rehabilitation. But it had been a long time since he'd used his skills purely to help somebody to remember, and after several recent cases in which he'd been forced to work on the front line, dealing with some of the world's most damaged men and women, it would be a welcome change to take a short assignment that would help him to remember why he had become a psychologist in the first place.

He sent a brief response to Ryan's message, then leaned back against the seat and closed his eyes, wondering what they might find inside a little girl's mind.

CHAPTER 33

Wednesday, 5th June 2019

After a disturbed night, Samantha slept late the following morning, and MacKenzie and Phillips were happy to let her. It delayed the inevitable task that lay ahead, which was to inform her that her father had died. They'd discussed the best way of doing it, the form of words they might use or the places they could go, to make it better for her.

But there was no way to sugar-coat it.

First, her mother, and now, her father.

"I have an idea," MacKenzie said, as she heard the girl's footsteps coming down the stairs.

"Morning."

Samantha was still embarrassed by the side-effects of her nightmare, the previous evening, but MacKenzie had already washed and dried the sheets. They were folded away in a linen cupboard—out of sight, and out of mind.

"Are you hungry?" Phillips asked, but, for once, she shook her head.

"No, thank you," she said, still hovering in the doorway.

It was as though she already knew something was wrong, MacKenzie thought. Perhaps she had sensed it, in the atmosphere.

"Can I show you something, Sam?"

The girl looked across, instantly curious.

"What is it?"

"Come with me," MacKenzie murmured.

A door led from the kitchen to their attached garage and she paused beside it to check Samantha had something on her feet—in this case, fluffy slippers in the shape of unicorns—before pushing it open. Inside, part of the garage had been converted into a home gym area, with a boxer's punchbag hanging in the centre of it all.

"Cool!" Samantha said, and went across to look at it. "My dad knows how to box, but he's never shown me. He says it's only for boys."

On another day, MacKenzie might have cracked a joke about that, but not today.

"It's because of your dad that I brought you here, Sam," she said softly, and looked across to where Phillips had seated himself on an old garden chair. "I'm afraid we have some very bad news."

Samantha looked down at the foamy matting beneath her feet.

"What is it? Was he—is he the one who killed my mum?"

MacKenzie was thrown off guard, unsure of how to answer. The fact was, Charlie O'Neill might still have been responsible for his wife's murder, but now they may never know.

It was bad news, whichever way you looked at it.

"We don't know that yet," she answered, then ordered herself to look the girl in the eye. It was a mark of respect she afforded the family of any victim of crime, and now was no exception. "Something else has happened that we need to tell you about. I'm so sorry, Samantha—your dad died last night."

As they'd expected, the first emotion she felt was anger, not grief.

"How? How did he die?" *We're not finished, yet! You can't leave me, too!*

"We're looking into that," MacKenzie said, having judged it inappropriate to go into the gory details. There was a time and a place for everything.

"Here," MacKenzie said, handing her the smallest pair of boxing gloves she could find. They were too big, but they'd protect her hands. "Try taking a swipe at the bag. It won't change what's happened, but it might help."

Samantha looked at the gloves and then shoved them on, strapping them at the wrists.

She stood in front of the bag, staring at it with tear-glazed eyes.

Then, she went for it, pouring out all her fury, her grief, her disappointment. MacKenzie held it steady for her, watching for any signs of injury, while Phillips looked on at the two women in his life and remembered his own childhood. Just like Samantha, he'd gone down to the boxing ring whenever life became too much and there was nowhere to put all the anger, nowhere to expel it without hurting somebody else.

There were many times in life when the world was not fair; people didn't always play by the rules they'd made, and there was often nothing you could do about it. Not a blasted thing. But, usually, a person reached a certain age before life robbed them of both parents, especially with such brutality. There was only one other person he knew who had lost both parents, in equally sad circumstances.

Anna.

He decided to call her, as soon as he could. At times like these, they needed friends around them, and so did Samantha. Especially ones with a unique understanding of what she might be going through.

In the meantime, they waited while Samantha worked it out of her system as best she could, knowing it was the start of a long, rocky journey that might get worse before it got any better.

But right here, right now, she was cared for.

She was not alone.

* * *

Ryan had scheduled a briefing for nine o'clock and, this time, the Major Incident Room was looking more like its usual self. A bank of printers hummed against the back wall while representatives gathered from the forensics, analytics and tech teams to go over the information they'd gathered the previous day. Although the crime scene suggested that Charlie O'Neill had taken his own life, and therefore would not warrant the services of the Criminal Investigation Department, Ryan was a firm believer in the old adage that there was no such thing as a coincidence. There were too many questions that remained unanswered, and too many inconsistencies for him to overlook. He'd therefore taken the executive decision to treat Charlie's death as 'suspicious', and to investigate it beneath the umbrella of 'OPERATION SHOWSTOPPER'.

Ryan was in the process of reviewing the CCTV from the ticket office camera, when Phillips walked into the room.

He didn't beat around the bush.

"How'd she take it?" he asked, handing his friend a coffee.

"As well as could be expected," Phillips replied, taking a grateful swig of milky coffee, sweetened to his taste. "Thanks."

Ryan saw the shadows beneath Phillips' eyes and something else, too.

"The Social Worker, whatsherface—"

"Mrs Carter," Ryan supplied.

"Aye, that one. She rang this morning, asking for an update and wanting to come around for tea and biscuits. What am I s'posed to tell her? The kid's had the worst week of her life, and people keep proddin' and pokin' at her when she just wants to be like any other ten-year-old."

"Gregory's on his way," Ryan felt honour-bound to say. "He's catching the first flight out of Paris and hopes to be here by lunchtime, but if Samantha isn't up to it, we'll call it off."

"We'll let her decide," Phillips agreed.

"You and Denise are helping her through it," Ryan said quietly. "It isn't an easy thing, but you're making it look easy."

Phillips was taken aback.

"W'hey, it's nothing…just giving her a bed to sleep in and a bit of grub—"

"You know it's a lot more than that."

Phillips sighed.

"Aye, I know. To tell you the truth, son, it's getting harder every day to imagine what the house'll be like without her in it."

"Quieter, probably."

Phillips managed a small laugh.

"Aye, trouble is, I'm starting to wonder if it'll be too quiet," he said, and set his coffee down again. "After we broke the news to her about her dad, she asked whether she could stay with us."

Ryan gave him a searching look.

"And? What did you tell her?"

"What could I tell her? She's still got an uncle and, now he'll be running the circus, he's got the means to look after her. He's not going to set the world alight, but he's not violent, as far as we know. It'll be up to Social Services to decide."

"We're still investigating Duke O'Neill," Ryan reminded him, and nodded towards the whiteboard, where a row of photographs had been added to signify Persons of Interest. "Let's not strike him off the list, just yet."

Phillips ran a hand over his chin, then let it fall away.

"Howay, let's get on with doing what we do best," he said. "Somebody out there's laughing at us, and I want to know who."

Ryan nodded and came to his feet, but had a final word to say before they turned to business.

"You'd be good at it, Frank."

"Good at what?"

"Being a father. Just in case you were wondering."

CHAPTER 34

It was shaping up to be another blazing hot summer's day, but Ryan wanted no distractions in the room and so he let down the cheap window blinds with a rattle of clinking metal.

"Sorry, folks," he said. "Hopefully, the sun will still be shining by the time we wrap this thing up."

Lowerson and Yates had left to keep their ten o'clock appointment with Rochelle, so Ryan moved to the front of the room to get the briefing underway.

"Thanks to all of you for coming in," he began. "For those who aren't up to speed, we're investigating the suspicious death of a thirty-four-year-old male by the name of Charles O'Neill, who was the owner-manager of *O'Neill's Circus*. He was discovered shot dead in his caravan, late last night, on the Town Moor."

He rapped a knuckle on the timeline he'd drawn out, beneath a picture of Charlie taken from his driving licence.

"These dates and timings are in your packs but, for the sake of simplicity, I've drawn a visual aid, here," Ryan continued. "The key timescale is sometime between nine and nine-thirty p.m., which is when Charlie died. Before then, he was in full view of the arena, where he was the ringmaster at the late show. After then, his body was discovered by two of his employees, Marco and Leonie D'Angelo."

He watched their faces, and raised a hand to greet Tom Faulkner, as he slipped into the room with a mouthed apology.

"At the moment, it appears to have been a suicide," Ryan said. "The body was found with a gunshot wound, apparently self-inflicted, and there were no signs of a struggle. The caravan door was locked from the inside and the windows are small, with the main pane fixed permanently closed. There are no other obvious exits—"

He paused, as Faulkner raised a hand.

"Did you find something when you were going over the place?" Ryan asked.

Faulkner felt several pairs of eyes swivel in his direction.

"Ah, right. Well, yes, I was going to say we spent some time at the deceased's caravan, and we came across a kind of trap door."

Ryan frowned, wondering how they'd missed it.

"Where was it?"

"Beneath a faux-fur rug and a glass coffee table, which was quite chunky," Faulkner replied. "It gives access to the underside of the caravan."

"How big?" Phillips asked. "Large enough for someone to slip through?"

"For an average-sized person, yes, it's more than big enough. However, it was locked from the inside."

Ryan digested that bit of information.

"Anything else?"

"Well, there was only one set of prints on the gun, and they belonged to Charlie," Faulkner said. "His hand also displayed some gunshot residue, consistent with him having fired the pistol—which we've identified as an old Russian-made Biakal pistol. It's an obsolete weapon, originally a low-powered gas pistol, but it appears to have been adapted to fire live ammunition."

"I'm guessing it's unregistered," Phillips said, and Faulkner nodded.

"It's not on the system," he said. "I'd have said this was a gang weapon, not the kind of thing an ordinary person with a legitimate firearms license would own."

Ryan nodded, and his eye strayed across to the opposite wall, where Lowerson had tacked up three images in his own murder investigation.

"The question is how it came to be in O'Neill's possession," he said.

"That's not all," Faulkner said. "There was no gunshot residue found in any of the other samples we took from the hands and arms of people who were in the vicinity last night, which reduces the likelihood of it having been some other person who fired the shot."

"But not impossible," Ryan murmured. "What about on the body?"

"Pinter's going over it now, but we've taken all the usual samples, so we'll get through it all as soon as we can."

Faulkner paused, considering how much to say without having the complete picture to hand.

"Something struck me, last night," he said slowly. "Looking at the position of the body in relation to the blood spatter, and the direction of the exit wound."

"Go on," Ryan said, thinking that he'd experienced a similar feeling of unease. It was why he'd refused to rubber-stamp it as a suicide.

"It's statistically less likely for someone to shoot themselves standing up," Faulkner said, echoing Ryan's thoughts the previous evening. "But, equally, it's not outside the realms of possibility, so let's set that aside, for now. I'm still concerned by the unusual spatter formation. Ordinarily, I'd expect a wide arc, spreading across a larger area at the general height of the deceased. That would reflect the height and direction, as he fell."

He paused, referring to the drawing he'd made of it, the previous evening. Faulkner was adept at using the most up-to-date forensic tools on the market and was a pretty decent photographer, thanks to all his years snapping death shots, but sometimes the act of committing a scene to paper was the most useful in helping to visualise a murder.

Because, like Ryan, that's what he firmly believed it was.

"In this case, there was a much smaller arc of blood spatter, concentrated in a much smaller area and at a height of less than a metre above the floor."

Phillips cast his mind back to the caravan the previous evening, and nodded.

"You said something about the exit wound?"

"Yes, that struck me as unusual, too," Faulkner said. "But the pathologist is really the man to ask—"

"Oh, bollocks to that," Phillips said roundly. "You've been doing this job for as many years…if you've seen something, spit it out."

Faulkner laughed.

"Fair enough. In that case, I'll say the angle of the head wound looked all wrong. The pistol was found beside the victim's right hand, as though it had fallen after the shot was fired—in fact, it should have fallen a lot further, given usual trajectories and recoil. But, let's say the victim is right-handed, you'd expect him to raise the pistol to his mouth like this," Faulkner held up his right hand, two fingers fashioned to look like a gun. "We could say Charlie O'Neill was in a highly agitated state, that he was disordered, but whichever way you try it, the direction of the shot would have gone straight through the back of his head, or slightly to his left."

Ryan nodded his agreement.

"The wound was on Charlie's right-hand side, elevated to the crown area. It would have been difficult for him to have angled the pistol in that direction, whilst still firing in the ordinary way with the forefinger of his right hand."

"And that's the print we found on the pistol," Faulkner assured him. "I can't, for the life of me, figure out how it got there."

But they would, Ryan thought, and before the week was done.

If they were right, and Charlie O'Neill's body had been staged to look like a suicide, somebody had gone to an awful lot of trouble to make it look that way.

The question was, why had nobody heard a gunshot?

CHAPTER 35

Corbridge was a historic market town nestled in the scenic Tyne Valley, twenty miles to the west of the city and on the way to Cumbria. It was a pleasant drive as the motorway wound its way through Northumberland and, as they passed over the peaks and troughs of the valley, Lowerson reflected that it was an incongruous choice for the girlfriend of one of the rising stars of the criminal underworld.

"What do we know about Bobby Singh?" he asked Yates, who'd insisted on doing the driving, this time.

"He's relatively young," she replied. "Early thirties, runs *Singh Holdings,* a property development company. He was flagged up a while back by the Financial Investigation Unit in connection with Martin Henderson, the bloke up at Cragside, remember?"

Lowerson pulled a face, then it cleared again.

"Right—I'm with you, now. The one when Ryan and Anna were staying in a cottage in the grounds of Cragside? How did Singh come into the frame?"

"The FIU suspected Henderson was one of Singh's employees, hired to help launder money through a series of shady property deals. Unfortunately, when they tried to chase the money down, it was too well hidden. It's an ongoing case, for them."

"They might want to look at *Rochelle Interiors,*" Lowerson said. "But let's wait until after we've spoken to her."

Yates came off the dual carriageway at the turning for Corbridge, and they followed the winding country road leading to the town centre.

"The Drugs Squad have their eye on him, too. Since Jimmy the Manc is no longer on the scene, there's been a bit of a turf war ongoing across Newcastle, Gateshead and Sunderland, with a spate of gang-related murders over the past couple of years. According to the DS, things had died down a bit until recently, which led them to think the war had been won."

"By whom?" Lowerson asked. At one time, there had been twelve or thirteen distinct gangs operating in the North East.

"A gang calling themselves the 'Smoggies'," she said. "They don't know who the leader is, but the name suggests a Teesside connection."

Lowerson made a sound of agreement, then bit the bullet.

"Alright, smarty-pants, why does it suggest a Teesside connection?"

"Because 'Smoggie' is short for 'smog monster', of course," she replied. "It started out as an old derogatory football term used by the Sunderland supporters, when they were playing Middlesbrough. It's a reference to the air pollution that used to be quite heavy around Middlesbrough, back in the day."

Lowerson looked at her as though she'd grown another head.

"How do you *know* all this stuff?"

"Common knowledge," she said, maddeningly. "Heads up, there's the petrol station."

* * *

It was just shy of ten o'clock, so Yates found a parking space opposite the petrol station which afforded them a good view of the forecourt. Luckily, her research the previous day had included a picture of Rochelle, taken at a recent charity benefit that had—irony of ironies—been held to raise money for several charities working against drug addiction.

Time ticked by and, twenty minutes later, they started to worry she wouldn't show.

"God, I hope nothing's happened to her," Lowerson said. "If my phone call put her in danger—"

"Over there," Yates interrupted him, and pointed towards a new white Jeep with blacked-out windows turning into the petrol station.

Instead of moving into one of the petrol pump spaces, it reversed into an area to the side of the air and water terminal. Its engine was turned off, but nobody exited the car.

"Are you sure it's her?" Lowerson asked, and Yates gave him a sideways look.

"Check out the plates," she said. "They've been personalised to 'CHELLE 1'."

"Ah," he said.

They got out of the car and walked at a normal pace across the street, not wishing to draw any undue attention to themselves. As they neared the Jeep, its engine started up again, as if its driver was getting ready to bolt.

Lowerson took a good look around, making sure they were not being watched, then tapped on the driver's window.

After a moment, it was lowered so they could see the top of a woman's head.

"Rochelle?"

"Get in," she said. "I can't stay long."

* * *

Rochelle White was not what they had expected.

She was a quietly attractive woman of around twenty-five, with highlighted blonde hair, perfect nails and understated jewellery to match the classy linen summer dress she wore. In fact, she looked very much like the woman who might have decorated the late Daniel Hepple's home, but not at all like the sort of person they expected to find attached to a serious gangland criminal.

It took all sorts, they supposed.

And, to Yates eternal annoyance, Lowerson was clearly impressed with what he saw.

"Thanks for coming to meet us, Ms White," he said. "As I said on the phone, we're from Northumbria CID. I'm Jack, and this is Mel."

"You said you found my number on Dan's phone?"

She came straight to the point, because there was no time for pleasantries. She'd needed to fabricate an excuse as to why she was heading out, and had come up with a last-minute consultation with a client in Corbridge, just in case she was seen around the town. She'd found that it was best to stick to the truth as far as possible; it reduced the likelihood of being found out.

"Yes, we found the phone at his address in Whitley Bay," Lowerson told her. "We understand you were…close with Mr Hepple?"

She smiled at that.

"If you've had a look on the phone, you probably saw some of the pictures," she said. "So, yes, you could say Dan and I were close."

She shoved her sunglasses back on her nose, in an effort to hide the glint of tears. He'd been no prince, but Dan Hepple had loved her, and he'd been her lifeline. Now, he was gone, and she was alone again.

"You said on the phone you were in fear of your life?" Yates prompted.

"I said too much," she replied. "In fact, I don't even know why I came here—"

"Because you're scared," Lowerson said. "And you need our help."

"You can't help me, now," Rochelle said, resting her head briefly on the steering wheel as she tried to pull air into her panicked lungs. "Do you know who my boyfriend is?"

"Bob Singh," Yates replied shortly, from her position on the back seat. "We know the rumours."

"It's not just rumours. He's a dangerous man. Bobby found out about Dan and me, and that's why he murdered him. I'll be next, I know it. He's toying with me, waiting for the right time."

Lowerson opened his mouth to deny it, but the fact was, he didn't know for certain that she wasn't the reason.

"We could offer you police protection, if you come forward," he said. "Go on the record about Bobby and we'll protect you, Rochelle."

She let out a watery laugh.

"Protect me? He has police in his pockets. How do you think you'll be able to protect me?"

A terrible thought suddenly came to her mind.

"Are you one of them?" she asked, tremulously. "Are you one of Bobby's?"

"No—"

"Please," she begged, starting to cry. "Please, don't hurt me, I—"

"Get a grip on yourself," Yates said, shocking everyone in the car. "We're not one of your boyfriend's dirty coppers, alright? We're the good guys."

As a technique, it worked to snap Rochelle out of it.

"Right. Okay," she mumbled. "Sorry, but you all look alike."

"Thanks," Lowerson chuckled, but decided then and there that he needed to know which of his fellow officers were on the take. It might take days, weeks or months to win this woman's confidence, but he was prepared to do it, if it meant cleaning up shop.

Yates had come to a similar conclusion, herself.

"If you don't want police protection, and you won't leave of your own volition, what is it you want, Rochelle?"

The woman had recovered herself and was even re-applying lipstick in the rear-view mirror. Her hand stilled, as she caught Yates' eye.

"I want to bring him down," she said softly. "I want him to pay for everything he's ever done."

"We can definitely help you with that," Lowerson said. "If you'll help us, in return."

She lowered the lipstick and then held out one of her perfectly manicured hands, which he took.

"It's a deal," she purred.

CHAPTER 36

Back at CID Headquarters, Ryan was replaying the footage they'd seized from the circus ticket office. The footage came from a single, high-level camera that had been fixed on the corner wall, so it would capture rolling images from two sides of the office: the front desk and the side wall, where a narrow door was cut out to give access to the ticket seller. Presumably, it was intended to capture images of anyone attempting to steal across the counter, or anyone who tried to force their way in through the staff door. As an unexpected bonus, the camera also managed to capture the frontage of Charlie O'Neill's caravan, on the extreme edge of its wide-angle lens.

The camera had been fitted next to a security light, with a motion sensor to conserve its bulb. Ryan thought it was unfortunate the light wasn't permanently illuminated, because that would have provided them with much clearer images. As it was, they were heavily reliant on the stretches of footage where somebody had happened to walk within range of the sensor, activating the light. Outside of those times, the footage was simply too dark and grainy, even after considerable help from the tech team.

"There he is," Ryan said, as they watched Charlie pass beneath the camera at exactly 21:03.

He paused the screen to look at the ringmaster's expression, as he'd glanced up at the light, searching the black and white image for the smallest clue, but there was nothing to read on Charlie O'Neill's face. As he'd walked towards his own death, he looked just the same—as if it were any other night.

"He's not running, he's not stumbling, he's not walking with his head bowed, and his shoulders slumped. I'd say he was walking with purpose."

"Aye, but some would argue the purpose was that he planned to top himself," Phillips pointed out.

Ryan clicked another button and the footage continued to roll.

They watched Charlie move off quickly towards the gate leading to his caravan and, a moment later, they watched him on the very edge of the screen, pausing by the doorway.

"What's he doing?" Phillips asked.

"He's looking up at something," Ryan murmured, but the angle of his chin was too high for it to be anything other than the night sky. "Stargazing, apparently."

"Didn't seem the type," Phillips said, reaching for the packet of custard creams he'd squirrelled out of the house that morning.

Ryan let the tape continue to roll for the next twenty minutes, while they watched the tape closely and munched through half the packet of biscuits, stopping occasionally when the light was activated by another figure entering the screen and, once, when a cat wandered beneath the sensor.

"There's Marco and Leonie," Ryan said, coming to attention again. "They first pass beneath the motion sensor at 21:24, which is almost exactly when they estimated."

A moment later, their figures disappeared in the direction of Charlie's caravan and they leaned forward to scrutinize the action playing out on the edge of the screen, which Ryan had maximised as much as he could. They were disappointed to note that everything happened as the D'Angelos had described: they watched them knock on the door several times, then saw Marco angling his taller body to see inside one of the living room windows. A moment later, he jerked away in shock, and Leonie rushed across in concern. Soon, she was seen hurrying off the screen, in the direction of Charlie's neighbour and they saw Marco trying the door handle again, before giving it a couple of hard kicks. They watched him edge inside, then a few moments later, he rushed back out again, bent over double as he threw up onto the grass.

He was leaning against the edge of the caravan when Leonie returned with the neighbour in tow.

"Nothing they didn't already tell us," Ryan muttered, pausing the footage before standing up to pace around a bit. "If only it captured sound, we might have heard when the shot was fired."

"Is this the only camera?"

Ryan nodded, then wandered over to look at the murder board. He scanned each of the faces on the wall.

"What I can't understand is why nobody heard the shot."

"Silencer?" Phillips suggested.

"Not found anywhere with the gun," Ryan replied. "And, if Charlie's death was made to look like suicide, they couldn't use a silencer, could they? A man who intends to kill himself doesn't care whether anybody hears the shot."

Phillips clucked his tongue.

"Well, the fireworks didn't start until around half-past nine," he said. "And Marco and Leonie found him *before* then, behind a locked door. If Charlie didn't off himself, the killer had to get inside sometime after nine, but there's nothing on the footage—"

"Maybe there is, but we can't see it."

"What do you mean?"

"I mean, they must have approached the caravan from the opposite direction without activating the motion-sensor light," Ryan said. "If they avoided the ticket booth, the footage would stay dark, so we can barely see a bloody thing."

Phillips gave a long whistle, running a hand over his chin in a nervous gesture.

"That's reaching, lad."

"Is it? It's the only way I can think that somebody got inside without it being captured on the screen."

"Aye, but how did they lock the door from the inside, and get out again?"

Ryan sighed heavily.

"I'm still working on that part," he admitted, turning back to look at Phillips. "But I've been thinking about that trapdoor, Frank. Remember what Samantha said, about her mum seeming to disappear from the floor, without going through the door? We wondered how the hell anyone could dispose of a body in broad daylight, without being seen. But what if they didn't have to? What if—"

A picture was forming in Phillips' mind, and it turned his stomach.

"You think somebody killed that poor lass, then shoved her underneath the caravan for safekeeping, using the trapdoor?"

A muscle in Ryan's jaw clenched, but he nodded.

"Yes, I do. Then, I think they returned to the scene later, once things had died down, and disposed of the body under cover of darkness."

"That's cold," Phillips said, his button-brown eyes darkening with anger. "Cold, and pre-meditated."

Ryan gave a slow nod.

"You know what I think, Frank? I think somebody wants us to believe Charlie killed his wife and was driven to suicide rather than facing prosecution for murder. At first, I wondered whether Esme was killed in the heat of the moment. But now, I realise something important: she was killed for a reason, that day in 2011, and we must be getting close to finding out what that reason was. Staging a suicide is a desperate act, and it must have taken some thought and planning to orchestrate, so I'm starting to wonder whether the reason for killing Esme is more important than the murder itself."

"And Charlie's a kind of collateral damage?"

"Maybe. We haven't figured out exactly *how* they managed to lock Charlie inside, to mask the shot and make it look as though he was the only one who fired the weapon. But we will."

"How are we going to do that?" Phillips asked. "Faulkner confirmed that the door was broken in, just as Marco described, and just as we saw on the tape. The CSIs went over the door with a fine-toothed comb, and it wasn't tampered with."

Ryan gave his sergeant an enigmatic smile.

"I'm going to start by asking the pathologist to expedite time of death," he said. "If Charlie's body has any more secrets to tell us, I want to know about it."

Just then, the telephone in the incident room began to ring.

"Ryan."

"Sir, this is the Duty Sergeant on the front desk. There's a gentleman to see you, here in the foyer, a Doctor Alexander Gregory? He says he's expected."

"Thanks, I'll be down in a minute."

Phillips slipped his phone out of his pocket.

"I'll let MacKenzie know he's here," was all he said.

The rest would be up to Samantha.

CHAPTER 37

As he made his way downstairs to greet Alexander Gregory, Ryan wasn't sure how he would feel seeing the man again. Two years ago, he had turned to Gregory for help in finding the notorious serial killer known as 'The Hacker' to the press, but to Ryan as the man who had killed his sister, Natalie, and who had almost claimed him, too.

The government's attempt to set up a think-tank to rival the FBI Behavioural Science Unit in America had been shut down following a series of systemic failures, and Gregory was now the closest remaining thing Britain had to a criminal profiler. Unlike so many of his colleagues, who had peddled unsubstantiated profiles to police forces far and wide, Gregory had preferred a more cautious approach that relied on science and method. For that reason, he remained in high demand from police forces around the world, travelling and working on a freelance basis to help those who sought to draw upon his unique insight. All the same, when he'd first made the call, Ryan had been sceptical.

That is, until he'd helped them to refocus on the most important key to unlocking The Hacker's personality: his mother.

Facing Gregory was like facing the past all over again; and, if he hadn't trusted the man's abilities—both as a clinician and as a human being—he wasn't sure he would have sought his help a second time.

It was just too painful.

A version of the same line of thought was running through Gregory's mind, as he awaited Ryan's arrival in the reception foyer downstairs. It was a difficult thing for someone to overcome their own prejudices, and he admired Ryan for his ability to do so, when the occasion called for it. Two years ago, every ordinary line of police enquiry had dried up and his team was giving up hope, but, rather than lose his own nerve, Ryan pursued another line that ultimately confirmed his own accurate deductions about the man he hunted.

He was not there to replace solid police work, Gregory thought; he was there to supplement it, or provide a useful focus where none existed before.

That was all.

The security door to the executive suite buzzed, and Gregory came to his feet as Ryan strode out into the foyer. There was an awkward moment of recognition, and then Ryan held out a grateful hand.

"Thanks for coming in, at such short notice," he said. "Long time, no see."

Gregory smiled, and shook his hand warmly.

"I was glad to hear from you, Ryan, and glad I was able to come."

"Well, don't thank me too soon," he replied, leading the way back towards CID. "We've got a tall order for you, this time."

Gregory had read the brief but preferred to hear it from the man in charge.

"Your message said the girl was a witness to her mother's murder, but she seems to have blocked most of the detail out?"

"Either that, or she was just too young to remember," Ryan said, shouldering through the double doors leading to the incident room. "That's also possible."

"She was two years old?"

Ryan nodded.

"Factoring in the trauma, and the fact everybody told her the mother had left, she's spent the last eight years believing an alternate version of the truth. Then, one day, it all came rushing back to her."

"What was the catalyst?" Gregory wondered.

"Something on the radio," Ryan said. "A jingle from Tyne Radio."

Gregory nodded, thinking of all the other cases he'd seen where a particular sound or other sensory trigger held such importance.

"I presume you have some evidence to corroborate her memory?"

Ryan nodded again.

"We had an unidentified DB, just no name. Once Samantha came forward, we were able to match the DNA. Her memory of what her mother was wearing is correct, as is the cause of death by strangulation. But there are details we need to know more about," he said, and held the door open. "But, before we get into that, I'd like you to meet my sergeant, Frank Phillips."

Phillips stood up as they entered, and turned to face a pair of assessing green eyes.

"Good to meet you, Frank," Gregory said, extending a hand.

Phillips tried not to feel unnerved by the sensation that he was being catalogued, and couldn't help wondering if it was his own paranoia rather than anything else.

"Dr Gregory," he said.

"Alex," the other man corrected. "I don't think we ever got a chance to meet, the last time I was in town."

"No, but your reputation precedes you," Phillips replied, thinking that his notion of what Alex Gregory would look like had been way off base. After learning a bit about the man's background and experience, he'd expected to meet a man in his fifties, like himself, or perhaps even older. Instead, Gregory was of a similar age to Ryan, with a light tan from his travels abroad and the kind of polished manners and transatlantic accent that came from international schooling, or something of that ilk.

"As does yours," Gregory said, returning the compliment. "Ryan spoke very highly of you, the last time we met."

Phillips blustered a bit, caught off guard.

"Aye, well. This 'un needs all the help he can get."

Gregory laughed appreciatively, then spread his hands.

"So, tell me how I can help."

* * *

Dark storm clouds were gathering overhead, casting long daytime shadows across the Tyne Valley as Lowerson and Yates made the short journey from Corbridge to the nearby town of Prudhoe. Their most recent victim, whose body had fallen from the upper level of a multi-storey car park, had since been identified as Evan Parker, a twenty-three-year-old handyman by day and drugs-pusher, by night. His last known address was one he shared with his mother, which killed two birds with one stone.

"Do you want to inform the mother, or do you want me to do it?" Lowerson asked, as Yates drove towards their next destination with a certain enviable panache.

"Why don't we both do it?" she replied, in cool tones.

"Right. Sure."

Lowerson drummed his fingers against his knees, then asked the burning question all men wanted to know.

"Is there anything the matter?"

Yates flexed her hands on the wheel, and, for a moment, he wondered if she was imagining the smooth leather was his neck.

"Why would there be anything the matter?" she said, overtaking a lorry with a swift jerk that sent him crashing against the car door.

"Ouch," Lowerson muttered.

"Sorry," she said, cheerfully.

"Did I say something?" he asked. "Look, I'd rather know—"

"It doesn't matter. It's not important."

"It sounds important, if you're upset."

"Upset?" she squeaked, in protest. "I'm not *upset,* I'm just disappointed."

Oh, God, he thought. *That was much, much worse.*

"For starters, I don't know why I'm even *surprised* that you'd go for someone like Rochelle," she said, throwing caution gaily to the wind. "She's got that sad, vulnerable look about her—and she smells nice…"

"She does?"

"Of *course*, she does! She can afford to wear Chanel!"

"Ah—"

"How d'you think it felt, having to watch you with that—that *woman* for all those months?" she stormed on, referring to his ill-fated relationship with their former boss. "And then, waiting for you to come back to life again, hoping you might see me...but instead, you turn into a salivating mess for the same kind of woman!"

"Stop the car for a minute, Mel."

"Well, I'm—I'm not bothering anymore," she said, and to her mortification, her lip began to wobble. "I'm not going to waste my time waiting for you to see what's been sitting there, right under your nose, because I've got my own life to live."

"Will you just stop the car for a minute?"

By that time, they were already in Prudhoe, so she pulled into a residential side street and turned off the engine.

"Sorry," she said, straight away. "Just ignore me, I shouldn't have said anything. This case is obviously getting to me—"

"Did you mean all that, about hoping I might see you?" he asked, shifting in his seat to look at her.

She lifted her chin and thought about denying it all, then decided she'd come too far to back down, now.

"Well, of course, I bloody did! What kind of rock have you been hiding under, all this time? It's been hell, trying to stay professional around you, and now I'll probably have to request a transfer because I've jeopardised our working relationship..."

"Or, we could just do this."

Before she had time to think up a token protest, his lips were on hers, searching, demanding, full of passion. His fingers speared through her hair while hers ran over his face, his chest, plucking at the shirt he wore. Eventually, he drew back, his face hovering inches away from her own.

"But what about Dante-Dennis?"

"Who?" she muttered, then tugged him back.

CHAPTER 38

At Gregory's suggestion, the three men made their way to Phillips' house to conduct the session with Samantha, so she would feel safe and secure in surroundings that were familiar to her but held no negative associations. It was agreed that they might use the living room, with Samantha lying comfortably on the sofa while Gregory took a chair across the room and either MacKenzie or Phillips would sit in with them, but remain silent throughout.

All of that rested upon Samantha conducting her own assessment, a fact Gregory understood and admired. *His* interview took place around the kitchen table, where the little girl sipped a cup of milk when she wasn't reeling off a series of quick-fire questions.

"Have you seen a lot of mad people, then?"

Gregory grinned.

"All the time," he answered. "Especially in my bathroom mirror."

She giggled.

"That's funny," she said. "Who's the craziest person you've ever met?"

There were several that sprung to mind, but there were some things that shouldn't be spoken of with a child, and some he was prevented from discussing because of his professional obligations as to confidentiality.

However…

"There have been several politicians," he replied, drawing smiles from the adults in the room. "Have you heard of something called 'Brexit'?"

Samantha licked her milk moustache, and nodded.

"When you hypnotise me, what if I don't wake up again?"

"It's just a state of deep relaxation," he replied. "You won't get stuck there; I promise."

"Okay. What if I say the wrong thing?"

"What do you mean?"

"I dunno, what if I swear or something?" Her eyes slid across to where MacKenzie and Phillips stood beside Ryan, and Gregory realised that a strong bond had already been formed between them if she was worried about disappointing them by repeating bad language.

"There's no such thing as saying the 'wrong' thing, while we're talking," he said. "Everybody knows that you wouldn't normally say a swear word, so you won't get into trouble if you accidentally say one while you're half-asleep."

"So long as you don't say you're an Arsenal supporter, there's nothing you could say that'll upset us," Phillips added, with a wink.

"What about if I can't remember anything else?" she said softly. "I want to help, but what if I can't?"

"Think of this as the icing on the cake," Gregory said. "If you can remember anything else, no matter how small, that's great. If not, it doesn't matter."

Samantha nodded.

"I remember more when I hear the radio jingle," she admitted. "I don't like to hear it because it brings it all back, but now my mum and dad are both gone, I think I need to hear it again to see if I missed something important."

Gregory looked into her small face and wondered how one so young could be so strong.

"We'll be right here, beside you all the time."

"You promise?"

"Scout's honour."

* * *

The living room curtains had been closed and the side lamp turned on, to create a warm, dimly-lit room that was conducive to relaxation. Gregory set up his smartphone to record the session, as well as an old-fashioned tape recorder as a back-up. When MacKenzie had settled Samantha on the sofa, and herself on the chair, he asked one last question.

"Who's your favourite character from *Harry Potter*?" he asked, correctly assuming she had read the books already.

"Um, Dumbledore. Why?"

"Okay. If you feel you need to stop at any time, or if you're getting worried about something, just say 'Dumbledore' and I'll know. Alright?"

"Alright," she agreed.

"Then, let's get started. Samantha, first of all, I want you to close your eyes. Imagine every muscle in your body is relaxing. Concentrate on listening to my voice. First, your eyes, then your mouth and the rest of your face is starting to relax. Feel the tightness draining out of your body, out of your arms, then your hands and each of your fingers."

He spent considerable time helping Samantha to relax every muscle in her body, his slow, melodic voice circling the room and having a soporific effect on MacKenzie, who almost fell asleep in her chair.

"Imagine you're floating on a cloud, which takes you to your favourite place in the whole world," he was saying.

Samantha felt her body grow lax as she listened to his soothing voice, imagining herself bobbing on a cloud and then waking up inside Pegasus' stall, with his soft, wet nose nudging the top of her head.

"Where are you, Samantha?"

"With Pegasus," she whispered.

"Is anybody else with you?"

She shook her head.

"It's just us."

"Is there a radio nearby, Sam?"

The girl nodded, growing restless as she thought of it.

"Why don't you listen to the radio while you groom Pegasus?"

"Don't want to," she murmured. "It'll come back."

"What will?"

"The monster in my memory."

"What does the monster look like?" Gregory asked.

"Big," she said. "And red. It has a red body."

This last part was new information, and MacKenzie frowned, at first thinking of Charlie O'Neill's red ringmaster's coat.

"Alright, Sam. You're back on that cloud. Can you feel it?"

He took the girl back to a safe place, a neutral zone where nothing could hurt her. It was just the beginning and he knew the value of patience.

"Imagine the cloud takes you to your parents' caravan, Sam. It's floating there, now…"

"I don't want to go there," she said, plaintively, but did not say 'Dumbledore'.

"We're only going to stop in there for a minute, then we'll be on our way, Sam. You can leave at any time."

"No, no. I can never leave," she said, brokenly.

CHAPTER 39

At the same moment Samantha stepped through the metaphorical door into her parents' caravan, Ryan took a call from Tom Faulkner. The sunshine had given way to rain, which fell in a light shower at first, then graduated to heavy raindrops that tumbled from the skies and drenched the people of the North East, who had been spoilt by three consecutive days of sunshine.

Ryan watched the puddles form, from his position beside Phillips' kitchen window.

"What is it, Tom? Got an update?"

"Yes, and, before I tell you what it is, I asked for the results to be verified and checked three times."

"Understood," Ryan said, intrigued as to what could be so important to warrant the special treatment. "What did you find?"

"It's the charm bracelet—the one that was discovered in the grave beside Esme O'Neill's remains."

"I remember."

"We're still going through all the Low Copy Number DNA," he said, referring to the tiniest samples of DNA they were able to work with. It accounted for the smallest of skin cells but was notoriously difficult to rely on in court, owing to the high risk of contamination.

"Ryan, we found a match, but it's not what we thought."

"Tell me."

"The LCN DNA profile we managed to isolate was a fifty per cent match to Samantha's DNA profile, but it doesn't belong to Esme—we already checked."

"It must be Charlie, then."

"No, that's just it," Faulkner said. "When we compared it with the profiles we took from everybody at the circus, we found the match. It's not Charlie, it's Marco D'Angelo."

Ryan was quiet for a moment, taking in the enormity of what that meant for the little girl next door, and what it might mean for her mother's killer.

"You're sure?" he said, while Phillips looked up from his paperwork with a curious expression.

"As sure as we can be, yes. We applied the same process to the fresh DNA samples we took from Charlie's caravan, last night, to be sure it wasn't a fluke result. The samples we found in the caravan were much larger and easier to work with, and we got the same result. Charlie's DNA bears no genetic similarity to Samantha's, except the tiny percentage we all share as fellow human beings. When you compare it with Marco's profile, the connection is undeniable."

"Have we got our smoking gun, after all?" Phillips asked, after the call ended. "Let's hear some good news, for a change."

Ryan looked at his friend and wondered whether the news he was about to impart would be considered 'good'.

It was a breakthrough, at least.

"It turns out, Samantha's father isn't dead, after all," he said bluntly. "He's alive and well, and goes by the name of Marco D'Angelo."

Phillips stared at his friend for an endless moment, then injected a note of false cheer into his voice as he thrust upward from the kitchen table.

"Well, what are we waitin' for? Let's go and speak to the new father."

Ryan knew that his friend had begun to hope that, now Samantha had been orphaned, there might have been a possibility of them adopting her for the long-term. Phillips had never spoken of it, but he didn't need to. Ryan had seen it coming, the first moment his friends had laid eyes on the little red-headed monkey with the mile-wide grin.

But now, it appeared there was somebody else to contend with, and their hopes were scuppered.

Nobody wanted an ageing murder detective with a receding hairline, when they could have a handsome acrobat for a father, Phillips told himself.

* * *

Oblivious to the latest piece of news set to rock her young life, Samantha lay on the sofa in the living room, while her mind stood just inside her parent's caravan as it had been eight years ago.

"Turn to your right, Sam. What do you see?"

"It's my mum, doing the dishes at the sink," she replied, in a dreamy voice. "The radio's playing."

Gregory looked across to MacKenzie, who gave a nod and prepared to press 'PLAY' on a pre-recorded version of the radio jingle they'd procured earlier, to jog the girl's memory.

"What's playing, Sam?"

"It's a radio presenter talking, I think. I can't remember."

At Gregory's nod, MacKenzie pressed 'PLAY' and the sound of the Tyne Radio jingle surrounded them.

Samantha's body tensed, and her feet began to push against the cushions on the sofa as she grew more agitated.

"Remember, Sam, you're safe," Gregory said, nodding again for the recording to stop playing. "You can step back outside and leave the caravan, at any time."

"Okay," she whispered.

"Tell me what your mum's doing now, Sam?"

"She's blowing a kiss to a baby in the pen," Sam said, not fully aware that the baby had been her, which made it easier to continue. "She's drying her hands, now."

"Then what does she do?"

"She's disappearing into the corridor," Sam whispered. "I can't—I can't see her, anymore."

"Does she come back?" Gregory asked.

Samantha nodded.

"She's carrying two bags," she said.

This was also new information, and MacKenzie strained to hear the girl's softly-spoken account of what they looked like.

"One was black, a rucksack," Sam explained. "The other's the baby's changing bag. Pink with white stars on it."

MacKenzie listened with wide-eyed attention, already knowing that this new information would be life-changing for Samantha. It meant that her mother had been intending to leave, but not without her baby. There had been two bags, not one.

The question was whether she had intended to leave on her own, or with somebody else.

"That's great, Samantha," Gregory was saying. "What does your mum do, after she carries the bags through?"

"She puts them on the sofa," the girl replied. "Then she's turning around, because somebody's coming through the front door."

"Who is it?" Gregory said, in the same even tone. He knew that breaking the rhythm now could ruin everything.

But Samantha shook her head from side to side, fighting the knowledge, fighting the memory.

"The monster," is all she would say. "The one with the white hands."

"Tell me about the hands," Gregory said. "Are they big, or small?"

"They can wrap all the way around her neck," Samantha said, in a distant voice. "I can see them."

"Are they white, like your skin is white, or white, like the cloud?"

"Like the cloud," Sam said. "Bright white."

MacKenzie nodded in the dim space, knowing now that the girl had been speaking literally when she said her mother's attacker had 'white hands'. Possibly, because they were wearing gloves.

The problem was, almost everyone in the circus wore gloves as part of the show.

"Focus on the hands, Samantha," Gregory was saying. "Can you see anything else?"

"Yes," she replied simply. "They're white cotton gloves, with little gripper things on the edges."

CHAPTER 40

Given the sensitivity of the case, and allowing for the fact he had a wife in the later stages of pregnancy, Ryan rang Marco D'Angelo to set up an immediate appointment at CID Headquarters, rather than turning up at his motorhome unannounced. It was a judgment call, because there was every possibility Marco would decide to run, but the man apparently had a conscience because they found him waiting for them in the foyer at Police Headquarters, a short while later.

"Mr D'Angelo, thanks for coming in," Ryan said, and went on to recite the standard caution. "This is a formal interview in connection with the murders of Esme and Charles O'Neill, so if you would like to exercise your right to have a legal representative present, you're entitled to do so."

"I don't need a lawyer," Marco said.

Ryan wasn't about to argue the point. He led the way to the interview suite and selected a room, flipping the sign to 'OCCUPIED'.

"Please, have a seat."

"Chief Inspector, you said this was in connection with two murders, but I thought Charlie committed suicide?"

"We are treating his death as murder," Ryan said shortly. "But the reason we've called you in here today concerns Esme's disappearance."

Marco looked between the pair of them and lifted his hands in a mute gesture of apology. "I'm sorry, I don't know what else I can tell you."

He lied so flawlessly, Ryan thought, it was almost possible to believe the DNA results could be wrong.

And yet, the statistical probabilities said otherwise.

"You can start by telling us why you lied in your statement, when you stated you had no reason to believe Esme had been having an affair."

Marco laughed, and looked away.

"I don't know what you're talking about."

"I'm talking about your relationship with Esme O'Neill, sometime around 2007 and 2008."

There it was, Ryan thought, as a flicker of panic skidded across the other man's face.

"How long did it last, Marco?"

The other man raised a hand to his mouth, then scrubbed it over his eyes, trying to think.

"It was always Esme," he said, after the silence had stretched for over a minute. "It was always her, from the first time I saw her—but I was already married to Leonie."

"Go on," Ryan urged.

"She didn't believe me, when I said I would divorce Leonie," Marco continued. "In Esme's world, a marriage was meant to be for life. She'd been brought up Roman Catholic, and felt bad enough about committing adultery. She couldn't stand the thought of having my divorce on her conscience, especially as Leonie was her friend."

"So, what did you do?"

"She called it off," he said. "It came as a shock, out of the blue. The next day, I saw her with Charlie, and I thought"—he laughed, and shrugged a muscular shoulder—"I thought she'd transferred her feelings. I felt relieved not to have done anything drastic, if what she felt for me was so superficial.

"It seemed like they were married overnight, and the baby followed straight away, so I figured she'd been playing around with both of us. I was angry about it, and she kept her distance and tried to make things work with Charlie. She was loyal to him, at first."

"What changed?" Phillips asked.

"He wasn't cut out for marriage," Marco said. "He didn't like the responsibility of a family, and he wanted her all to himself. He didn't want to have to share her with the baby. From what I heard, he slapped her around a few times."

He shifted in his seat, clearly unhappy at the thought.

"I don't remember exactly when it happened, but I went across to visit her, one day while Leonie was away and Charlie was off somewhere. It was while the circus was in Edinburgh, I remember that," he said softly. "Everything rekindled again, and we saw each other almost every day after that, around the same time."

"What happened, the day she disappeared?"

"I don't know, I swear," he said, in a shaking voice. "We planned to go away together and take the baby, but she disappeared before that could happen. We'd planned to meet at her caravan, at the usual time, and we'd take my car. But Duke found the baby crying about an hour beforehand, so I never got there. When I heard Charlie had found that note, and people started to say she'd left with someone else…I'm ashamed to say it, but I believed them. It was easier to believe it."

He took a tremulous sip of his water.

"How did you find out?" he asked.

"Through your daughter," Ryan replied.

Marco's mouth formed an 'O' of surprise, then his brows drew together in an angry line.

"My *what*? What are you telling me?"

"Samantha O'Neill is your biological daughter," Phillips said, very calmly. "A comparison between her DNA profile and yours has confirmed a parental match. From that, we were able to deduce that you obviously had an intimate relationship with her mother."

Marco leaned forward, resting his head in his hands.

"Is it—is it really true?"

Both men nodded.

"She never told me," he said, softly.

"Does your wife know about your affair, and the plan to leave with Esme?" Ryan asked.

Marco shook his head.

"Of course not. Do you think she would have stayed with me, if she'd found out? Leonie never knew a thing. The two of them carried on as friends, and our marriage continued as normal."

He swallowed, imagining what she would say now, and what harm it might do the baby if she were to find out.

"Please…does she have to know? Can't we carry on as we are, for the baby's sake?"

"And what about Samantha?" Phillips asked. Not once had this man thought of anyone other than himself. "Don't you care about her, and what she might want?"

"Look, she's a good kid, but what difference would it make to tell her? She thinks her father is dead; can't we leave it at that?"

Ryan looked at him with extreme distaste.

"No, Mr D'Angelo, I'm afraid we can't avoid telling your daughter that she has a father. It will be her decision whether she wishes to have any contact with you."

With that, Ryan terminated the interview and let the man go home, to break the news to his wife. Marco D'Angelo had confessed to having an affair with Esme, and that they intended to leave together, but he'd made no further admissions. Without that elusive smoking gun, there were no charges to bring against him—it wasn't a crime to have fathered a child.

CHAPTER 41

Lowerson and Yates recovered themselves sufficiently to continue with the day job, first in delivering the news of Evan Parker's death to his mother, and then, in speaking with the drugs squads across several command divisions and, in particular, with their colleagues down in Middlesbrough. It seemed that the trend of male bodies being found with their fingertips sliced off was spreading, with two further bodies being found in Richmond and Berwick-upon-Tweed.

The pathologist had already sent a preliminary report on Parker's body, confirming what they had already surmised: Evan had died long before his face hit the pavement, and even longer before his brains spattered young Emi-Lee's freshly tanned legs. The lack of blood upon impact, combined with a series of deep stab wounds to the man's torso, suggested he had died and bled out elsewhere.

The additional information helped to confirm a consistent MO across the three known killings and, once they received the reports from their colleagues in the other divisions, they may find more victims whose bodies displayed the same signature markings.

"Do you think it's the same person doing it all, or several people contracted to make it look the same?" Yates asked, as they made their way back into Police Headquarters.

"Could be either," Lowerson said. "But there's another consistency, which is that two potential witnesses state they saw a very tall, very broad man with distinctive facial features in the area around the time two of the bodies might have been dumped."

"What was so distinctive?"

"Apparently, his skin was heavily pock-marked and scarred."

Yates frowned, wondering why that description was setting off a distant alarm bell.

"I'll run it through the system," she decided. "Is there anything else you want me to look into?"

"How about looking to see if there's anything playing at the theatre, next Saturday night?" he asked. "I was thinking we could go on our first date, if you're not busy."

Yates sent him a slow smile.

"I love the theatre."

"I know," he murmured. "I do listen, sometimes."

* * *

He might listen, but Lowerson didn't always think things through before deciding to act.

While Yates took herself off to find out why the description of their unknown assailant was so familiar, Lowerson placed a call to their new informant, this time using her work number which he'd found on a Google search.

"*Rochelle Interiors*, how may I help you?" A voice tinkled down the line, but it was not the lady herself.

"May I speak with Ms White, please?"

"What is it regarding?"

"I, ah, met her the other day to talk about the décor for my study, and I've had a change of heart," he improvised. "I just wanted to run my ideas past her."

"Ms White will be leaving the office soon," the receptionist told him. "But I'm sure she can spare a couple of minutes. What name shall I give?"

"Mr—ah, Mr Lowerson."

There was a brief pause, then a click on the line as the receptionist transferred the call.

"Rochelle?"

"How dare you call my office," she whispered furiously. "Do you have any idea how *stupid* that is?"

Lowerson swallowed.

"I wanted to call and let you know that there's been another murder with the same MO, which makes it less likely that Dan Hepple was murdered because of you," he said. "I thought you'd want to know; in case it puts your mind at rest."

At the other end of the line, Rochelle let out a long breath.

"Thank you," she said. "What was the name of the other one?"

Lowerson hesitated.

"Parker. Evan Parker."

Rochelle made a small sound of recognition, and he jumped on it.

"If you know anything about what happened, you need to tell us," he said.

"I don't need to do anything," she replied coolly. Now that the danger had passed, she felt stronger.

But Lowerson had other ideas.

"Don't you have any kind of conscience?" he muttered.

"Don't start that crap with me," she hissed. "If Bobby finds out I've talked to you, I'll be the one lying down at the mortuary, next time."

With hindsight, that was the turning point in their conversation. Up until then, Lowerson might have walked away; he could have left Rochelle and wished her good luck.

But he didn't.

He'd come too far to let his only chance of unveiling the criminal underworld slip away, like sand between his fingers. In the back of his mind, he saw himself uncovering widespread corruption, as Ryan had done. He saw himself toppling criminal overlords, as Ryan had done.

He wasn't about to let that opportunity go to waste.

"Listen, Rochelle," he said tersely. "Unless you meet me at the petrol station tonight, I'll bring Bobby Singh in for questioning. I can't promise I won't ask him whether he killed Dan Hepple because he was having an affair with you."

He heard a sharp intake of breath.

"You—you wouldn't."

"Try me."

"Fine," she said, quickly re-working her schedule to cover it. "But I can't stay long, or I'll be missed. I could meet you on my way back from work."

"Okay," he agreed. "I'll be at the petrol station at five-thirty, sharp."

There was another short silence, then a cynical laugh.

"When I first met you, I thought you were sweet," she said mockingly. "I was wrong, wasn't I? You're not a sweetheart, at all."

Lowerson hardened his heart.

It would be worth it, he told himself. The ends justified the means.

"Five-thirty," he repeated, then hung up, feeling sweat trickle down his neck.

He leaned back against the taupe-coloured wall of the corridor outside CID. Several out-of-date posters hung limply from a noticeboard on the opposite wall, as well as an open copy of the police newsletter and a large, plain black and white A4 sheet of paper from the police chaplain with two simple words: 'HEAL THYSELF'.

With an angry expletive, he pushed away from the wall and hurried off, already planning his next move.

CHAPTER 42

By the time Ryan and Phillips made it back to the house in Kingston Park, Gregory had finished his session with Samantha and was enjoying a bowl of MacKenzie's excellent fish chowder and soda bread, a recipe that had been handed down from her Irish mother, and her mother before that.

When she caught sight of her husband's face in the doorway, MacKenzie turned to Samantha with a smile.

"Would you like to watch a movie for a while, darling? Just while we talk over a few things to do with the case."

She had no intention of lying to the girl, but neither did she want to speak of things unless they were certain.

"Have you got *Chitty Chitty Bang Bang*?" Samantha asked, and MacKenzie's face was a comical mask of confusion.

"Chitty Chitty What Now?"

"Why don't I help you look for it?" Gregory suggested. "I'll be back in a minute."

After they left, MacKenzie took a seat at the table beside the others, who had since helped themselves to a bowl of her soup.

"What have I missed?" she asked, after the first couple of spoonfuls. "You were gone a while."

"It's Marco," Phillips said, keeping his voice barely above a whisper. "He's Samantha's father."

MacKenzie looked away quickly, making a show of smoothing out the tablecloth.

"You're sure? Of course, you're sure," she muttered, answering her own question. "What did he have to say about it?"

"Marco claims that he and Esme had planned to run away together, and that they'd planned to take the baby, too—although he also claims she hadn't told him it was his. But, when he found out about the note and that she'd disappeared, he assumed she'd abandoned the idea and gone off with someone else. He seemed to have no idea about the baby," Phillips said. "About Samantha, that is."

"It would tie in with what she told us, during the session with Alex," MacKenzie said. "She spoke of her mum having packed two bags: a black rucksack, and a pink baby changing bag. That would suggest she planned to leave with the baby, and with Marco."

"What else did she say?" Ryan asked.

Just then, Gregory returned.

"Sam's happily set up with *Bedknobs and Broomsticks*," he said. "It was the closest thing I could find."

"How did it go, during the session?" Ryan asked.

"She did incredibly well," Gregory said, pulling up a chair. "We managed to draw out quite a bit of detail which will hopefully be of some use to the investigation. She's a bright child, and she's been through a lot, so it took some time until she could let her mind go, but we got there in the end."

MacKenzie had taken a note of everything during the session.

"Samantha described the monster as having a red body, which made me think of Charlie's coat, at first," she said. "But it could have been any kind of costume. We'd need to go back and check what people were wearing during the show in 2011, which may be a bridge too far."

Ryan nodded.

"She talked about there being two bags, as I said, and she mentioned the 'white hands' again. This time, she was clear about them being gloves. White cotton gloves, with little grips on the underside."

Ryan felt something skid inside his chest, because he'd seen those gloves somewhere before.

"What about the gender? Was it a man or a woman?"

"She couldn't say for certain, but she did say their hands were big enough to wrap around her mother's throat."

Ryan knew that, statistically, a handspan like that tended to suggest a male assailant, but it could have been any of the people he had in mind.

"The gloves," he muttered, and brought out his smartphone. "He was wearing them on the camera footage, but he wasn't wearing them when he came out of the caravan again."

"Who wasn't? What gloves?" Phillips demanded.

"*Marco,*" Ryan told him. "He wears white gloves with tiny grips on the underside, all the acrobats do. They're different to the plain ones that Charlie wore, or Duke, for that matter. I need to check..."

He brought up an e-mail containing the CCTV footage as an attachment, and played it on the screen of his mobile.

The others waited, and then Ryan smiled fiercely.

"He has the gloves on as he walks towards Charlie's caravan, beneath the ticket office," he said. "But when you scroll ahead to when he stumbles out again, supposedly horrified by what he's found, his hands are bare."

He looked up as pieces began to fall into place.

"It's been smoke and mirrors, all along," he said, and felt a hard burst of anger at the thought of how they'd all been duped. "Phillips, check the inventory from Charlie's caravan to see if a pair of white gloves were recovered. In fact, there should be at least two pairs: one plain set, belonging to Charlie, and one set belonging to Marco which he'll have hidden in plain sight, probably amongst Charlie's other gloves or in a white sock drawer. If you can't see it on the list, call Faulkner and ask him to send a team back down to look at Charlie's caravan again. We need those gloves, because they'll have the gunshot residue all over them."

Phillips nodded, but still hadn't quite caught up.

"I still don't see how he could have got into the caravan, if it was locked—"

Ryan shook his head.

"We need to work backwards. Let's start by thinking about the fatal shot that killed Charlie, that nobody heard. We were led to believe it must have been fired before the fireworks display, but that's an elaborate piece of showmanship I'll get to in a moment. If we look at things objectively, the most obvious answer is that the shot didn't happen beforehand—it was masked by the fireworks display."

"But Leonie and Marco found the body—"

"No, they didn't. If we agree that the shot was fired after the fireworks began, that puts Charlie's death at more like nine-thirty or thereabouts. It means he was still alive when Marco and Leonie arrived at the caravan."

"I don't follow," MacKenzie said. "You're saying he was disabled, before then?"

Ryan nodded.

"It's the only thing that makes sense. When we looked at the gunshot wound on Charlie's head, I thought it was strange that the angle of the gun had fired on the right side of his skull, because it's a hard angle for a right-handed person to achieve, if they're putting a gun in their own mouth. Then, I started to wonder, if it wasn't Charlie, why a killer would choose to fire at that angle. What did it achieve?"

"It would hide an existing wound," MacKenzie realised.

"Bingo," Ryan said. "It completely obliterates the evidence of a previous attack, which I think happened soon after Charlie came back to his caravan, not long after nine o'clock."

He could almost hear the cogs whirring.

"So, let me see if I have this right," Phillips said, leaning his elbows on the table. "You're telling me somebody snuck across to the caravan to lie in wait for Charlie, so that when he went inside his caravan he was disabled by a blow to the head. We didn't see this on the tape, because they avoided setting off the motion-activated light and just walked around the back of it, so the tape would stay dark. Right?"

"Right."

"The doors are always open, as we already know, so that's no great surprise. But how did they lock it..." Phillips trailed off. "Ah, wait, now I see."

He shook his head, almost in admiration.

"That's bold," he said. "Very bold."

"Hang on! Some of us haven't read the case papers," Gregory protested, dunking the last of his soda bread. "Then what happened?"

"The person who disabled Charlie could have used a rock, a kettle, anything. The CSIs haven't finished going over every item in the caravan, so we'll wait to see what heavy object they find that fits the bill. But they brought the pistol with them, for later, and left it inside the doorway, or they already knew where Charlie kept his own. I think we're going to find our Mr O'Neill had some side ventures, so it's likely he kept some protection in the caravan."

"And so, they left again, under cover of darkness?" Gregory asked.

"Yes, they left the door unlocked as they went, because it serves a purpose later. That's another very high-risk move," he said. "Anybody could have come along to see Charlie in that time, and could have stepped inside. But there was a tight turnaround and they had to take the chance."

"They," MacKenzie murmured. "Aye, I see what you mean."

It was like they were speaking a different language, Gregory thought. One where each followed the other's train of thought, and needed only to say a couple of words to be understood. "Marco and Leonie walked deliberately beneath the lights because they wanted their little drama to be captured on camera. They wanted us to see them trying the door, apparently finding Charlie dead, then Marco kicking the door down. In all fairness, I think the vomiting part was genuine," Ryan said.

"What really happened was, Marco tried the door—which was actually *unlocked*—and then clicked the latch before breaking it down, for show. When he ran inside, he picked up the pistol that had already been left waiting for him, and staged the rest of the so-called suicide. He had his gloves on, but there's nowhere to stash them in a leotard, so he had to hide them somewhere inside. I think they're still there, and he was hoping they'd never be found if we believed the idea of it having been a suicide."

"So, it was never locked," Gregory said. "And they waited until the fireworks started before running for help and completing the rest of their plan. That's cunning."

"Yes, and planned to the finest detail, given the time constraints," Ryan said. "They had to act quickly. I think, when Pinter's report comes back, we'll find that Leonie exercised enough force to kill Charlie from the off. There was no assurance that he'd stay down, otherwise."

"But are you saying Marco was the one to kill Esme, too? I thought they were going away together?"

"No, I think that was Leonie," Ryan said. "Contrary to what her husband said, I think she found out about his plan to leave her, and went around to confront Esme about it. When she saw the bags already packed, a terrible fight started, and Leonie saw red. She wasn't pregnant back then, and she's very strong, so it would have been easy to gain the upper hand."

There were nods around the table. It took the strength of a world-class gymnast to perform acrobatic displays of the kind they'd seen at *O'Neill's*.

"Samantha remembered the trapdoor opening during our session," Gregory put in. "It seems that's where the killer—Leonie—bundled Esme's body for safekeeping. The rucksack went that way, too, and then she put everything back as she found it. Samantha remembers the coffee table being moved around, to cover the edges of the trap door so as not to arouse suspicion."

"Poor kid," Ryan said, as they heard the dulcet tones of Angela Lansbury wafting through from the living room.

"But why did Marco stay with Leonie after she'd killed Esme?" MacKenzie wondered. "I know, there's the argument that they're as bad as each other, but—"

"I don't think he ever knew," Ryan replied. "When we spoke to him today, I think he was telling us the truth about that part."

"Why would he help her to get rid of Charlie, then?"

"We'll have to ask them, but my guess would be that Leonie lied, and told Marco that she'd found out Charlie was the one to kill Esme. Maybe she said she'd acted in the heat of the moment, whacking him around the head, and they needed to make it look like a suicide—otherwise, their baby would be born in prison."

Through this last part, Gregory grew more concerned.

"Ryan, you're not dealing with a garden variety killer here, as I'm sure you know. She's crossed a tipping point, this one, and the lines of acceptable behaviour no longer apply. She'll kill whoever threatens her, now."

He did not say it to create panic, but to make them aware of the very real danger.

"What if she's found out about Marco being Sam's—" Phillips jerked his head towards the living room. "If he was telling the truth about not having known before, Leonie wouldn't have known about it, either. It might send her over the edge."

Ryan nodded, coming to his feet.

"Let's get down there now, Frank, and bring them both in before the early evening show starts."

Before they left, Ryan took Gregory's hand in a firm grip.

"Thanks for everything," he said. "And don't be a stranger."

"I appreciate what you did in there, and the care you took with her," Phillips said. "Where are you off to next?"

"Upstate New York."

"Oh," Phillips said. "Well, that'll be lovely. Denise and I were thinking of touring the Highlands—"

"Frank!" Ryan called from the hallway, and—with a quick peck for MacKenzie—Phillips hurried off.

CHAPTER 43

The rain had eased to a light drizzle by the time they reached the Town Moor, but it was slow going on the roads and the journey took longer than expected. Consequently, they arrived just as the show was about to start, rather than before.

"We'll just have to wait for the interval," Ryan said. "Might as well go inside."

They were about to walk through the main entrance to the arena, when a broad Cockney voice stopped them in their tracks.

"'Ere! You got a ticket?"

They looked around to see a burly, red-faced woman leaning over the counter in the ticket office.

Ryan retrieved his warrant card and held it up.

"What's that s'posed to do? Looks forged to me."

His lips twitched.

"We're from Northumbria CID," he explained, very slowly. "I'm Detective Inspector Ryan, and this is—"

"Yeah, and I'm the Queen of Sheba. Look, son, I've seen it all before, so let's stop messin' about. I've got a stack of ones just like that, back in the caravan. Three for a fiver, if you're interested."

Ryan opened his mouth to start taking her to task about dealing in forged goods and the folly of impersonating a police officer, then realised he'd been had.

Her face broke into a wide grin.

"Only joking, gorgeous," she cackled. "I'd never forget your face. Might forget yours," she added, for Phillips' benefit.

"Same to you, n'all," came the cheerful reply.

"Go straight in," she said, waving them on. "The acrobats are about to start."

"Well, we wouldn't want to miss that," Ryan murmured.

* * *

The arena was resplendent, filled with families who'd hurried to catch the show after school. Their excited faces beamed as unicycles danced on tight-ropes, jugglers kept a dozen clubs flying in the air, and a woman balanced on top of a beautiful white horse as it trotted around the arena, switching between handstands and side-flips, to gasps and applause from the audience.

"Now, then! Now, then! Prepare to witness the most death-defying feats of all!"

The lights lowered around the main arena and spotlights illuminated the top of the tent, where four acrobats waited to begin their routine.

From their position in the gangway on the edge of the arena, Ryan and Phillips strained to see who had taken over from Charlie as the circus ringmaster.

"I don't believe it," Phillips said. "That's Duke."

And it was; the former circus clown had morphed into a butterfly, holding court in an arena filled with hundreds of people who were all looking at him in admiration and wonder.

He was in his element.

"Prepare to be dazzled and amazed by our acrobatic display, led by the one, the only—Marco the Magnificent!"

The arena erupted into applause and the flame-thrower roared into action as a single acrobat flew across the tent, swinging like Tarzan from one suspended bar to the next in a perfectly synchronized action. He wore a bright red, full-length leotard, as his wife had done eight years before, and seemed to dance across the air. Even knowing what Marco had done did nothing to diminish the spectacle.

They watched the display and thought that, since it was the last show Marco was ever likely to do, they hoped it was a good one.

And they were not disappointed.

A moment later, Duke's loudspeaker rang out again.

"And now, ladies and gentlemen, boys and girls, it's time for the most dangerous flight of all…remove the nets!"

With another fire burst, the safety netting fell to the ground.

"Now, in his most daring feat yet, Marco will attempt to make his way across an obstacle course of fire without a safety net!"

There were gasps from the crowd, which always made Marco smile. In reality, he was supported by a lightweight harness with a springy, flexible cord that followed his progress through the air. If anything were to happen, it would break his fall.

"Ready, darling?"

At the top of the platform, Leonie kissed her husband and gave him the thumbs-up.

"I love you," he said. "I'm sorry about—"

"I've already forgiven you," she said, putting a protective hand on the bump she carried. "I'll see you on the other side."

If he thought it was an odd choice of words, Marco put it out of his mind and prepared to do a routine he'd practised many times before. Leonie made her way carefully down the ladder, pausing occasionally to catch her breath.

She wanted to see the full effect, from the ground.

The drumroll began, a deafening crescendo leading up to the moment when he would take his first leap. On the other side of the tent, on the opposite platform, his fellow acrobats began to swing the rope-bars, keeping time so he could judge the best moment to push off.

The drumroll stopped.

* * *

From the gangway, Ryan and Phillips waited for Marco to perform the last part of his routine. It was an impressive sight, and there was a hush amongst the crowd as they waited for the drumroll to stop. When it did, they watched him take the first leap, swinging back and forth to gain momentum and then, at exactly the right moment, Duke rallied the crowd to begin a countdown.

"FIVE!"

Marco's legs pumped, to gain the height he needed.

"FOUR!"

Leonie reached the ground, sweating from the added exertion, and then hurried around to watch her husband's last flight.

"THREE!"

The flame-thrower threw up an enormous fireball and there was another gasp from the crowd.

"TWO!"

Ryan's eye strayed across the arena, to where Leonie's face was briefly lit up by the light of the fire. The expression she wore was caught somewhere between love and madness.

"Frank—" He grabbed Phillips' arm, but there was nothing he could do.

"ONE!"

Another huge fireball was timed to fill the gap just below the spot where Marco would perform a flip in mid-air, before catching the next rope-bar that was swinging towards him. But, this time, he never made it that far. As soon as he detached from the first swing, he felt his harness snap, and the distraction was enough to throw his coordination off. He flipped, but when he stretched out his hands to grasp the next swing, he found only air.

And then he was falling—twisting and tumbling into oblivion, with the safety harness plummeting to the floor by his side.

* * *

The crowd's cheers turned to cries and then screams of terror. Mothers shielded their children's eyes and scrambled to leave as panic spread. Duke ran out into the arena, calling for people to leave in orderly lines, trying to reassure them—telling them that an ambulance had been called.

But there was nothing anyone could do for Marco, now.

Ryan and Phillips pushed their way through the crowd, moving against the flow of people who were rushing to get out, and made their way into the arena where they found Duke in a state of shock.

"What happened?" Ryan demanded.

"The safety harness failed," Duke said, sweating beneath his top hat. "It must have done, it's the only thing I can think—"

"Who's responsible for it?"

Duke wiped the sleeve of his jacket over his forehead to stem the flow of sweat that was dripping into his eyes.

"Marco checks it himself, or Leonie does. He says she's the only other person he trusts to do it right."

Ryan thought back to her maniacal face and scanned the arena, but there were too many people.

"Do you know where she is?"

Duke shook his head.

"Oh God, I hope she didn't see that—"

"Never mind that, now," Ryan said. "What's the quickest way out of here?"

"Exit C," Duke muttered. "Everybody forgets it's there."

"Frank, you stay here with the body, I'll find Leonie."

"Careful, lad. Remember what Gregory said."

Ryan nodded, and then took off at a run.

CHAPTER 44

"Where are you off to?"

Yates caught Lowerson as he was heading out of the door, at the end of his shift.

"Don't you want to come over for some…dinner, or something?" She gave him a winning smile.

"Ah, I'd love to, but I can't tonight. I've got a few errands I need to run." He was surprised at how easily the lie rolled off his tongue, and his neck began to redden as his conscience battled against it.

Yates was disappointed but shrugged it off. There would be other days.

"I'll see you tomorrow morning, then."

After a quick check to make sure nobody was there to see, she leaned in to brush her lips against his, and was pleased when his arms came up to wrap around her waist.

"'Night, Mel."

"'Night, Guv."

He rolled his eyes to make her laugh, then slung his blazer jacket over one shoulder and headed off to keep his appointment with Rochelle. He'd always been a straight-up sort of person; the kind of man who did things strictly by the book. But bringing in a new informant required some bending, he realised, and it was proving difficult to know where to draw the line, especially now that his relationship with Yates had just become a lot more complicated.

* * *

Ryan battled through the crowd until he reached the opening marked 'EXIT C' and it didn't take too long before he emerged back onto the moorland outside. The crowds were disorientating, and he took a moment to get his bearings before jogging around to the other side of the tent, where the caravan park was located on the far side. The ground beneath his feet was slippery after the deluge earlier, and a couple of times he almost lost his footing, but he vaulted onto the side of a nearby stall to get a better view above the crowd.

He spotted Leonie immediately, heading in the direction of the black motorhome she'd shared with her husband.

Ryan put a call through to the Control Room to send immediate support, then cut between two tents and sprinted along the back of them, avoiding the swathes of people who milled around or fought to get back to their cars. He made swift progress, that way, and eventually reached the boundary fence separating the circus area from the caravan park.

He relayed his position back to Phillips, and then prepared to face the monster Samantha had seen, all those years ago.

* * *

Ryan knocked on the door to the motorhome and called out a warning.

"Mrs D'Angelo! This is Detective Chief Inspector Ryan! Can you open the door please?"

He waited a moment and, when there was no response, hammered on the door again.

"Leonie! Open the door please, or I will force entry!"

Conscious that the woman was volatile, and possibly armed, Ryan turned the door handle and pushed it open exercising extreme caution.

"Leonie?"

He spotted her straight away, because she'd made no attempt to hide. She was seated on the floor, legs outstretched and with her back against the kitchen units, clutching what appeared to be an open bottle of window cleaner.

"Hello, Chief Inspector," she said, in a friendly voice. "I'm sorry, things are a bit topsy-turvy, at the moment, but you're welcome to come in and have a seat."

He eyed the large knife block on the countertop, clocked the heavy brass pan sitting on the hob, and then scanned the room for anything else that could be used as a dangerous weapon.

Then, he stepped inside.

"You must be uncomfortable on the floor there, Leonie," he said quietly. "Wouldn't you like to sit on the sofa, here?"

"I'm fine, thanks. Besides, it won't be for much longer."

Ryan looked between the bottle of toxic fluid and the baby bump, and felt his heart begin to pound.

"I knew it would be you," she said, after a minute. "I could see it in your face, all that *tenacity*."

Ryan said nothing, then slid to the floor to sit cross-legged in front of her. Within range of being able to wrestle the bottle from her hand, if need be—and far enough away to take evasive manoeuvres if she attacked him.

"Do you want to tell me what happened?"

Her eyes were wild and unfocused when she looked up.

"Ha! I had you fooled for a while, didn't I? Go on, admit it."

"Yes, you had us fooled."

She smiled at that, as if they were discussing something much more trivial than murder.

"I like your home," she said, suddenly. "I drove up there, the other night, in case that's where you had Samantha stashed away. Your wife is very beautiful."

Ryan felt sick at the thought of this crazed woman having watched her from the shadows of the hedgerows.

"Why did you go up there, Leonie?"

She turned coy.

"Well, I know I shouldn't have, but, if you'd only let me take care of it, things would have been so much easier. Now, look what's happened."

Ryan looked away, so she wouldn't see the fury in his eyes.

"You killed Esme, didn't you?"

"Yes."

No denial, no remorse—just a simple acknowledgement.

"Because of Marco?"

She nodded.

"Esme had a sort of aura around her. She was the type of woman who turned heads, even when she didn't mean to. She couldn't help it, and we used to laugh about it. But then, I started noticing the changes in Marco. He was distracted, less affectionate with me. He'd be as excited as a puppy whenever she came over, or even walked by. It was pathetic, but I knew it was just a passing thing. If she'd only go *away*, he'd have time to get over it and come back to me."

"What happened?"

"He didn't say anything, and I kept it to myself while he worked her out of his system. He thought I was so stupid," she said, shaking her head. "He thought he'd kept it all so secret. But a woman *knows*, chief inspector.

"I wasn't going to let it go on much longer. They'd had their fun, and I'd been a good friend in sharing him, for a while. That's what I told myself, that I was being a good friend. But then, something changed in him. It wasn't just that he was sneaking about, it was as though he was detaching himself from me, emotionally. That was a step too far."

"You went to speak to her?"

Leonie nodded, twisting the bottle between her fingers.

"She looked surprised to see me," she said, with a harsh laugh. "She was surprised her *stupid* friend, Leonie, had noticed that something was going on. I told her she was nothing but a common whore, and that she should keep away from now on. I told her our friendship was over.

That's when I saw the bags sitting on the sofa, and I knew. I knew they were planning to leave together, that day."

"You put a stop to it?"

"I don't know what came over me," she said.

She thought of the terrible power she'd felt with her hands around Esme's throat. If she closed her eyes, she could see the way her eyes had bulged, her mouth gasping for air.

"I hardly noticed the baby, at first, but then…afterwards, when it was over, it was just staring at me and crying. It wouldn't shut up."

It, Ryan thought. She had dehumanised Samantha, not even referring to her by name.

"Afterwards, I was so panicked, I almost called the police," she said, laughing. "But then I managed to find a way. I shoved her underneath the caravan and moved my car, so it was closer to Charlie's caravan, then waited until after dark. It must have been two or three in the morning. It was hard getting her across the grass without waking anybody up, and she'd started to smell, by then. I had a map in the car and I just looked up somewhere with plenty of woodland and drove out. It was exhausting, all the lifting and carrying. I lost my bracelet somewhere along the way, and that cost me some sleep. I went back to search for it, a couple of days later, but I never found it. At least it was easier for me to get around back then, without all this extra bulky cargo."

She looked down at the bump and, before their eyes, her baby gave a kick.

"It won't make a difference," she told it. "Not anymore."

Ryan didn't like her tone, nor the way she was cupping the bottle of neon blue liquid, ready to knock it back.

"Everything went back to normal, after Esme left," she continued. "Marco came back to me, just as I knew he would. Out of sight, out of mind. It's incredible, really, what people will believe, if it suits them."

Yes, Ryan thought. It really was.

"Samantha worried me, for a while. When she was little, she used to avoid me, wouldn't go anywhere near me, and it was quite obvious. I worried about people noticing. But I just broke her down, gave her sweets and toys, played games, that sort of thing. Eventually, she forgot why she'd been frightened. It was easy enough to drop in a little something here and there, to see if she remembered."

"She did remember."

Leonie's face shifted into something hard, and dangerous.

"She's ruined everything. *Everything*!"

"Did you know she was Marco's daughter?"

She shook her head, and started to knead her temple, to ease the throbbing behind her eyes.

"When he told me this morning, I can't describe how I felt," she whispered. "And, after he came back from the police station, he was talking about adopting her, making her part of our family…*imagine*, Esme's brat, living here with us! The thought of it made me sick. He made me sick. I knew it was the end."

Ryan's eyes flicked to the window above the sink, where he could see flashing blue lights approaching.

Not long now.

"Marco never knew what I'd done," she said, in a low, almost inaudible voice. "When I decided Charlie had to go, I needed help, and there was no way Marco would have done it, if he'd known the truth. So, I told him the version he wanted to hear; the version everybody expected. Charlie had killed Esme and I'd found out. In fear for my own life, I clubbed him with the back of that ugly marble statue he has sitting on the shelf in his caravan. I managed to work up some tears, and, once Marco was over the initial shock, he understood what we had to do. Charlie was the guilty one, after all, and I'd been acting in self-defence."

She snorted.

"Like I said, it's amazing what people will believe, if they really want to."

She raised the bottle of window cleaner in a toast.

"Here's to you, chief inspector. I gave it my best shot and, for a while, I almost managed to pull it off, didn't I? But you played the trump card. You found out Samantha was his."

Ryan's body tensed, as he prepared to lunge.

"Put the bottle down, Leonie. Think of your baby."

"I am! Don't you get it? I'm saving it the pain of the life it'll have, if it's born. This way, it'll never have to live with strangers, and eventually find out what its mother did. It'll never have to know the pain of loving someone, so much, so badly, that you'd do anything to keep them. I wouldn't wish that on my worst enemy. Can't you understand? This is for the best."

They heard the sirens approaching outside, and knew that the time for talking was almost over.

"Did you see him fall, chief inspector? Did you see the graceful way he fell? It was like watching an angel, falling from heaven."

Her eyes had grown wide again, and tears ran freely down her cheeks and onto her shirt.

"Time's up," she whispered.

As she raised the bottle to her lips, Ryan surged forward to snatch it from her hands. He would never have imagined he'd be caught in a wrestling match with a heavily pregnant psychopath, and it didn't rank high on his bucket list, but he was not afraid of exerting whatever force was necessary to protect her, and the life she carried inside her.

He managed to knock the bottle out of her hands and its contents chugged onto the floor, pooling on the cream linoleum.

"No! NO! Look what you've done!"

She turned on him, fingers curled into claws as she went for his face. Ryan grasped her forearms to hold her away, half sitting on her legs, so she couldn't thrash about and hurt herself further. She was surprisingly strong, and he was more than relieved when he heard voices outside.

"In here!" he shouted.

A moment later, Phillips burst inside, with several officers in tow. He made a swift assessment of the situation and came to the only conclusion he could.

"Looks like you've got everything under control here. Howay, lads, let's leave him to it!"

CHAPTER 45

For the second time that day, Lowerson awaited the arrival of Rochelle White at the petrol station in Corbridge. It was almost half-past five, and the high street was busy as people made their way home for the day. The sun had broken through the clouds again and turned the stone buildings a warm sandy brown, but the streets were still slicked with rain from the downpour earlier in the day and his smart black shoes skidded against the tarmac as he ducked inside the petrol station shop for a can of coke and a flake. It was hardly fine dining, but he'd had very little to eat all day, and was starting to feel the effects.

Unfortunately, Lowerson was forced to abandon the purchase when he spotted the white Jeep pulling into the forecourt once again.

"Don't you want your coke?"

Lowerson ignored the shout and hurried outside to tap on the driver's window, and its tinted glass was rolled down a crack, just as before.

"Get in," Rochelle said, from behind the wheel.

Lowerson walked around the side of the car and pulled open the passenger door, before jumping inside.

Before he'd had time to put on a seat-belt, she put the car into gear and accelerated onto the main road.

"Hey! Where are we going? That wasn't the agreement—"

Only then did Lowerson realise there was a large, angry bruise forming on Rochelle's face and her left eye was swollen.

"What happened to you?"

"I'm sorry," she mumbled, looking dead ahead.

"What for?"

"I hear you've been looking for me."

Lowerson spun around and caught sight of the most wanted man in the North East.

"Wh—"

He never saw the blow coming. From his position in the back seat, the man known as 'Ludo' knocked him out with a single punch to the side of his skull.

"Keep looking straight ahead, princess," he told Rochelle, who started to shake badly. "We'll be there, soon."

As the sun fell deeper into the horizon, the car motored further into the wilds of Northumberland, away from anyone who might come looking for the young detective constable who'd forgotten the first rule of his training: *never leave your partner behind.*

CHAPTER 46

Later that evening, MacKenzie, Phillips and Samantha had settled themselves on the sofa and were pleasantly engaged in a debate over whether to watch *Black Beauty* or *The Railway Children,* which was Phillips' own personal favourite on account of its star, Jenny Agutter, who had been the object of his teenage affection throughout the 1970s.

"How about *Black Beauty*?" MacKenzie said, being fully aware of the prior claim on her husband's affections.

But, before any decision could be made, the front doorbell rang.

"Wonder who that could be," Phillips said, and hurried to answer it.

And wished he hadn't, when he found Mrs Carter standing there.

"Detective Sergeant, I'm sorry to trouble you at this time of night, but given everything that's been going on, I wanted to stop in and check how Samantha's coping."

Phillips pasted a friendly smile on his face.

"Of course, come in," he said, and ushered her inside. "We were just about to watch a film."

"Oh, how nice," she gushed. "Did you ever see *Thomasina*?"

Phillips gave her a blank look.

"It's told from the perspective of a ginger cat…"

"Really? Well, I never," he said, wishing he had a whistle and a flare to call for help.

"Hello, Samantha," Mrs Carter said, as she came into the living room. "Hello, Detective Inspector."

She nodded to MacKenzie, who excused herself to put the kettle on, and prepare herself for what was to come. A moment later, Phillips joined her in the kitchen and put a gentle hand on the small of her back.

"She wanted a minute alone with Sam, to ask how she's been doing," he explained. "But how are *you* doing, love?"

MacKenzie selected four cups from the cupboard, then dropped a teabag in each of them.

"To tell you the truth, Frank, I feel like I hardly know myself anymore. It's only been a few days, but life seems—"

"Richer? Brighter?"

She turned to him and put gentle hands on his face.

"I never wanted children," she said clearly. "But then, I'd never met anybody I'd want to have them with. Then, I met you, and my heart started longing for them, for the first time in my life. God knows, life was good before Samantha came into it; we love each other, we laugh, we travel, and we have successful careers. That's more than many people could wish for."

"But?"

"But she came into our lives like a tornado, shaking the foundations. She's been through hell, and she's still smiling. She likes her food even more than you do—"

"Now, just a minute—"

"—and she's bright, Frank. Funny, kind and smart as a button. It's like she was made for us."

Phillips' eyes crinkled as he smiled.

"I know, love. It's like being shown a whole new world."

"She might want to stay with a younger couple," MacKenzie said.

"Speak for yourself," Phillips said. "I'm in the prime of life."

"That you are," she agreed, patting down the wispy salt-and-pepper hairs on the side of his head. "So, what do you say?"

"I think we should ask Samantha," Phillips replied. "If she'd like to stay here with us, then we'll put up a fight for her."

* * *

When they stepped back into the living room with a trayful of tea and biscuits, they found Samantha fighting back tears.

"She says the investigation's over now, so I need to go into a long-term home!"

"I don't want to go to another family. I want to stay here! Can I, Denise? Can I, Frank?"

"I don't think—" Mrs Carter began, but MacKenzie's soft Irish burr interrupted whatever she'd been about to say.

"Would you like that? Would you want to stay here, with us?"

Samantha nodded, and then shuffled off the sofa to run into MacKenzie's arms.

Mrs Carter watched it all and couldn't help but feel moved; she was only human. But there would be forms and applications to be made, discussions to be had…

She looked across at the girl's smiling face, and at the little unit that had evidently grown to three.

"I'll have a word with my boss, and come back tomorrow morning," she conceded, gathering up her papers.

A moment later, she almost jumped as a pair of slim arms gave her a brief, hard hug.

"Thanks," Samantha whispered.

"There, now," Mrs Carter said, blinking furiously before giving her an awkward pat. "I'd best be off."

CHAPTER 47

Thursday, 6th June 2019

The following morning, Ryan and Phillips looked on as the circus packed up and moved out of the Town Moor. Duke O'Neill had disappeared sometime during the night, amid rumours that the circus was deeply in debt and had only survived as long as it had thanks to a lucrative side-line in drugs smuggling as it toured the various towns and cities of the UK. Now, its various acts scattered to the four winds, their caravans, trucks and motorhomes heading off to pastures new.

As they stood watching the Big Top slowly being dismantled, a woman approached them across the grass.

"Sabina?"

"I know, it's a different look," she said.

Gone were the long dark locks and floating skirts. They had been replaced by a shorter, stylish cut and ordinary blue jeans.

"I've been offered a job at a local estate agent," she said, ruefully. "It's not quite Hollywood Boulevard, but the pay's good."

"That's great," Phillips said. "Congratulations."

"What about all your psychic skills?" Ryan asked, and she grabbed his hand before he could stop her.

"You'll lead a long and happy life," she said, with a smile. "You'll be married to the love of your life until both of you are old and grey. You'll get into scrapes almost every week in your constant quest for justice, but you'll be remembered as the best friend this city has ever known."

She let his hand fall away again, then waited a beat.

"See? Total bollocks, really."

The three of them laughed, and then Sabina came around to the real reason she was there.

"Look, Duke asked me to pass on a message before he left."

"Oh? Did he leave a forwarding address, n'all?" Phillips asked, pointedly.

"No, but he did leave the horse. He says it's Samantha's, anyway, and he thought she might want to keep him."

"Horse?" Phillips asked, turning slightly grey around the gills.

"He's called Pegasus," Ryan remembered, as they followed Sabina in the direction of a blue-painted horsebox.

Inside, stood the most beautiful white Arabian horse they'd ever seen. Not that Phillips knew much about them—as they'd learned during a memorable case in Kielder—but Ryan had ridden a few in his day.

"He's a beauty," he remarked.

But Phillips still looked shell-shocked.

"Look, I'd love to be able to give the lass her horse back, but I don't know the first thing about looking after them—and then, there's the time and the money…"

Ryan had an idea.

"We have a bit of land, a few acres, that we lease out to the equestrian centre at the bottom of the hill. I could have a word with them and see if we could come to an arrangement? That way, Sam can come and visit whenever she likes, but you'll know the horse is being looked after in the meantime. I'll pop in, whenever I'm around, and you'll probably have a hard job trying to keep Anna away."

Phillips looked at his friend with sincere gratitude.

"Thanks, son. Let's surprise her, at the weekend, eh?"

Sabina ticked that problem off her list, and then, always being able to spot an easy mark, decided to mention the next item, too.

"Duke also left his caravan," she said, pointing to the old VW Campervan. "It needs a lot of work, but if you settle the last of the rent on the land, here, he'll call it even."

She mentioned a figure that was very reasonable.

"Frank," Ryan cautioned. "Think of your health."

"I am," the other man declared, already dreaming of Highland walks and al fresco stotties.

"You've already gained a daughter and a horse, this week," Ryan tried again.

"Three's a charm," Phillips said cheerfully, and shook on it.

* * *

Later in the day, once Pegasus had been delivered into the safe hands of the Elsdon Equestrian Centre and Phillips had arranged for the delivery of the campervan he intended to call the 'Mystery Machine', they called in to Police Headquarters and set about the lengthy business of Tying Up Loose Ends. There were statements to be filed and checked, pathology reports and forensic records to order and date, and any number of administrative tasks before Leonie D'Angelo could be successfully prosecuted for her crimes. Following her arrest, the former acrobat had been admitted to a specialist, secure mental health ward, for the remainder of her pregnancy and while the experts came to a decision as to whether she might enter an insanity plea.

When Ryan and Phillips entered the incident room, they found Yates already hard at work on her own caseload.

"Morning, Mel!"

She looked up with a ready smile and, if they weren't very much mistaken, a definite glint that had not been in her eyes the previous day.

"Have you seen Jack, anywhere?" she asked, checking the clock on the wall, as she had done for the past hour.

Ten-fifteen.

It was unusual for him to be so late, and even more unusual for him not to call in to let her know about it.

"No, sorry," Ryan said. "Does he have a meeting?"

"He didn't mention it," she replied, and tried to dispel a nagging sense of worry.

"How's it all going?" Ryan asked, wandering over to the murder board she'd set up. It featured the images of three male victims, all of whom had been found with similar injuries. A picture of Bobby Singh had been added to the wall, and she was in the process of pinning lines between his various enterprises and the three dead men.

"Well, it's looking as though there may be a connection with the circus," Yates said, confirming his own suspicions. "The working theory is that these three victims were 'Smoggies' employed by Singh, but started moonlighting on the side when a new supply channel presented itself."

"The circus," Phillips guessed.

"Yeah, we think so," Yates said. "Hard to do anything about that, now that Charlie O'Neill is dead."

"You can still go after the brother," Ryan said. "But I agree, it's more likely he was Charlie's stooge rather than any kind of mover and shaker."

"It's possible that these three, among others, wanted to set up a rival gang and take over some of Singh's turf," Yates said. "Obviously, he put a stop to that."

"Makes sense," Ryan agreed. "Do you have a line on who did the dirty work for him?"

"Actually, yes," she said, reaching for the picture she'd recently printed. "This guy, goes by the street name 'Ludo'—"

"We know him," Ryan said, taking the picture from her outstretched hand. "He was Jimmy the Manc's right-hand man. He's been on the 'wanted' list for two years. You have reason to think he's back in the area?"

"Two witnesses report seeing a very distinctive man, matching his description."

"Once seen, never forgotten," Phillips put in. "As I recall, the man's built like a brick shit-house."

Ryan swore beneath his breath.

"If he's back, it's because he needs money," he said. "He's ruthless, organised, and has a talent for violence. He's the last person we want roaming the streets."

"Let's hope nobody else runs into Ludo before we have a chance to track him down," Phillips said.

"God help them, if they do," Ryan breathed.

DCI Ryan will return in

Penshaw: A DCI Ryan Mystery

If you would like to be kept up to date with new releases from LJ Ross, please complete an e-mail contact form on her Facebook page or website, www.ljrossauthor.com

AUTHOR'S NOTE

Like many people who grew up in or around Newcastle upon Tyne, the Town Moor played a very special part in my childhood. Not only did it serve as the route for many a chilly, early morning cross-country run when I was at school, but it also played host to an annual travelling funfair known as 'The Hoppings'. As my character Phillips has already mentioned in the book, the funfair comes to town at the end of June each year and local people pile in to enjoy themselves. However, I think it is important to mention that the fictional circus I have created in these pages is not based on that funfair. For this reason, you will not see any of the usual dodgem cars or ghost train rides at *O'Neill's Circus,* which is intended to be modelled on traditional showmanship, including old-fashioned costumes, nostalgic stalls, clowns, magicians and illusionists. Naturally, it also goes without saying that any suggestion of nefarious activity surrounding my fictional circus is limited to these pages and does not relate to any other real travelling circus that may or may not visit Newcastle.

The character of 'Samantha' came to me one day after watching the old movie, *Oliver!* and I began to imagine a little girl who shared some characteristics with the Artful Dodger, albeit to a much lesser degree. I hope that I have been able to channel some of his loyalty and playfulness through the new character of Samantha, whilst sketching out a better life for her than Dodger was forced to lead.

L J ROSS

April 2019

ABOUT THE AUTHOR

Born in Newcastle upon Tyne, LJ Ross moved to London where she graduated from King's College London with undergraduate and postgraduate degrees in Law. After working in the City as a regulatory lawyer for a number of years, she realised it was high time for a change. The catalyst was the birth of her son, which forced her to take a break from the legal world and find time for some of the detective stories that had been percolating for a while and finally demanded to be written.

She lives with her husband and young son in her beautiful home county of Northumberland.

If you enjoyed *The Moor*, please consider leaving a review online.

If you would like to be kept up to date with new releases from LJ Ross, please complete an e-mail contact form on her Facebook page or website, www.ljrossauthor.com

ACKNOWLEDGEMENTS

The Moor is the twelfth book in my DCI Ryan Mysteries, and the ninth of my books to have captured the coveted Number One spot in the Amazon chart in the United Kingdom. I am often asked whether the process of writing and releasing a new book has lost some of its verve, now that I have a good number beneath my belt. However, I can say, very emphatically, that this is never the case. Each time I begin to write a new book, there is a frisson of excitement at where the story might take me, and returning to characters I have grown to love is always a joy.

None of this would have been possible without the love and unstinting support of my family, and in particular my husband, James. The "J" in "LJ" is taken from his name as a permanent 'thank you' for the part he played (and continues to play) in making my writing dream a reality.

I am grateful also to the many readers, book bloggers and bibliophiles who have read and enjoyed my stories and have been kind enough to recommend them to others. I never underestimate the value of your kindness and goodwill, and I am thankful to every one of you.

Finally, I would like to thank my five-year-old son, Ethan, for being wonderful. Now that he is a proficient reader himself, he is growing curious about the 'grown up' books that his mummy writes, and it would not surprise me to find him leafing through the pages of a DCI Ryan novel in years to come. In the event that he manages to scale the bookshelf to nab a copy of this before he reaches the appropriate age, I'll take this opportunity to tell him that the *Secret Seven* collection is an excellent alternative until he is ready to go on a journey of discovery with Ryan and Co.